DARKBLOOD ACADEMY

Book 1: Half-Blood

G.K. DEROSA

Print ISBN: 9781070402239

Cover Designer: Sanja Gombar www.fantasybookcoverdesign.com

Published in 2019 by G.K. DeRosa LLC
Palm Beach, Florida
www.gkderosa.com

❀ Created with Vellum

To the little squiggly baby in my belly that was my constant companion as I wrote.

~ GK

CONTENTS

PROLOGUE

A scream tore through the silence, echoing down the halls of the quiet hospital. The essential first breath was drawn. It was over. Jacquelyn squeezed her eyes shut and with a final pant of exhaustion, slumped back against the pillow. Beads of sweat lined her brow, her body sore and every muscle screaming in agony. She kept her eyes closed not ready to meet the wailing creature the nurses were fussing over.

"Ms. Bennett?"

She recognized the midwife's soothing voice but ignored it. The cries moved nearer, slowly dwindling to low whimpers the closer they got.

"Ms. Bennett, it's perfectly normal to feel overwhelmed after what you've been through. Please, open your eyes. Don't you want to meet your daughter?"

Jacquelyn resisted the urge to whip her head back and forth and shout, "No!" She clenched her teeth, her jaw clamped shut as she peeked through slitted lids.

The tiny pink baby wriggled in the midwife's arms, her gray eyes latching onto her mother's. A flash of gold eclipsed the newborn's irises, and Jacquelyn's breath hitched. Her heart

G.K. DEROSA

stilled. Was she seeing things? She ran her hands through her sweat-slicked hair, her shaky fingers catching in the tangles. She shook her head from side to side, the slow movement making her head spin. This wasn't her daughter; she never would be.

A crash of thunder exploded outside and lightning crackled across the pitch sky, the flash illuminating the dim hospital room. Her eyes shot to the window, the brewing storm providing something—anything—to distract her attention from the tiny swaddled infant the woman held out to her.

"Ms. Bennett, are you all right?" The midwife handed the baby over to a nurse, and the two stood side-by-side staring at her.

Jacquelyn continued to shake her head, her glassy gaze locked on the window. Unease churned her stomach, acid crawling up her throat. She swallowed hard, but it did nothing to quell the anxious stirrings. A shudder tattooed up her back, the thin hospital gown no match for the chill overtaking her bones.

He was here.

The air thickened, and pops of electricity skimmed her skin, raising every hair on her body. She could almost feel his dark magic clogging the room like thick, oily tar invading every crevice.

The midwife and nurse's expressions went blank before they froze, along with the other two hospital personnel bustling around the room. The slap of heavy footfalls resounded in Jacquelyn's head, pounding in time with her erratic heartbeats.

The baby's wails doubled in intensity.

Jacquelyn knew she should take the child out of the motion-less nurse's arms. The baby wasn't safe. What if she dropped her?

Would that really be so bad? A dark voice echoed in her mind. *Then she wouldn't be your problem anymore.*

The baby continued to squirm, her chubby, round face

2

growing redder by the moment. Jacquelyn sat there too para-lyzed by fear and exhaustion to move.

A blonde man in hospital scrubs strode in, his intense gaze settling over her before moving to the child. His mere presence sucked all the oxygen out of the room. Jacquelyn's lungs constricted and she forced in short, ragged breaths.

He loomed over her. His perfectly angelic looks reminded her exactly what drew her to him in the first place. "You thought you could keep her from me?" His gruff voice was equal parts sinister and enthralling.

She summoned every last ounce of courage remaining in her frail body and hissed, "I don't even know if she's yours."

The man moved toward the child, snatching her away from the nurse's arms. Cradling the baby against his chest, a shadow of a smile curved his lips. He offered her his thumb and she stopped crying, her tiny fingers curling around his big one. "She's mine all right." Golden sparks lit up his irises.

Jacquelyn's lungs tightened further until even shallow breaths were a struggle. *It can't be.* My child cannot be like him.

"You will raise her as a human," he began, moving toward the foot of the bed, "many half-bloods never show supernatural abilities at all."

She shook her head, all the blood draining from her face. "I can't," she spat. "I won't."

The man's light brows knit, his thin lips twisting into a frown. "You'd forsake your own child for no fault of her own?"

"That's no child of mine. She's a monster just like her father." She squeezed her eyes shut, refusing to look at the baby or the man that plagued her nightmares. How could she have done something so stupid? One night of pleasure to be bound to these unholy creatures for a lifetime? No, she wouldn't do it.

His eyes frosted over, the icy blue colder than the fiercest snowstorm. He turned to glance out the window, and Jacquelyn followed his gaze to the full blood moon breaking through the clouds. The deep crimson hue sent a wave of goose bumps over her flesh.

The baby cooed in the man's arms, and another smile lit up his stern features. "I will call you Luna," he whispered, "and one day you will hold more power over the elements than the moon itself."

The newborn's fingers tightened around his thumb, her lids beginning to droop. He turned to Jacquelyn once more. "This is your last chance, woman. I'm offering you the opportunity to raise your child without any interference from me. This is not the first human child I've sired, and I assure you it won't be the last. I take care of my offspring, but I do not interfere if I'm not needed. You and the girl can have a normal life together."

She shook her head furiously, her lips pinched. "I don't want her. I don't want anything of yours." Snapping her eyes shut, she leaned her head back against the pillow shutting them both out.

The tendon in his jaw quivered as darkness overcame his handsome features. "So be it."

CHAPTER 1

"Come on, Jay!" I shouted over my shoulder as I climbed the rickety chain link fence. "If Principal Greenfield catches us we're screwed." Reaching for the aluminum cross pole, I tugged myself over the top and braced for the fall.

My Converse slapped the blacktop, a tremor snapping up my legs as I landed. But my ankles held. Last thing I needed was to sprain something right before graduation.

I drew in a long breath to slow my racing heart. A balmy breeze brushed over my skin, sweeping blonde strands of hair across my face. Only a foot on the other side of the fence of Crestwood High, and I already felt free.

"What's got you in such a hurry, Luna?" asked Jay as he dropped to the ground beside me.

"I don't know. Do you ever feel like you need to move? Like if you spend another second in your skin, you'll explode?"

His light brows furrowed as he scrutinized me like I had three heads.

"Okay, I guess it's just me then." I adjusted the straps of my backpack and turned toward the train station.

"Must be senioritis." He stepped up beside me and ran his hand through his thick auburn curls. "So where to?"

Excitement swirled in my gut inciting a swarm of butterflies to take flight. "I was thinking we could check out that new coffee shop I was telling you about."

"The Supe Café?"

I nodded quickly, chewing on my lower lip. It had been a year since the supernatural world came out of the closet, revealing its existence on primetime television no less. I, along with millions of other Americans, had watched stupefied at the revelation. But even now, an entire year later, supernaturals weren't that common. Not in the suburbs anyway. I didn't get into Manhattan that often, and according to the news most had settled in the Lower East Side and Alphabet City which was pretty far from our small town of Crestwood.

"I don't know, Hallows." Jay shook his head. "Why are you so obsessed with meeting one of them anyway?"

I shrugged. Because I found them fascinating, because the idea of escaping into a magical world and leaving the group home I'd been trapped in for four years seemed like a dream, because, because, because... I stilled my wandering thoughts and speared my friend with my best pout. "Are you scared? Jay McMasters... are you scared of a big, bad supernatural?"

He frowned, folding his arms against his chest. "Of course not. I just don't get what the big deal is."

I shook my head and picked up the pace toward the train station. The café was in the neighboring town, and I would go whether he was coming or not. Timing my escape from study hall had been no easy feat, and I was not letting this opportunity pass me by. Today was my eighteenth birthday, and it was the only present I'd get. Not even Jay knew. I'd had a pretty crappy track record of birthdays over the years so it wasn't something I liked sharing. "Fine, I'll just go by myself."

Jay's footsteps only slowed for an instant before he sped up and appeared next to me once more. "Like I'm going to let you go by yourself. What if you get eaten by one of those things?"

I laughed, weaving my arm through his. "President Lazaris doesn't let just any supernatural into the human world. There's like a whole series of background tests they have to pass. It's worse than what it was for human immigrants back in the early days after 9/11."

William Lazaris had just become president when our two worlds collided and though he was all for unification, he'd been keeping a tight leash on things. The newest mandate called for any human with supernatural blood, or half-bloods as they were affectionately called, to be sent to special academies in Azar—the supernatural realm where the rest of the supes lived.

The Supernatural Intelligence Agency or SIA had sent agents from Azar to comb the schools one by one. All human students were forced to take a blood test to determine their paranormal status. Even kids with a tiny percentage of demon, faery, witch or shifter blood were compelled to go. Some didn't even have magic. They hadn't made it to Crestwood yet, but I couldn't wait to see who had supe blood in them. So freakin' cool.

"I don't know. I still think some are sneaking in through the wards. My dad said there's been an increase in weird animal attacks lately. Everyone knows that's code for supe attacks."

Jay's dad was the sheriff of our sleepy little town and overly paranoid if you asked me. "Whatever... it's not like one is going to attack us in broad daylight at a café."

"Fine," he grumbled as he hurried to keep up with my pace.

The quick train ride on the Metro North had us on the outskirts of the city in no time. As the train pulled out of the station, I glanced at the GPS on my phone. Just a five-minute walk to Supe Café.

"So have you figured out what you're doing after graduation?" he asked.

I shot Jay a narrowed glare and resisted the urge to snarl. "I already told you a million times. I'm not going to any crappy community college to get some B.S. two-year degree. Now that I'm finally eighteen, I can get a full-time job so I can afford my own place. Getting out of Astor Home is priority number one."

"You can always take a few classes on the side. And there's nothing wrong with community college."

Ugh. Why couldn't I ever keep my trap shut? The urge to stuff my old red Converse in my mouth was suddenly overwhelming. Jay was starting at CC in the fall. His parents were thrilled he'd gotten in at all.

I stopped and turned to him, fidgeting with my backpack strap. "I'm sorry. That's not what I meant. It's just not for me. You know how much I suck at school."

"Right, because I'm so much better?" He smirked and started walking again. "Come on, I think that's it." He pointed at a stretch of shops off the main street.

At the very end, a neon sign hung in the window of a red brick building. The curtains were pulled shut, but the words Supe Café set my nerves a tingling—in a good way. I sprinted the last few yards with Jay panting to keep up.

My fingers wrapped around the old doorknob, but it didn't budge. I wiggled it a few more times, but it was locked tight. My heart plummeted. "What the heck?"

Jay peered in through the window, but the heavy crimson curtain blocked any view of the inside. "Guess it's closed."

I scanned the sign on the door and huffed. "It shouldn't be. It says it's open till midnight." Lifting my knuckles to the dark timber, I knocked lightly. Nothing.

Jay shrugged, turning back the way we'd come. "Come on, let's go. We can try again another day."

"No way." When Mrs. Sanderson, Astor Home's friendly custodian, found out I skipped out on school early, I'd be grounded until graduation. I couldn't give up that easily. I knocked again, louder this time. Jay fidgeted beside me, bouncing from foot to foot. I didn't know why he was so freaked out by the supes. From what I'd seen on TV, they seemed pretty cool.

Footfalls shuffling toward the door sent my heart rate skyrocketing. Jay's wide eyes shot to mine, and we stared at the door until a hidden slat opened in the dark wood.

"What do you want?" A gruff voice seeped through the opening first, then a pair of crimson eyes peeked through.

My throat suddenly went dry. "Um, we..." I curled my fingers into fists and steeled my nerves. What was wrong with me? *I'm not scared of them.* "We just wanted to come in and check the new place out."

The piercing gaze scanned over me, an unearthly glow illuminating his ruby irises. The man's eyes whipped toward Jay for a moment before returning to settle on me. "It's just the two of you?"

I nodded, and Jay elbowed me in the stomach. "I mean, some friends might come meet us later. They know we're here." I chewed on my lower lip, realizing how stupid I sounded.

The lock clicked, and the door creaked open.

Jay shook his head, his big eyes wider than I'd ever seen them. I grabbed his arm and tugged him in behind me.

The scent of roasted coffee beans swirled in the air as I crept into the dimly lit café. Something else tickled my nostrils —something smoky and sweet, but I couldn't place the odor. As my eyes adjusted to the low lighting, the quaint coffee shop came to life. Cute chairs and tables were arranged around the small space, brick walls on all four sides. Framed landscapes filled the walls, each one looking like it came right out of a fairy tale—ice castles, stone fortresses and towers floating on clouds. A large bar with a few stools overlooked the fancy coffee machine where the barista whipped up a frothy concoction.

It was only after turning back to Jay that I noticed the

dozen or so eyes glued to us. I was so busy taking in all the details that I'd missed the glaring patrons. Eyes of all shapes and freakish colors bored into me, and goose bumps prickled my skin.

"Now what?" hissed Jay.

I scanned the room, my eyes landing on the barista. He gave me a warm smile, and my feet moved toward him. He was cute and young, probably only a few years older than us. As I got closer, he waved and then tucked a longish curl of black hair behind his ear—his very pointed ear.

I froze, my feet halting of their own accord and Jay smacked into my back. He propelled me forward, and I practically barreled into the bar, knocking over two barstools in the process. The loud crash sent my pulse spiking once again.

"Watch it, human." The crimson eyes from the slat through the door appeared once again, attached to the body of a WWF wrestler. Jay's eyes bulged out beside me as he stepped back from the hulking figure looming over us.

I did my best impression of a smile and squeaked out a "Sorry." Bending down to pick up the stools, embarrassment rolled over me. I could practically feel the heavy glares on me once again. When I straightened, a pair of mossy green eyes were only inches from mine.

"I can get that," the barista said with a smile.

"Oh, no, I should. I'm sorry I was so clumsy."

After all the stools were returned to their proper places, Jay and I sat at the bar, dropping our backpacks on the floor. The burn searing my skin from heated glares lessened, and I sucked in a breath as I stared up at the chalk menu board.

"What can I get you guys?"

I tried not to gawk at the cute guy's pointy ears, but no matter what I did, somehow my eyes ended up there. "Um, I'll take a mocha latte."

"Same for me," yelped Jay.

The guy spun away, a grin pulling at his lips. As soon as he turned, I twirled to my friend lowering my voice. "Well, this is going well."

"I told you it was a stupid idea to come here," he grumbled.

Whatever. Now that the stares had subsided, I took the opportunity to check out the other patrons. Were they all supes?

A couple sat cuddled on a couch, whispering to each other. They looked pretty normal—no pointy ears or weird eyes. A big group of men sat in a corner booth, dark tattoos swirling from beneath their sleeves. Their arms were the size of my thighs, but besides that, there was nothing about them that screamed paranormal. They could've just been a regular human biker gang.

A wisp of air brushed my hair across my face, and a man appeared beside me, leaning against the bar. Whoa, where the heck had he come from? He cracked his cherry-colored lips, and two pointy fangs protruded from his upper lip. Deep crimson streaked across his pitch-black irises, and I couldn't tear my eyes away. A part of me knew I should be afraid, but I felt nothing, a giddy sense of calm swimming over me.

The guy finally released my gaze, and I slumped back onto the barstool like a puppet whose strings had been cut off. He wiggled his fingers at the barista. "I'll take another shot, please." His voice flowed like honey, smooth and saccharine.

"I'll bring it to your table." The cute barista leveled him with an icy glare and shooed him away.

As quickly as he'd appeared, the man was gone. My skin tingled as my brain fought to process the unbelievable. Was that a freakin' vampire?

A moment later, the barista returned with our lattes, a smile still curling his lips. I kept my eyes down to keep from staring at his ears.

"So I take it you guys have never met any supes before?" His light-green eyes sparkled.

"Nope," I answered. "Is it that obvious?"

He chuckled. "Just a bit."

I glanced at the golden nametag on his burgundy apron, finally more at ease. Riordan—such a cool name! "I'm Luna, and this is Jay by the way. Sorry for all the weirdness earlier. What's up with the tight security, Riordan?"

"Not everyone is happy about us being here—in the human world, I mean. People have gotten used to us in the city by now, but whenever we move into the small towns, we meet some resistance. When the café first opened, we had a few incidents so we hired Trevor to handpick the clientele." He jerked his head toward the towering giant manning the door.

How had I missed the towering giant when we first came in? The man melted into the shadows a second later, answering my own question. Wow.

"What is he?" I whispered.

"Strixa demon."

I gulped. According to President Lazaris, most demons and other Underworlders weren't allowed entry. Maybe Jay's dad had been right, and some were sneaking in.

"It sounds worse than it is," said Riordan, our friendly barista. "They're mostly harmless, just big and burly with a penchant for dark spaces and grape jelly beans."

I couldn't help the laugh that bubbled out. "See, Jay, supes aren't scary."

My friend raised his hand at me, showcasing his three middle fingers. "Read between the lines, Hallows."

"We're really not," added Riordan, interrupting our stare down. "So spread the word, huh?"

"Sure thing." I leaned in closer, whispering, "So what are you Riordan? Or is that a totally uncool and newb thing to ask?"

He laughed, the thin lines around his eyes crinkling. "Nah, it's no problem. I'm a sprite."

When my expression remained blank, he continued, "We're from the Fae realm—you know, faeries, pixies, trolls, etcetera."

"Like Tinkerbell." Jay snorted on a laugh.

Riordan shook his head with a rueful smile. "No, not like Tinkerbell. The land of the Fae is nothing like Neverland." He turned to me. "You should go one day, you'd be amazed, but stay away from the kingly courts. Those royals are not friendly."

After some more chitchat with our outgoing barista, I finished off my latte and pulled out my wallet. "Thanks for the advice, Riordan. Before I venture anywhere near Azar, I'll be sure to come by for a visit to get the supe 411."

His fingers closed around my hand, and sparks of electricity shot across my skin. My mouth went dry as he shook his head. "Don't worry about it. The coffees are on me."

I guessed I was wrong about not getting any birthday presents after all. "Th-thanks," I croaked. What the heck was that tingling? I shook off the errant thought as Jay jumped off the barstool—*must be a sprite thing*.

"See you soon, Luna."

CHAPTER 2

I trudged up the street, the dilapidated old brownstone finally coming into view. *Crap*! Mrs. Sanderson's beat up Corolla already sat in the driveway. Glancing at my watch, I readjusted my backpack and climbed up the steps. *Just play it cool, Luna.* Maybe no one had noticed my epic escape from study hall, and no one would ever be the wiser. Astor Home's custodian, Mrs. Sanderson was not a fan of the paranormal. She'd skin my hide if she knew I'd cut school to venture into the supernatural world.

I slowly turned the doorknob but the old hinges betrayed me, creaking sharply as the door swung open. I crept toward the stairs as my housemates' muffled voices spilled down from the second floor.

"Oh, good, Luna dear, you're back from school." The familiar hoarse voice sent ice rippling through my veins.

I froze, immobile in the middle of the entryway. *Great, I'm in so much trouble.*

Mrs. Sanderson jumped up from the couch, faster than I'd ever seen the plump old woman move. And Luna dear? What was that about?

As she walked toward me, her full bosom exploding out of her pink muumuu, the figure of a young woman coalesced behind her. "There's someone here to see you." Mrs. Sanderson tipped her reading glasses up so they perched atop her head and rested against her silver bun. She placed her hand on the small of my back and led me into the sitting room.

The pretty blonde stood and gave me a warm smile. Her hair was pulled back into a messy ponytail, a thick sweater and heavy corduroy pants completing her winterish wardrobe, which was odd for late spring in New York. Something about her seemed so familiar...

She opened her mouth to speak, but Mrs. Sanderson cut her off to pester me. "Go on, Luna, introduce yourself to the beautiful lady. She came just to see you." Her dull gray eyes sparkled with an excitement I didn't think the cranky woman possessed.

I dropped my backpack on the chair and extended a hand as I moved closer. "Hi, Luna Hallows. And you are?"

Mrs. Sanderson's pudgy elbow jabbed me in the ribs. I winced for a second before schooling my expression back into a smile. The girl's gaze never deviated from mine, and now close up I was certain I knew her. Closing my eyes I imagined her in a fancy ball gown and pounds of makeup with a gorgeous guy on each arm. The long blonde hair, bright blue eyes, killer bod—

"O.M.G., it's you—you're Kimmie-Jayne Starr from *Hitched*!"

A big smile lit up her face and she took my hand, pulling me into a hug. My body froze, completely not expecting the intimate contact. I couldn't remember the last time anyone had hugged me. Jay wasn't exactly a hugger, and I didn't have many girl friends. My mind wandered back to Mrs. Hallows, the woman who'd raised me until I was thirteen. Her floral perfume swirled in my mind, a warm fuzzy feeling coming over me. She was like my grandma, and probably the last person that really cared about me. When she passed away, I bounced around foster care for a year before I ended up here.

"So nice to meet you, Luna." Kimmie-Jayne's voice drew me from painful memories. I relaxed into her for a moment before she released me and held me out to arm's length. Her blue eyes rolled over me as if searching for something. She finally tore her gaze from mine and turned to Mrs. Sanderson. "Is there somewhere Luna and I can speak privately?"

My friendly custodian clasped her hands together. "Oh, well, yes." She glanced upward as more shouts echoed across the house. "I suppose I should go check on the other little hellions, and I can leave you two to speak alone here. I'll make sure the others don't bother you."

My mind whirled with questions as I tapped my foot waiting for Mrs. Sanderson to leave us alone already. What would a TV star want with me? *Hitched* was the hottest reality show on television, not to mention it had been the show that revealed the supernatural world to the human one. Kimmie-Jayne had been a normal human girl sent on a dating show with twenty-five eligible bachelors. The big twist was that they were all supernatural. In the end, she'd chosen one to marry after finding out the truth about everything alongside the rest of America. It was freakin' nuts.

Mrs. Sanderson extended her hand, squeezing Kimmie-Jayne's. "It was a pleasure to meet you, Ms. Starr. I'm truly a fan of your work, and I can't wait to see your next movie."

"Thank you. I really appreciate that." She smiled, and it actually reached her eyes. She didn't seem like one of those typical fake Hollywood actresses—either that or she was a *really good* actor.

Mrs. Sanderson reluctantly trudged up the stairs, her head spinning back to look at us until she finally disappeared around the corner.

"She seems nice."

I rolled my eyes. "Yeah, she's a real barrel of laughs."

Kimmie-Jayne moved toward the couch and folded down, motioning to the spot beside her.

My eyes widened, but I just couldn't get my feet unstuck from the floor. Seeing her in my living room was too insane to get my head wrapped around. I was totally fangirling. Wait until Jay heard this. He'd never believe it.

When I remained frozen to the spot, Kimmie-Jayne loosed a breath and pinned me with her clear-blue gaze. "You must be wondering what I'm doing here."

I nodded quickly, tucking my arms over my chest.

"I think you should sit down for this."

Nothing good ever came after those words. I crept over to the opposite side of the tattered couch and sank down.

Kimmie-Jayne fiddled with her fingers in her lap before finally looking up at me. "There's no easy way to say this so I'm just going to spit it out. I'm your half-sister."

My jaw dropped as all the air siphoned from my lungs. I urged my brain to put together a sentence, but the words jumbled in my mind. "How? What?" I spewed out the only words I could muster. I didn't even know who my biological parents were so how did this Hollywood celebrity?

"It's crazy, I know. Believe it or not I was in your shoes just over a year ago. I only found out who my biological father was while I was filming *Hitched*."

My brain synapses suddenly started firing again. "Wait a second. Your father is President Lazaris." A week after the season finale, the president made the shocking confession.

She nodded, snagging her full lip between her teeth.

"Please tell me we share the same mom."

Kimmie-Jayne shook her head. "Nope. President Lazaris is your father too—which is how I found you."

"Seriously?" I sucked in a breath, my mind swirling with this unbelievable information. "So he sent you here to come get me?

I'm going to meet him?" Hope fluttered in my chest, excitement spilling through every inch of me. After all these years of imagining what my biological parents were like, I couldn't believe I was finally going to meet my dad—the flippin' President of the United States!

Her expression darkened, the smile pulling at her lips fading. "Not exactly." She drew in a breath, clasping her hands together. "There's more... You see, our dad, he's not exactly who he seems to be."

"Huh?"

"Oh man, I'm so bad at this. I'm sorry. Now I know how my mom felt when she told me." Kimmie-Jayne reached out and squeezed my hand. "Our dad's real name is Garrix and he's a warlock—a really powerful one that can change his appearance to look like anyone he wishes. He assumed the persona of Vice-President and then when President Turner died last year, he took over for him. It was all part of dad's plan for the great supernatural revelation."

What the freak? This was absolutely insane. The president of the U.S. is a supe? I shook my head furiously. "It can't be. This is a joke, right?" I jumped up and searched the corners of the shabby living room. "This is some sort of new reality TV show, right? Where are the cameras?"

Kimmie-Jayne took my hand and pulled me back to the couch. "I'm sorry, Luna. I can't imagine how hard this must be for you, but I swear it's the truth."

I slumped back against the sofa, leaning my head on the worn cushion. "So my dad is a warlock and my half-sister is half-warlock?"

She nodded. "Technically, I'm considered a witch; only men can be warlocks. And don't forget I'm married to a dragon shifter too."

"Oh, right." Her words suddenly registered as my hazy brain began to process the information. "Holy bagels, I'm a supe."

"You are. That's why I'm here. You see, our father is kind of what you'd call a ladies' man. He's had quite a few affairs with humans over the years. With his most recent proclamation about half-bloods—"

I cut her off, my brain finally fully functioning. "No sugar! You're here to send me off to some supe school? That's why you came to find me." A hint of disappointment swirled in my chest.

"That's one of the reasons. The other is that I really wanted to get to know my half-sister." She gave me a warm smile and though I wasn't sure I believed her, I wanted to. My whole life I'd wished for family. Be careful what you wish for, right? And I'd thought this birthday would be just as boring and sad as all the ones before.

I wiped my sweaty palms on my jeans and inhaled a slow breath. "So what happens now?"

"Tomorrow I take you to Darkhen Academy."

CHAPTER 3

I t took me less than half an hour to pack all of my earthly
possessions into two duffel bags and a backpack. *Sad, I
know.* Kimmie-Jayne had returned first thing the next
morning to escort me to this mysterious supernatural academy. She sat at the end of my bunk bed watching quietly.
Every so often she'd make a comment about a cute shirt or
nice boots. She was definitely trying—I'd give her that much,
because there was nothing cute or nice about anything I
owned. Not compared to the fancy things I'd seen her wear
on *Hitched*.

About a million questions zipped around my mind but with
all of them fighting to get out, I hadn't been able to ask my half-
sister a single question. I'd spent half the night up trying to
process everything she'd told me yesterday. My father was a
warlock; more than that, he was the freakin' president. And I
was part supernatural—a half-blood like a tiny percentage of
the human population. Apparently, they hadn't done such a
fantastic job of keeping our worlds separate before the big
supernatural revelation.

"How come I don't have any powers?" The question surged

to the surface, winning out against all the others battling for attention.

Kimmie-Jayne shrugged. "From what I understand, sometimes magic skips a generation in half-bloods like us." She shot me a wry smile. "Or other times, it just takes awhile to make itself known."

"Do you have any special abilities?" Her half-blood status had never been revealed on the show. According to the rest of America, Kimmie-Jayne Starr was an innocent human girl thrown into a supernatural world who just happened to fall in love with a gorgeous supe.

"I didn't until about a year ago. Right around my twenty-first birthday I started getting visions. It was also right after I arrived in Azar. Sometimes I wonder if that's what triggered it."

"So I could get visions too?" Images of me seeing the winning lottery numbers and scoring the million-dollar jackpot danced across my mind. How cool would that be?

"Maybe. Our father has a wide variety of powers, and you never know which one you'll inherit."

"Or none at all." I gnawed on my lower lip, suddenly realizing I'd be disappointed if I didn't get any.

I zipped up the final bag and glanced up. "I guess that's it."

"Oh, you might want to keep a winter coat out."

I glanced out the window at the bright sun. It was nearly seventy degrees out, and I'd just swapped out my sweaters for sundresses. "It's going to be cold in Azar?"

She nodded. "It will be where Darkhen Academy is located."

"And where is that exactly?"

Her lips twisted, and I could almost see the gears grinding in her head as she considered answering my question. I'd always been good at reading people and so far, my half-sister hadn't given me a reason not to trust her. "It's in the Fae realm—the Winter Court to be exact."

Yuck, winter again? I yanked my only thick coat from my

duffel and tossed it on top of the bag. Darkhen better be pretty freakin' cool. I couldn't believe I never had to go back to Crestwood High again. Kimmie-Jayne said my graduation would be taken care of, and I didn't have to take my finals—score! Jay was going to be so jealous.

Crap, Jay. I couldn't leave without saying goodbye to him. I never would've survived four years of high school without him. "K.J., can I call you that?" Kimmie-Jayne was just way too long.

A big smile lit up her face. "Sure. It's actually what my favorite uncle calls me."

"Great. So um, do you think we could stop by my friend's house before we go?" I had no idea how we were even getting to Darkhen Academy. I'd heard there were portals to Azar, but their locations weren't exactly common knowledge. The two governments were doing their best to monitor all travelers between the two worlds.

She glanced at the clock over my bed and grimaced. "I'm sorry, Luna, but we're kind of on a time crunch. We're meeting the headmaster at Darkhen in an hour. He's a busy guy as you can imagine, and I'd hate to keep him waiting."

My shoulders drooped. I had no idea when I'd see Jay again. With how tight security was between the realms, I doubted I was allowed visitors.

K.J.'s eyes lit up. "I'll tell you what; I promise once you're all settled in, I'll bring you back here myself so you can see your friend."

"Okay, thanks." I slung the duffel bags over each shoulder, tossing my heavy coat over my arm and Kimmie-Jayne surprised me by grabbing my backpack. She definitely didn't act like a normal celebrity.

"Fenix is meeting us outside. We can let him carry the heavy stuff." She winked, and my stomach dropped.

"F-Fenix Skyraider? Like the Alpha of all the dragon shifters in Azar?" I froze on the top step of the staircase. My body broke out into an all-out sweatball at the thought of the drop-dead gorgeous bachelor. I'd forced Jay to watch every single episode with me. Poor guy had to sit by and watch me drool over the ridiculously hot bachelors on the show. Before Kimmie-Jayne picked the final two, I was totally team Ryder— a breathtakingly gorgeous demon bad boy. But once I'd seen her and Fenix together, I couldn't deny she'd made the right choice.

"Yup—my husband." She laughed.

Heat crawled up my neck and settled over my cheeks. *Way to go, Luna.* Nothing like coveting your half-sister's hubby to make things super awkward. I swallowed down the embarrassment, unable to stop the next words from popping out of my mouth as I continued down the creaky old staircase. "I can't believe you got to ride a dragon! And fly with an angel and spend time at Winter Court with the prince... It was all so unbelievably cool."

She smirked. "Yeah, I guess it was. Except for when I was kidnapped and almost killed a few times."

Oh my... what was wrong with me? Sometimes I thought my foot should be permanently shoved inside my mouth instead of dangling at the end of my leg. K.J. had almost died on numerous occasions thanks to some dark forces that tried to sabotage the show. "I'm sorry, that was a really stupid thing to say. When I get nervous, I babble."

She squeezed my shoulder as we stopped at the door. "You don't need to apologize. I can only imagine what you're feeling right now. I kind of dropped a pretty huge bombshell on you."

The weird thing was how not weird it all seemed. I should've been freaking out right now. My dad was a flippin' warlock, and I was about to get sent off to some paranormal prep in a magical world. Why wasn't I freaking out? I considered as my half-sister held the door open for me. Maybe it was because my life kinda sucked, and I always wished there was more out there for me. And now there was—a hell of a lot more.

We walked out, and I barely looked back at the home in which I'd spent the last four years of my life. Mrs. Sanderson had run out for groceries so I didn't even get a chance to say goodbye. I left a note though. There wasn't much love between us, but things could've been worse. Much worse from what I'd heard from other foster kids.

Speaking of bombshells, a dark, tall handsome one stood in front of the walkway as we stepped off the porch. Holy dragon hottie! Fenix was more gorgeous in real life than on TV.

Golden irises pierced mine, a shock of dark hair tumbling over his forehead. "Hey there. You must be Luna." A cute smile pulled at his lips as he extended his hand, and heat coursed through my veins. *OMG, stop that!* This was my brother-in-law for crap sakes.

I placed my hand in his and he gave it a firm squeeze, all the bones in my fingers scrunching together. I tried not to wince, but Fenix's expression fell and he quickly released me.

"Sorry about that." He rubbed the back of his neck, a light crimson dusting his cheeks and making him even hotter. "I guess I've been spending too much time in Draeko lately. I've forgotten the lighter touch necessary with humans."

I shook out my hand and tucked it behind my back. "No worries." I was lucky my brain was still able to form sentences being this close to the steamy bachelor.

"Here, let me take those for you." Fenix grabbed both my duffel bags and turned toward the train station.

"I hope you're okay with a little walk?" asked Kimmie-Jayne.

"We're walking all the way to Azar?"

They both laughed. "No, we just need to grab a train into the city," explained my half-sister. "The nearest portal is in Grand Central Station."

"Seriously?" That's so not what I would've expected.

Fenix nodded and took K.J.'s hand. "We could fly"—he tipped his head up to the sky— "but I don't think that would go over well in these parts."

My eyes widened, and I couldn't help but bounce on my toes. "Oh please, can we?"

He laughed, his big chest rumbling beneath the tight black shirt. "Don't worry, you'll get to do plenty of that at Darkhen. I happen to know a dragon shifter or two I can introduce you to."

Excitement spilled through my veins like a live wire. I couldn't believe this was really happening. I was about to travel to another realm where dragons, faeries, witches and warlocks roamed the streets like nothing. More than that, I was about to live with and go to school with them. I didn't know much about Darkhen—I added it to the list of a million questions to ask— but I assumed I'd be learning to use magic with other half-bloods. It was all unreal.

The train ride passed in a blur with all the wild thoughts clamoring around in my brain. K.J. and Fenix told me a little about Darkhen Academy, but I still had so many questions. My bio dad, Garrix, was a bit of a mystery even to my half-sister apparently.

"We're working on our relationship," said Kimmie-Jayne. "Garrix isn't an easy man to get to know." Fenix squeezed her knee, a reassuring smile on his handsome face. Man, they were as cute and in love in real life as on TV. A part of me wondered if it had only been for the cameras, but seeing them here together wiped out every doubt I'd had.

I still couldn't believe K.J. was my half-sister. I covertly glanced at her from across the aisle. We definitely shared a similar shade of blonde hair, but whereas her eyes were bright blue mine were a darker hue. And she was like supermodel gorgeous. I was okay, but definitely not Hollywood material.

"I'm sure Garrix will come visit you as soon as he gets the

opportunity." Kimmie-Jayne's sweet voice pulled me from my inner thoughts.

"Um, yeah sure, whatever." I shrugged nonchalantly. If this guy hadn't cared to come see me once in eighteen years, I didn't need him either. "The man's the president so I'm sure he's got more important things to do than meet one of his many offspring." How many of us were there anyway?

Kimmie-Jayne opened her mouth as if to say more when the sharp keening sound of the brakes cut her off. The train slowed and we pulled into the tunnel, darkness blotting out the windows.

"This is our stop," said Fenix. He stood and grabbed my duffel bags from the overhead rack.

"I can take them." I felt bad letting him carry all my stuff. Not that there was that much, but still.

"No way, Luna. I got the bags."

K.J. ran her hand over his bulging bicep and smirked. "Yeah, let the guy get his workout in for the day."

"If you say so." I threw my backpack over my shoulder and followed them off the train. "So now where to? Is there a special magical train that takes us to Azar?" I totally felt like I'd just stumbled into a Harry Potter movie.

"Not exactly." Fenix led the way down the platform, but instead of following the hordes of people heading up toward ground level, he pivoted in the opposite direction.

He led us through the dimly lit corridor until we reached what looked like a dead end. He stopped in front of a gray cinder block wall and whispered, "Apertum." The stones creaked and groaned before shifting and falling away. I stared with my mouth hanging open.

"After you." Kimmie-Jayne motioned me forward, but my feet were planted to the ground.

Fenix ticked his head through the magical doorway. "Maybe you should go first, treasure."

"Right, of course." Kimmie-Jayne walked through and I followed after her, willing my legs not to embarrass me again.

We emerged onto another platform, nearly identical to the one we'd just arrived on. The rumbling of trains passing overhead filled the uneasy silence as I trailed behind them.

"Well, this is it." Fenix stopped and peered down the dark tunnel. A headlight flashed in the distance, the tremor of an arriving train making my knees tremble.

"You should put on your coat now," said Kimmie-Jayne, eyeing the old black jacket slung over my arm.

I shrugged into it and glanced down the dark tunnel. "So we just get on the train that's coming?"

K.J. shook her head. "There's no train actually coming. It's an illusion to keep intruders away."

I arched a brow. "So how do we get to Azar?"

"Jump." Fenix's lips twitched.

I stared down at the six-foot drop to the train tracks below. A rat skittered across the railway, sending a wave of goose bumps rippling over my flesh. "You've got to be joking."

"There's a hidden portal," explained Kimmie-Jayne. "When you jump you'll get sucked right in. It's kind of like leaping into a vat of jell-o. Totally painless, I promise."

I peered down the black tunnel and cringed. The train horn blasted in the not-so-far distance, the bright headlight flashing ominously. I'm going to jump and get squashed by a freaking train—that's what was going to happen.

"Um, I don't know about this, you guys." I tightened the straps on my backpack, clenching on for dear life.

K.J. held out her hand and threw me a reassuring smile. "Come on, we can go together."

My knees rattled, threatening to give. Every nerve in my body screamed at me not to take her hand. This was insane—jumping onto railroad tracks with a train approaching? Totally certifiable. But then again, until a year ago, dragon shifters, faeries, and demons were all things that had only existed in fairy tales.

What the hell, right? I took her hand, wrapping my fingers tightly around hers. For someone that didn't trust easily, I was surprised how much Kimmie-Jayne put me at ease. "Okay, let's do this."

"On the count of three," said Fenix. "One..."

I sucked in a breath.

"Two..."

My fingers clenched around K.J.'s hand as a horn blasted in the distance.

"Three!"

I squeezed my eyes shut and jumped.

CHAPTER 4

Yup, it was just like what I'd imagined diving into a vat full of jell-o would feel like. A thick, viscous liquid slid over my skin cocooning every inch of me. I opened my eyes but could barely see to the tip of my nose in the endless black. My body lurched backward like it was hurtling down the sharp descent of a rollercoaster but in super slow motion. Only the feel of Kimmie-Jayne's fingers wrapped around mine grounded me from the never-ending free fall.

Suddenly everything sped up, and a brilliant light bathed the interminable darkness. Squeezing my eyes shut from the blinding flash, I tumbled out of a crack in the atmosphere and landed face first in powdery snow.

"Son of a biscuit!" My fingers dug into the softest snow I'd ever felt as I pushed myself to my knees. Towering pine trees encroached upon the small white clearing we'd landed in. The glistening snow covered the giant pines, catching the brilliant rays of the dipping sun.

Fenix held out his hand to help me up, a small smile tugging at his lips. "Are you okay?"

"Does a bruised ego count?" Somehow he and my half-sister had managed to land on their feet.

He chuckled as I brushed the snow off my jacket. I was suddenly very thankful Kimmie-Jayne had suggested I wear it. My teeth chattered, and I hugged my arms around myself.

My half-sister's gaze lingered over me, the line between her brows deepening. "Don't worry, you'll be issued a uniform coat when we get to Darkhen—along with shirts, sweaters, pants and skirts."

"Seriously? I have to wear a uniform? I thought this was like a university."

"It is, but you'll see it's not so bad. They're kind of cute. I wished I'd had a uniform at community college." She squeezed my hand and turned me onto a path between the endless rows of pines and evergreens.

"It makes it much easier to roll out of bed right before class and throw on a uniform than having to pick what to wear." Fenix winked.

"Yes, take it from my husband, the expert in fashion."

I smirked, then turned to scan the forest, searching for something—anything—in the vast wilderness. "So how far do we have to walk till we get there?" I could already feel icicles forming on my toes. My beloved Converse weren't really made for trudging through snow.

"Just a few more steps," answered K.J.

Steps? We were in the middle of a frozen tundra. "Huh?" I stared at the thick copse of trees in front of us.

"Darkhen Academy is warded for the students' protection," she continued. "Just like at Grand Central, we don't want just anyone getting in."

"But who'd want to hurt some college kids?"

Fenix and Kimmie-Jayne exchanged a furtive glance. "It's just precautionary. The headmaster likes to err on the side of caution," she explained.

Fenix snorted. "Damn, overprotective angel—"

She elbowed him in the gut, cutting off the rest of his grumblings and we trudged on. The tip of my nose throbbed, my icy breath swirling with each exhale. If we didn't get there soon, I was certain hypothermia would set in. Why would the faeries want to live in such a freezing climate? I'd always pictured them as lithe creatures in light airy clothing, not bulky giants in thick fur coats to protect against the frigid temperatures.

"We're here!" Kimmie-Jayne paused in front of a massive pine.

Thank the freakin' faeries!

She muttered a few words much too quickly for my ear to make out, and a scanner appeared, built right into the bark of the tree.

My eyes popped open, and I inched closer. "What the heck is that?"

"It's the best of both our worlds," answered Fenix. "High-tech human technology paired with good old witch magic."

A red light blazed from the scanner, running over my half-sister's face.

"Top of the line biometric recognition software," he whispered.

"Kimmie-Jayne Starr," a robotic voice droned. "Identity confirmed."

The dense forest stretching out before us shimmered and swirled until it completely fell away.

My jaw unlocked like one of those crazy snakes able to consume animals four times their size.

A ten-foot wrought iron gate soared before my eyes, the name Darkhen Academy atop a fancy crest fashioned right into the thick black metal. It loomed over us like a dark totem daring us to enter its hallowed halls.

Finally tearing my eyes away from the imposing gate, my gaze settled on the school itself. Or maybe fortress or castle were better terms for it. Massive gray stone walls soared high into the darkening sky, spiraling turrets and ominous towers shooting up against the deep green forest backdrop. The sprawling building looked like it had been torn out of medieval times with its arched windows and candle-lit torches. It was eerily beautiful.

A flag flew over the immense structure, jutting out from the tallest tower, its maroon, green and black hues whipping in the wind. The official flag of Azar.

My half-sister seemed almost as entranced by the school as I was. She finally tore her gaze away and swallowed, turning to me. "Welcome to Darkhen Academy, Luna."

"Thanks," I sputtered, my mouth gone completely dry.

The massive gate creaked open, revealing two men in black military uniforms. Each had a sword hung at their hip and a menacing twinkle in their eye. They nodded at our approach, clearing the way for us to enter.

"Pretty tight security, huh?" A nervous giggle bubbled out.

"It's for the students' safety," assured Fenix.

I wasn't so sure about that. Goose bumps puckered my skin. Once I was in would I ever able to get out? *Dammit.* I knew I should've said goodbye to Jay in person. The quick text I'd sent him didn't go into any of the important details. Now Mrs. Sanderson was the only one who knew where I was, and she wouldn't care less if I disappeared into a hidden magical school in the land of the Fae never to be seen again.

Why had I been so trusting?

Kimmie-Jayne appeared at my side as we trudged up the winding walkway to the entrance. She squeezed my shoulder and shot me a reassuring smile. "Relax, Luna. It's not as terrifying as it seems, I swear."

We walked up the stone steps, and my eyes landed on the pair of gargoyles perched on the ramparts on either side of the massive oak door. Their sharp-toothed grins sent shivers down my spine. Their cold gray eyes followed us as we neared the entryway. Before Fenix lifted his hand to knock, the door swung open.

A long, crooked nose appeared through the opening before revealing the rest of the tiny man. A pair of beady black eyes glanced up at us, thin lips twisted into a half-sneer. I wasn't tall, and I towered over the elderly, hunched figure before us. Two wrinkly hands emerged from the folds of his graying robes, and he motioned for us to enter. "The headmaster has been waiting," he grumbled before scurrying down the dark corridor, leaving us with no other choice but to follow.

Fenix shrugged and led the way behind the little man. Tufts of white hair shot out from the back of his head, and I couldn't help but stare at the pointy ears protruding from the balding sides. Kimmie-Jayne's heeled boots slapped the stone floor, echoing in the quiet corridor.

This wasn't like any school I'd ever been to... where were the rowdy kids? Slamming locker doors? The place seemed deserted.

We turned the corner and the hallway split, leading to a pair of doors. A golden sign hung over the one on the right with the word Administration stamped across the top in bold letters. The opposite sign said Elias P. Darkhen Hall.

A buzz of voices seeped through the thick door of the latter. My heart rate picked up. On the other side of that door were my future classmates—faeries, demons, vampires, witches and who knew what else. I wiped my sweaty palms against my jeans as our guide opened the Administration door, motioning for us to enter.

He ushered us through another hallway before stopping at thick oak double doors. The words Headmaster loomed over me. Man, I hoped this guy was better than Principal Greenfield. We'd gotten off on the wrong foot when I accidentally T.P.'d his car on freshman prank day. He'd hated me ever since. Who knew honey-coated toilet paper could do so much damage?

A rumbly voice from within shouted, "Come in," and our guide opened the doors just wide enough for us to sneak through. A hulking blonde in a suit sat at the massive mahogany desk in the corner, his wide shoulders bent over a laptop. Arched stained-glass windows made up the wall behind him, depicting flying dragons, freakish horned beasts and angels locked in battle. They stretched all the way up to the dark mahogany rafters crisscrossing the soaring ceiling.

When the man finally lifted his blue-eyed gaze to us, my heart stopped.

"Cillian, from *Hitched?*" The words flew out of my mouth before I could stop them.

He only spared me a moment's glance before turning his attention to my half-sister. The brilliant blue of his irises intensified, a heavenly glow illuminating them from the inside.

Sweet angels in heaven. How could I have not recognized him? Cillian had made it to the final two. He'd been this close to marrying my half-sister. Instead of a dragon shifter for a brother-in-law, I could have had this divine being—an honest to goodness guardian angel.

As all these thoughts scattered around in my mind, Cillian practically leapt across the room, pulling K.J. into a hug. A low growl reverberated in Fenix's throat until the two parted.

I fidgeted with my backpack straps, suddenly feeling like the fourth wheel on a very awkward vehicle.

"Cillian, I want you to meet my sister, Luna Hallows." Kimmie-Jayne's voice broke the uncomfortable silence, and I hazarded a look up at one of the most beautiful men I'd ever seen. Although the angel was older than dirt, he looked to be in his mid-twenties max.

I couldn't help the twinge of jealousy bubbling up inside me. K.J. had gotten to pick her future husband from some of the most gorgeous men on earth. And more than that, they'd all actually cared about her. Risked their lives for her even. My two high school boyfriends were just looking to get laid. Boy were they disappointed. Just because I acted a certain way didn't mean *I acted a certain way*.

Cillian finally turned his gaze to me, and a smile lit up his finely sculpted jaw. Extending his hand, his big fingers closed around mine. "It's a pleasure to finally meet you, Luna. Your sister went through a lot to find you. I hope that you'll make yourself at home here at Darkhen Academy."

I stared dumbstruck at the handsome angel, the feel of his warm skin against mine sending tingles up my arm. "Th-thank you," I muttered.

"She's kind of a fan of the show," said Fenix, rolling his eyes.

Oh geez, I sounded like a total fangirl. When he released my hand, I sucked in a breath, willing my erratic heartbeats to return to a more normal pace. I swallowed, moistening my dry throat so I could actually speak. "I'm really excited to be here." And terrified.

Cillian's jaw tensed, and he bent down to my eye-level. "I need to make something clear from the beginning. Since you're from the human world, you know me best as Cillian from *Hitched*. While the show was popular here in Azar, it wasn't anywhere near what it was in the U.S. As such, I need you to treat me with the respect you would a headmaster, okay?"

I nodded quickly, and he shot me a reassuring grin.

"Great then. We shouldn't have any problems."

"One more thing," said K.J. lifting her finger, "we should probably keep your—our father's identity between us for now. Not many Azarians know who the President really is, and we don't need any extra attention on him or Luna."

"Agreed." Cillian crossed his arms over his chest. "The fewer people who know who Luna's father is the better."

Kimmie-Jayne's hand landed on my shoulder, and I jumped.

"Don't worry, Cillian will take good care of you. Just like he did with me." She threw him a meaningful look, and I swear the imposing angel melted under her gaze.

A cool mask slipped back over the headmaster's face, and he turned to the little man that had brought us in. "Darby, will you take Fenix to see what we discussed earlier?"

The dragon shifter's eyes narrowed. "Must we take care of this now?"

Cillian nodded, his jaw set in a tight line. "I'd prefer you see it as soon as possible."

Fenix grumbled but followed Darby out all the same.

"Is everything okay?" K.J. asked.

"Nothing we can't handle." This time Cillian's smile didn't quite reach his eyes. "Come sit. We have a lot to talk about." He motioned to the two high-back leather chairs in front of his desk.

I followed Kimmie-Jayne and sank into the supple leather, dropping my backpack on the floor. Without the straps to keep my fingers busy, I clasped my hands together to keep from fidgeting as Cillian pulled out a maroon folder. Emblazoned across the front was the Darkhen Academy crest inked in green and black. It was the same as the one across the gate, but now close up I could actually make out the details. It was divided into seven sections—each one with a supernatural creature—a dragon, faery, angel, and a few others I couldn't quite make out before Cillian's voice drew my attention away.

"Are you familiar with the seven houses of Azar?" he asked.

Kimmie-Jayne shook her head. "I doubt they teach that sort of thing in human public school, Cillian."

I confirmed her guess with a headshake of my own.

"Right, then. We'll start with the basics." He sat back in his chair, his blue eyes turning pensive. "The seven main houses of Azar are: the Fae Court, the Brotherhood of Dragons, the Coven Council, the Sons of Heaven, the Shifter Pack, the

Ocean Realm and the Royal Vampires. All pretty self explanatory, right?"

I nodded when he paused.

"In addition, all the smaller supernatural communities elect one member to represent their minority interests. So eight members in total on the Etrian Assembly—each in theory equal. The Etrian Assembly is our governing body. Kind of like your Congress."

I pointed at the crest on the folder. "You said there were eight, but there are only seven represented here."

Cillian's brows furrowed. "As I mentioned, the eighth group is in the minority, and unfortunately not well represented. The Underworld, the final realm in Azar was also excluded. When the Darkhen family founded this academy, they chose to omit them from the official crest. But we do have a few minority members in attendance. None from the Underworld, however."

"Who are the Darkhens?"

"A very wealthy family of the Fae Winter Court. They're cousins to the Wintersbee royal family. You are familiar with Elrian Wintersbee, king of the Winter Court?"

My head bobbed. K.J. tensed beside me. Elrian was one of the final five bachelors on *Hitched*. He'd left the show before the second-to-last elimination when his father, the king, was murdered. He went from prince to king over night and chose his duties over remaining on the show. Judging by my sister's reaction, things still seemed strained between her and the new Fae king.

"Anyway, long before President Lazaris's ruling on supernatural academies came into effect, Darkhen had been providing instruction to the best and brightest young people of Azar. I only recently took on the role as headmaster last year." He paused, glancing up at Kimmie-Jayne. "I'm bound by duty, and now that duty has brought me here."

There seemed more to their unspoken exchange but with all the thoughts bouncing around in my mind, it was hard to focus.

"The Academy is divided by houses," he continued. "There are seven floors in the dormitories, each one corresponding to its respective supernatural grouping. Classes are mixed, but students each focus on their given magical ability plus choose an additional one to hone."

What if I didn't have any magical abilities? "Where do the humans live?"

K.J. shifted beside me, uncrossing her legs. "Well, you're the first..."

"What?" My eyes widened like some deranged cartoon character. "I thought the president said all half-bloods had to go to schools like this."

"They do, but Darkhen is a bit different. As Cillian mentioned, it wasn't built due to the mandate." She glanced at the angel, clearly looking for help.

He folded his hands on the desk, loosing a breath. "We're considering allowing humans to attend in the future. Let's say you're a test run."

The pieces of this crazy puzzle quickly assembled in my mind. "It's because of who my father is, right? That's the only reason I'm here."

"Only the best for Garrix's offspring." Cillian smirked.

Anxiety bubbled in my gut like one of those old school lava lamps. Being surrounded by supernaturals I'd expected, but I never thought I'd be the only human—or half-human anyway. How could I ever fit in a school full of elite supes?

He pushed a sheet of paper in front of me, the black letters and numbers taking shape to form my dreaded class schedule. "This is only tentative. We'll see how you do and can shuffle things around at any time. As I said, this is all new for us too. The rest of the students follow a predetermined schedule based on their kind. They then choose a secondary path of specialty."

I stared at the class list, feeling like I'd just fallen into the pages of a twisted fairy tale.

Potions and Poisons
Defensive Magic
Flying and Shifting 101
Spellcraft
Combat

You've got to be *shifting* me... "But I don't have a specialty."

"Maybe not yet," said K.J. glancing around the room, "but I have faith something will pop up. I'm sure being here will inspire something buried deep inside."

The only thing this creepy academy was inspiring so far was terror.

The doors to the office whipped open, slamming against the stone walls, and I spun as my heart leapt up my throat.

Bottomless onyx eyes bored into me for a millisecond before turning to my half-sister. Every single nerve in my body tingled to life for the moment his eyes were locked on mine.

A wry smile pulled at a pair of perfect lips. He ate up the distance between us, his intense gaze bouncing between my sister and me. A flash of yellow eclipsed his dark irises before he settled his attention on K.J. "So the rumors were true... You really are here, little minx."

CHAPTER 5

Holy hot bachelors! How was it possible to have so many gorgeous men under one roof? My mouth hung open as Ryder Strong wrapped my sister in a hug. It was him, it was really him... the demon bad boy that Kimmie-Jayne managed to wrap around her little finger on *Hitched*.

My eyes raked over his thick tattooed biceps peeking out from under his tight black t-shirt. His hair was closer cut than it had been while on the show, short gelled spikes completing his bad boy look. My gaze traveled down his broad chest to the tight dark blue jeans slung low on his hips. Damn, he really was every bit as sinful in person as I'd imagined.

I was so consumed with ogling him, I didn't realize it when he started speaking to me.

"Hey kid, you got a little drool right here." Ryder pointed at his chin, a smirk tugging at his full lips and revealing an irresistible dimple.

Blazing heat shot up my neck, spreading over my cheeks and ears. I swung my hair around hoping to hide behind the blonde curtain as embarrassment steamrolled over me.

"Don't be an ass, Ryder," growled Cillian.

I'd almost forgotten the angel was here.

Ryder approached me, a silly grin still lighting up his sculpted cheekbones. "Relax, uncle, I was just messing with her. After meeting you, I figured she'd need a little comic relief."

Kimmie-Jayne moved beside him, elbowing him in the side. "Ryder, meet Luna Hallows, my half-sister."

His pitch eyes roamed over me, scorching heat leaving its mark over every inch. After the longest seconds of my life, he extended a hand, wrapping his warm fingers around mine. "Always a pleasure to meet another one of Garrix's beautiful offspring." He glanced from me to my sister and back again. "I'll give him one thing, your father definitely knows how to pick 'em. Your sister is hot—"

"Don't even think about it, Ryder," Kimmie-Jayne and Cillian shouted in unison.

O.M.G., please kill me now. I wrapped my arms across my chest, hoping to keep myself from disintegrating into a pile of goo.

"What? I was joking..." He winked, and my heart flip-flopped. "How old are you anyway, kid?"

I forced my eyes to meet his and willed my lips to form words. "Eighteen."

His dark brow quirked up, his lips curling into a grin. "She's only a few years younger than you, little minx."

Kimmie-Jayne smacked him in the shoulder. "Hands off, Ryder. I mean it. She's here to study and learn, not get involved with someone like you."

"Ouch!" He made a stabbing motion into his chest.

"This is a moot point," interjected Cillian, fire lighting up his brilliant blue eyes. "Faculty and student relations are strictly forbidden. My dear nephew is well aware of our policies."

Faculty? Ryder is a teacher here? My heart fluttered at the thought of seeing him every day.

My new instructor raised his hands, grinning. "Everyone relax. Geez, I can't have any fun around here."

Cillian shook his head and snorted. "Well, since you're here, perhaps you can make yourself useful for once." He eyed his desk, the stacks of papers layered like the leaning tower of Pisa and shuddered. "I was going to give them the grand tour, but since you don't apparently have anything better to do, you can take them."

Ryder checked his watch. "Fine, but you're going to owe me an extra long lunch tomorrow."

It was only lunchtime? I rubbed my eyes, the lids suddenly heavy. I felt like it was almost bedtime.

As if reading my thoughts, Kimmie-Jayne chimed in. "It's a five-hour time difference here in Azar. You might be a little jet-lagged at first, but you'll get used to it in no time."

"Right."

Cillian handed Ryder a sheet of paper, and I noticed my name stamped across the top. "This will keep you on track for the tour and her rooming assignment is included."

"Yes, sir." Ryder saluted the headmaster, and I stifled the giggle from bubbling out. After seeing the pair interacting on the TV show, I was beyond surprised to see them working together. Ryder wasn't just any old demon; he was Lucifer's son —yes, that's right, as in the devil and the first fallen angel. Cillian and Lucifer were brothers so that made Ryder his nephew. My new instructor and I had at least one thing in common—we both had supernatural dads who loved the human ladies. Ryder probably had more half-siblings out there than I did.

"Okay, let's get this show on the road." He turned toward the double doors, and K.J. and I followed.

"If you need anything, just ask, Luna," Cillian called out as we crossed the threshold.

"Thanks," I answered over my shoulder.

As soon as we turned the corner out of the headmaster's office, Fenix and Darby appeared. The dragon shifter's eyes were dim, the brilliant gold opaque against his dark pupils. And something told me it wasn't only because of the demon standing next to me.

"I'm sorry, but we're going to have to cut this visit short." He looked to me then to his wife. "Something's come up that requires my immediate attention in Draeko."

"But we haven't even toured the academy yet," Kimmie-Jayne grumbled. "I don't want to leave Luna unsettled."

Ryder's arm came around my shoulders, and it was like a live wire snapping and crackling over my skin. I resisted the urge to shiver under his touch. His musky, sandalwood scent swirled around me, wrapping me in its spicy embrace. "Don't worry, little minx, I'll take care of the kid."

She rolled her eyes, stepping closer. "That's what I'm afraid of."

I stepped out from under his arm even though my traitorous body screamed at me not to. "I'll be fine, Kimmie-Jayne. I'm *not* a kid, and I appreciate you coming with me this far." I shot Ryder a snarky glare for good measure. I wasn't a kid. I was eighteen and had practically raised myself since Mrs. Hallows passed away when I was thirteen.

"I'm really sorry, Luna," added Fenix. "I wanted to introduce you to your new roommate, my little sister, Cinder."

A hazy image of a raven-haired girl with golden eyes scampered across my mind. We'd gotten to meet Fenix's family on *Hitched* when Kimmie-Jayne went to each of their homes. She'd seemed sweet.

"You'll love Cinder, mini minx. She's nothing like her brother." Ryder winked at Fenix, who shot him a good growl in return.

"Keep away from my sister, demon." The dragon's pupils elongated, the golden glow around the dark slits intensifying.

"Man, you guys are totally going to give Luna the wrong idea about me."

Kimmie-Jayne leaned in and pulled Ryder into a hug. She whispered something in his ear, and his teasing grin disappeared.

"Always," he muttered in return.

K.J. moved to me next, and I was surprised by the unexpected emotion that clogged my throat as her arms wrapped around me. "Take care of yourself, Luna, and I promise to come check in on you as soon as I can. If you need anything, go straight to Cillian—or even Ryder. You're going to do great here; I know you will."

"Thanks..." I leaned into her embrace, my tense body softening. "Thanks for everything." I'd only known my half-sister for two days now, but somehow it seemed much longer.

Fenix patted me on the shoulder with a reassuring smile. "Cinder will show you the ropes. You're in good hands here at Darkhen."

"Thanks, Fenix."

They turned to leave, and I couldn't help my gaze lingering on their backs as they faded into the darkening corridor.

"You ready for the tour, mini minx?"

My brows slammed together, not too fond of my new nickname, especially since it was a derivative of my half-sister's. "Just call me Luna, okay?"

"Whatever you say, kid."

He opened the door labeled Darkhen Hall, and I stepped through. Every muscle in my body tensed. I could feel it in my bones. Everything was about to change, and there was no going back now.

CHAPTER 6

S tudents spilled across the wood-paneled corridor, moving in packs. The high, arched ceilings multiplied every whisper and each footstep until it reverberated in my skull. Though the undergrads all wore the same crimson, forest green and black plaid uniforms, they couldn't have been more different. Eyes of every shape and hue bored into me, heads whipping around as we passed. The air smelled of smoky sweetness, instantly transporting me back to the day before at the Supe Café. It was magic; I was sure of it now.

Two boys passed by, their fangs popping out as they sniffed the air around me.

"Keep walking, Mace and River," Ryder snapped. "Nothing to see here."

I couldn't help the shudder that snaked up my spine. Vampires. My second encounter in two days.

Behind them three cute girls with translucent insect-like wings fluttered past. Their rainbow-colored hair stood out sharply against the dark uniforms. They giggled as their eyes landed on Ryder then me.

"Hi, Ryder," they said in unison.

"Good afternoon, ladies."

Curious gazes roamed over me as I continued to follow Ryder down the wide hallway. Five doors lined each side of the hall, class names labeled across the top. Some I'd seen on my schedule and others seemed like more advanced ones—*Dark Arts, Mastering Glamour, Elemental Manipulation.*

Geez, and I'd thought Geometry and Calculus had been rough.

"This is the second floor of the main hall. There are three others above us that hold classrooms. The level below is the banquet hall where you'll eat all your meals. Everything's included so don't be afraid to splurge."

I hadn't even thought about the financial aspect of attending Darkhen Academy. After years in public school, I'd taken free education for granted.

I glanced up at Ryder. "Is my father paying for me to be here?"

"Probably. You can ask Cillian. I don't really involve myself in that sort of thing."

"So what do you do here?"

"I'm the Combat instructor."

I swear his chest puffed out as he said it. With his massive pecs and thick arms, I didn't doubt it. Everything about his body screamed lethal weapon, and my stupid hormones wanted a taste.

Bad, Luna! I shook off the errant thought, and my mind focused back on the black words on my schedule. "I think I'm in that class."

"Yup. Your ass is mine."

My insides clenched at the rough edge to his voice, and heat swirled from my middle all the way up to my cheeks.

He chuckled. "Your sister used to do the exact same thing when she got embarrassed."

And it was gone. Ryder mentioning Kimmie-Jayne was like a

bucket of ice over the head. And it was probably for the best. This guy was my teacher now. I had to get these lusty thoughts out of my head fast.

"So anyway, you were talking about my classes..."

"Right. Since you're the first supe virgin we've had"—a ridiculous grin lit up his handsome face— "we'll start things out slow and see if any of your abilities surface."

Supe virgin was about ten times worse than mini minx. I really hoped that one didn't stick. I bit back the nasty retort, convincing myself I could handle his playful jokes and I needed to focus on why I was here. "What if they don't? I've heard that some half-bloods don't ever develop any powers."

"That's true, but I have a feeling about you, kid." He reached over to muss up my hair, but that's where I had to draw the line.

I swatted his hand away and shot him a narrowed glare. "Hey, I'm not your kid sister or something! I'm not even that much younger than you." I paused, not really sure how demons aged as opposed to other supes. "How old are you, anyway?"

"Twenty-two. Youngest instructor on staff."

"So you're like the same age as some of the upper classmen?" That had to get weird. I could totally see this guy trying to hook it up with some of the stunning girls I'd already seen.

"Most graduate by twenty or twenty-one. So yeah, I'm pretty close, but you heard what Headmaster Cillian said, right? Rules are rules."

"Yeah, you really seem like one of those sticklers to the rules."

He laughed, the smooth sound vibrating his big chest as he wrapped his arm around my shoulders again. "You get me, mini minx. I like that. I think we're going to have a lot of fun getting to know each other in the next few years."

We walked through the entire building from top to bottom before ending up at the banquet hall. Ornate wooden chandeliers hung the length of the vast room, illuminating the quiet space in an ethereal glow. Long banquet-style tables stretched across the hall—seven of them in total.

"So everything seems to be pretty divided by supernatural species—where am I going to fit in?"

His lips twisted as he scratched at his stubbly chin. "I guess wherever you want. Since you're rooming with Cinder, maybe the dragons will adopt you. They're a pretty easy going bunch."

Somehow dragon and easy-going didn't quite seem to fit.

A big yawn escaped through my clenching teeth, my efforts at suppressing it wasted. This had been the longest day of my life.

"Come on, why don't I show you to the dormitories? You can do some more exploring tomorrow." He turned me toward the far corner of the hall, and a doorway caught my eye. "I'm sure Cinder will show you all the ins and outs of Darkblood in the coming days."

"Darkblood?" I arched a brow at the demon.

"Huh? Oh sorry, it's a nickname for the school. Most of the students call it that."

"A pretty ominous one," I countered.

"Not really." He ushered me toward the door at the back, and as we neared I read the sign above it—Julias L. Darkhen Dormitory. "All supernaturals have both light and dark magic running through their blood. None of the houses are inherently dark or light—good or evil per say, however there are some that have a greater tendency to swing to one side over the other. Our sources of power differ. For example, all shifter magic is light, while the Coven Council and Fae are more gray, and the Sons of Heaven come from pure white light—the most uncontaminated of us all. Now, the Royal Vampires' power stems from dark magic as does the demons of the Underworld. Like me." He grinned. "They say that those with dark blood tend to be the most powerful and as this school is an elite one for the most gifted—"

"Hence the nickname Darkblood Academy."

"Exactly." Ryder held the door open, allowing me to go first.

"Do you think *I* have dark blood?"

He leaned in closer, his musky scent invading my space, and sniffed my neck. Goose bumps exploded over my skin as his warm breath brushed my collarbone, and my pulse skyrocketed.

He backed away with a mischievous grin. "How would I know? I'm not a vampire."

"You're such an as—" I quickly bit back the curse, reminding myself this was my instructor and not just some hot guy I was flirting with.

He waggled a finger at me, his dark eyes sparkling. "Watch it, mini minx. I do give out detentions, and I'm not above corporeal punishment." A wicked grin tugged at his lips as he turned down the next corridor.

Holy demon babies. This guy was going to be the death of me.

Ryder stopped at a massive spiral staircase and pointed up. "Dorms are this way."

"Let me guess, seven floors?"

"Yup! You're a smart one, aren't you, kid?"

"Luna. My name is Luna—not kid or mini minx and especially not supe virgin." I resisted the urge to stomp my foot because I didn't want to seem like a child throwing a tantrum.

"Right, sorry." He started up the steps before turning back to me. "Dragons are on the fifth floor by the way. I hope you're up for some exercise."

Ugh. I hitched my backpack higher up on my back and trudged up the stone stairs behind him. Luckily, he didn't try to engage in any witty banter while we ascended because I would've been too out of breath to respond.

When we finally reached the fifth floor landing, I sucked in a breath, my lungs burning. Damn, I was out of shape.

"Don't you worry, mini—Luna, I'll have you in tip top condition before long. We start each Combat class with a two-mile jog."

"You're joking, right?"

"Nope." He popped the P, and I couldn't help but smile even though my heart was still pounding from the uphill climb.

The fifth floor hallway looked much like the others we'd seen so far. Fancy mahogany doors, stone walls and candle-lit iron sconces—the medieval feel encompassed every foot of this old fortress. The only thing that set this floor apart was the navy blue banner stretching across the wall. A family crest was emblazoned on the left, and big bold letters were inked across the massive sign in a language I didn't recognize.

"What does that mean?"

"*Ex igne venite victoria.*" The strange words rolled off his tongue. "It's the dragon-shifter motto. Loosely translated it means from fire comes victory."

"That's pretty cool. Do all the houses have one?"

He nodded.

A question had been floating around in my mind since the demon bachelor appeared in Cillian's office. "How come the Underworld isn't represented at Darkhen or even in Azar?"

A rueful grin tugged at his lips so that he was almost smiling, but it also kind of resembled a sneer. "Because we don't count. We don't have a seat on the Etrian Assembly so our vote doesn't matter. The land of the damned was not deemed worthy of such honor."

"So how come you're here?" The second the words were out I regretted them. Dang, I had no filter.

His expression darkened. "Because being Lucifer's son does have some perks. And being a traitor to your own kind is worth more than sticking to tradition."

I opened my mouth to ask more, but Ryder stopped in front of a door about midway down the hall. "This is it." He knocked on the door before I could apologize. Something had obviously upset him because the fun, flirty instructor from a few minutes ago had vanished. A dark mask slipped over his handsome face.

Before I could think on it for long, the door swung open, revealing my new roommate. Cinder Skyraider. A year had turned the cute girl into a beautiful young woman. She pushed her bangs to the side, and her deep golden eyes flickered over me. Jet-black locks tumbled over her shoulders as her lips parted into a sweet smile. "You must be Luna. I'm Cinder, come on in." She scooted to the side, allowing me to enter.

I stopped midway across the threshold when I noticed my shadow had stopped moving.

Ryder cleared his throat, the tense set of his jaw making it clear something was still bothering him. "I'll let you two get acquainted. You're in good hands with Cinder, Luna. See you in class tomorrow."

I almost missed the stupid nicknames.

He spun around and disappeared down the hallway before I could thank him for showing me around.

I quirked a brow at my new roomie. "Is he always that moody?"

She rolled her eyes and laughed. "Yesss."

The dorm was a decent size with two double beds – one on each side of the room. My two duffel bags already sat next to my bare bed, and I dropped my backpack beside them. Matching mahogany desks, dressers, and nightstands stood on both sides of the chamber. My undecorated side looked markedly different from Cinder's, which was covered in pictures and posters and pink—lots of pink. A pile of books sat on her desk beside her light pink laptop.

Crap... I didn't have a computer. At Astor Home, we had a communal one that we all shared.

"That's your side, in case that wasn't obvious." She smiled, snagging her lip between her teeth. I couldn't imagine this girl as a dragon. She seemed sweeter than apple pie. Walking to my closet, she pulled out a cream comforter, pillow, and matching sheets. "You can use these for now. Until you get your own. They're kinda plain, but they work."

I took them from her and threw them on top of my bed. "Thanks." I couldn't imagine where I'd buy dorm stuff. I hadn't seen any Bed, Bath & Beyonds in the Fae forest. Not to mention I had no money.

She pointed at a third door in the middle of the room. "That's the shared bathroom. We split it with two other girls on the other side—Maxi and Alissa. They're pretty cool and not too messy."

"What happened to your old roommate?"

"I never had one. I just got here last week. Our calendar year isn't the same as the human one. We start in the spring and study through summer and fall. Then we have break during winter."

"Oh, that's interesting." But I guess it didn't really matter that much when you lived in a realm of permanent winter. I yawned again, unable to hold back the exhaustion.

"I was heading to dinner, but you seem like you're ready for bed."

"Yeah, I guess I'm more jet-lagged than I thought." I slumped down on the unmade mattress.

"No worries," she said, grabbing her pink purse and throwing it over her shoulder. "We can catch up in the morning. I'll introduce you to everyone at breakfast. I feel like I already know you anyway; Fenix caught me up before you arrived."

Oh man, I hope he didn't tell his sister I'd totally ogled him when we first met.

"Thanks, Cinder. I'll see you in the morning then."

She sauntered out the door with a wave, the short uniform skirt just skimming her mid-thigh. She was tall like Fenix, but slim unlike the bulky dragon. I thanked my lucky stars I'd gotten a decent roommate. From our short interaction plus what I'd seen on *Hitched*, I thought we'd get along just fine. It was weird because it seemed like I already knew her too.

Now I needed sleep. After a quick trip to the bathroom, I hastily made my bed and sank into the soft mattress. My mind whirled with everything that had happened the past few days— I turned eighteen, cut class, discovered a supernatural café then discovered *I* was supernatural. I met my half-sister and was whirled off to a magical school and met more supes in a few hours than I had in the past year. Oh, and I discovered my dad was not only a warlock, but also the President of the U.S. Tomorrow classes started, and I'd be tested against supes with actual powers. I didn't think sleep would come easily.

I was wrong.

CHAPTER 7

T he banquet hall was packed. The clatter of trays, books slamming down on tables, and chattering students reminded me of Crestwood High. Only difference was some trays floated to their tables, students levitated in the air, and I was pretty sure those tall bottles of crimson liquid at the vamp table were filled with blood, and not bloody Mary's.

I still couldn't get over how separated the houses were. Each of the seven banquet style tables were so clearly divided among the supe races—even to a newbie like me.

Besides the vampires, the Fae stood out the most. They were all gorgeous and perfect, plus the pointy ears were a total giveaway. They seemed to float across the floor, even those that weren't being propelled by translucent wings. The members of the Coven Council were more of a mixed bag as were the shifters. I didn't think I could pick them out of a crowd. The members of the ocean realm had a sort of chill vibe about them, and they seemed to move in slow motion. Like their legs still hadn't fully adjusted to life on land. Then there were the angels and nephilim, most didn't sit around with their wings out, but when they unfurled, a radiant heavenly glow shot out in a ten foot radius around them.

"Don't stare, sweetie." Cinder walked up beside me and nudged me toward a table on the far left of the hall. The Brotherhood of Dragons.

"Easy for you to say. They're all staring at me," I hissed.

"It's just because you're new."

"And human!"

She shrugged. "Yeah, okay maybe that too. They're trying to figure out what you are." She led the way, sitting at the end of a packed table. Two girls and a guy looked up and smiled at my roomie, until their gazes landed on me.

The two girls were our suitemates, Maxi and Alissa. Like Cinder, they were tall and slender, but both had light brown hair as opposed to her stunning deep raven color. Again, I couldn't imagine any of these cute girls turning into ferocious dragons.

I'd already briefly encountered my suitemates coming out of the shower this morning. I was half-naked so we didn't chat much as I scurried out of there to my room.

"Ladies, this is Luna Hallows."

They both gave me tight smiles.

"How about me? I don't get an introduction?" Emerald green eyes scanned over me, a cute grin lighting up the guy's face.

Cinder rolled her eyes, dropping her tray on the table. "Luna, this is my cousin, Ash. Is Luna the reason you're gracing our table with your presence today? Where are your friends?"

He ticked his head to a table at the far end of the dining hall. I followed everyone's gaze to the only round one in the place, where six others sat huddled together. There was one empty chair, which I assumed belonged to Ash. One of the guys spun around, catching my gaze. The most unusual lilac irises locked onto mine. I swallowed hard as a wave of goose bumps crawled over my flesh. Short, platinum blonde hair and a sharp angled jaw completed the guy's modelesque appearance. He was beautiful, but in a chilling way. His skin shone like porcelain and every perfect angle seemed to have been meticulously carved from the finest marble.

He nudged the guy next to him and before long the entire table had turned to gawk. It was like staring directly into the sun—their looks brilliant and scorching but deadly.

Dropping my gaze, I whispered to Cinder, "Who are they?"

"The Seven."

"Oh stop that, Cin," barked Ash. "You're going to freak her out. Those are my friends."

I scanned the table once again, and unlike each of the groups sitting at the tables around us, this one was markedly different. Power oozed from their side of the room, that sweet, smoky smell radiated from their table creating a wall which no one dare cross. The three beautiful girls and three uber-hot guys whispered among themselves, an intense aura shrouding them in power.

"Rule number one at Darkblood: Don't mess with The Seven." Cinder's hushed voice turned my attention back to her. Maxi and Alissa both bobbed their heads up and down.

"They're crazy powerful and don't talk to or hang out with anyone but themselves," added Maxi.

"That's totally untrue." Ash popped a French fry in his mouth and stood. "Everyone's just intimidated by us—them."

"You only talk to me because I'm your cousin," said Cinder, "and because my brother's the dragon alpha."

"Whatever. Come on, Luna, I'll prove it to you. I'll introduce you to them."

I glanced over once again, unable to keep from staring—especially at him. Those icy lilac eyes called to me. The guy raked his hand through his impossibly platinum hair, drawing my attention to his pointy ears. My mouth dropped, and he shot a scowl in my direction. I squeezed my eyes shut, blinking rapidly and forced my gaze to move on to anywhere else. Anyone but him. His frosty glare was melting my insides. The guy sitting next to him actually smirked when my eyes caught his. Unlike his unpleasant friend, he had warm amber eyes, shaggy light brown hair, and a more approachable expression.

"So are you coming, Luna?" Ash leaned across the table.

I'd been so distracted I hadn't even heard him speak. "Huh?"

"Do you want to meet my friends or what?"

I grabbed the breakfast sandwich from my plate and shoved it in my mouth. "Um, I'm just eating right now," I said around another bite, "super starved—maybe some other time."

Ash rolled his eyes at his cousin and stomped off to join his friends. I couldn't keep my eyes from trailing his broad shoulders the whole way across the breakfast hall. He folded down next to icy lilac eyes and whispered something that made the guy's frown twist into a grin.

Seven pairs of multi-hued eyes turned to me, and heat rose up my neck, spreading across my cheeks. Ugh, why me?

Of course they had to be gossiping about the new human girl.

"So what exactly is the story with The Seven?" I finally asked after my blazing skin cooled.

"Not sure if you've noticed," said Maxi, "but we tend to stick to our own kind." She ticked her head down the table, and I knew we were surrounded by other dragon shifters. It was going to take me some time to recognize the different species when they weren't all neatly divided into tables. The vampires were easy enough to spot because of their pale skin and fangs, Fae had the pointy ears, but shifters, witches, warlocks? How the heck was I supposed to know?

I must have been making my confused face because Cinder interjected. "We all wear different colored pins for our houses." She pointed at the small navy blue dragon pin attached to her brcast pocket. It was barely noticeable against the black uniform polo shirt.

"Oh... that should make things easier."

"I'll explain all the houses and their colors and symbols when we get back to our room tonight," said Cinder.

"Looks like I'm going to have a lot of studying to do." I shook my head and platinum hair whizzed across my peripheral vision. I refused to look at him again, forcing my gaze to Maxi. "So anyway, you were saying—about The Seven?"

"Right, so, the reason we call them that is they each represent one of the houses. It's just odd—they're tighter than any pack or coven in here. The blonde guy is Drake, he's a Fae and pretty much the leader, the one next to him is Ash, who you already met. He's the nicest of the bunch and most recent recruit. On the other side of him is Raine, she's a total b— witch. She and Aeria, with the neon blue hair are besties. Oh yeah, Aeria is a siren. You do not want to get on either of those girls' bad sides. Then there's Rafael and Triston, nephilim and werewolf, respectively. They're not too bad either but you don't want to be near Triston on a full moon. And lastly, the goth girl sitting off to the side is Scarlett. I bet even you can figure out what she is."

Her black hair, pale skin and crimson lined pupils were kind of a dead giveaway. "Vampire," I whispered. I didn't think I was ever going to remember all their names, but their faces were permanently emblazoned in my mind.

"Yup." Maxi took a sip of her cappuccino, glancing at me over the rim. "So those are The Seven. Do yourself a favor and avoid them at all costs. They're the ones that gave Darkblood Academy its nickname. Just stick with us for now until they start recruiting more humans."

I didn't know what to make of The Seven, but for now I'd follow Maxi's advice. Even though it all sounded a bit nuts. "So you guys really don't mix at all with the other students?" This was like some crazy racism. I mean sure there were cliques back in Crestwood, but they weren't divided by race or nationality. Not really anyway.

Cinder shrugged. "I'm new here and as soon as I arrived I was welcomed by my dragon pride. It was just natural. I talk to the other students in class and stuff, but I don't know, it's like that in Azar."

The eight houses of Azar weren't just political groupings, they were also territories. Each house had its own geographic area and apparently didn't cross over to visit each other often. I'd heard that a few hundred thousand humans had moved into Celestia—the angel territory—when our worlds were officially united. I wondered if they traveled around the other provinces.

A bell rang, tearing me from my inner musings.

"Breakfast time is up," said Cinder, finishing off her smoothie. "You ready for your first class?"

Ugh. "No, not really."

"Let me see your schedule again?"

When I awoke this morning, I found a shiny new laptop on my desk along with the official school tablet. And a pre-paid credit card. I almost fell out of my desk chair. There was a note from Cillian saying I'd get my books at each class and to let him know if there was anything else I needed. I had no idea how much money was on the card, but I'd use it sparingly for now. No online shopping for me... Did Amazon even deliver to Azar?

Shuffling through my backpack, I pulled out the tablet and flipped to my class schedule. Cinder, Maxi and Alissa all crowded around to get a better look.

Cinder's pretty pink lips turned into a pout. "Looks like we only have two together. Flying and Shifting 101 and Spellcraft."

"I'm in your Potions and Poisons class," said Alissa.

"Yup, me too." Maxi actually smiled.

Cinder straightened and picked up her tray. "So that means

you only have Defensive Magic and Combat by yourself. That's not too bad."

"Yeah, I guess." Too bad Combat was the first class of the day.

I lifted my tray and followed the girls to deposit our trash. As we neared The Seven, I kept my eyes trained to my half-eaten breakfast sandwich. It felt like a million tiny pinpricks stabbed my skin as we passed. Their intense gazes bored into me with more intensity than the sun on a scorching summer day. What the actual eff?

I picked up the pace, nearly barreling by Cinder to avoid their penetrating glares as I dropped my tray in the receptacle. She lifted her gaze over my shoulder and smirked. "Drake seems particularly taken by you."

"What?"

"Drake Wintersbee, the Fae prince. He's the blonde at *the* table."

"A prince?" I hissed. "Wait, I thought Elrian was the Fae prince—" My words cut off when I remembered their father, the king of Winter Court, was killed during the filming of *Hitched*. Elrian became king so that made Drake his younger brother. I should have recognized those icy lilac eyes. They were exact replicas of his brother's—who was totally in love with my half-sister. Geez, would I ever be able to escape Kimmie-Jayne's suitors? It seemed like reminders of them lurked in every corner of this school.

"I take it you were a fan of *Hitched*?" Cinder's lips tipped into a grin as she led the way out of the banquet hall.

"You weren't?"

"Of course I was, but my twin brothers were in it so I was personally invested. The show had a pretty limited release here in Azar."

"I can't believe that. It was insanely popular in the human world. Everyone is waiting for news on the next season."

"The Assembly likes to keep a tight leash on how much human programming comes into Azar. It's gotten better now with the unification, but we still don't have access to everything." She stopped in front of a door, and I realized we'd already reached the second floor. "This is me. Are you sure you don't want me to walk you to the gym?"

"Nah. I'm sure I can find it." I pulled out my handy dandy tablet and flipped to the map of the academy.

"Okay, I'll see you this afternoon in class then."

Glancing at the time on the sleek device, I spun toward the stairs. I had fifteen minutes until class started, but who knew how long it would take to find the gym. I hitched my backpack further up on my shoulders and took the stairs up a level. According to Cinder, there was an overpass on the third floor, which connected this building to the gym without having to go outside. I shuddered at the thought of the freezing temps beyond the door. My official uniform hadn't arrived yet. According to Cillian's note, I should get it by this evening. Which meant for now, I was stuck with my old crappy coat to brave the freakish faery elements.

A few students lingered in the halls, but as I made my way toward the overpass, the floor grew quiet. Without the hustle and bustle of students chattering, the old building was pretty creepy. With its dark wood, stone walls, and flickering candlelight, it had all the makings of a Hollywood thriller. Not to mention vampires, werewolves, and witches. Oh my!

I shook my head, chasing away the dark thoughts.

"You don't belong here." A raspy voice hissed from the shadows.

I spun around to an empty corridor, every hair on my body standing on end. "What? Who's there?" I took a step forward, and my fingers clamped around the handle to the overpass.

"You shouldn't be here. Get out while you still can." The

same voice whisper-hissed across the deadly quiet space. *Aw, hell no!*

I swung the door open and raced through, the slap of my Converse echoing off the thick walls. Another door stood at the end of the narrow hall, presumably leading into the gym.

Slow footsteps reverberated behind me, but I didn't dare glance back. Reaching the second door, I jerked the handle and it sprung open. I smacked straight into a rock-hard chest.

CHAPTER 8

I sucked in a breath, glancing up and found a pair of onyx eyes staring down at me.

"So nice of you to join us, Ms. Hallows." Ryder's lips curled into a smirk before he stopped to take in my crazed appearance. His smile vanished, and his hands settled on my shoulders as he looked me over. "Are you okay?" he whispered so only I could hear.

Over his massive shoulder I could make out the rest of the class gawking in our direction.

"Um, no. I mean, yes. I'm okay now."

He released me and I stepped back, my body immediately tensing. Geez, I'd practically been hugging my teacher.

"You want to tell me what happened?" he continued in a hushed tone.

Did I? Or would he think I was crazy? Maybe hearing voices was my magical power. That would be pretty sucky. I shook my head. "It was nothing. Sorry I'm late."

His dark brows dipped, but he didn't press any further. "Fine then. The lockers are that way. Go get changed, and you can join the class when you're ready."

I nodded and ran off in the direction he'd pointed. Walking into the ladies' locker room I was relieved to see a girl crouched in front of a locker. I so didn't feel like being alone right now.

The girl spun around, pulling her jet-black hair into a high ponytail. Oh crap. I'd recognize that pale face and dark ruby lipstick anywhere. She was one of The Seven. How'd I get stuck in a confined space with a vampire on my first day?

Hurrying over to an empty locker, I tugged my t-shirt and sweats out of my bag, hoping my Converse would be okay for now. I just needed to get out of here ASAP. As I tore off my long sleeve shirt, I could feel eyes boring into the back of my head.

It was like spiders crawling up my spine. When I couldn't take another second of it, I whirled around.

The locker room was empty.

So weird...

Once I was fully clothed, I dashed out of there faster than an Olympic sprinter. Either I was losing it or someone was trying to freak me out. I hated to admit it, but it was working.

I walked out onto the parquet floor where Ryder stood in the middle of the basketball court, his back to me. In front of him, two rows of students practiced with long wooden staffs.

Wow, they weren't kidding when they named the class Combat.

As I neared, I recognized a few more faces. Seven of them to be exact. Sh—nickerdoodles! How did I end up in *their* class?

Ash, Cinder's dragon-shifter cousin lifted a hand, wiggling his fingers at me with a cute smile. I did my best to smile back, but my stomach was roiling.

Ryder turned, following Ash's gaze toward me. "Oh good, our newest addition has arrived." He motioned with his index finger for me to come forward.

I crossed my arms against my chest and moved stiffly toward my instructor. "Maybe I could just watch for today."

He chuckled. "I don't think so, but nice try." Sliding his foot under a staff on the floor, he kicked it up and it landed perfectly in his hand. "Have you ever used one of these before?"

"Um... No. I grew up in New York, not Japan. Knives are a little less conspicuous."

A few students snickered behind me.

Ryder didn't even crack a smile. "Good. Then let's see what sort of natural talents you have." He pointed at one of The Seven—Raine, I thought. The gorgeous redhead sauntered toward me with her staff clenched in her long, delicate fingers. "Be nice," he warned her.

Awesome.

Handing me the staff, Ryder took a step back. "Attack her."

I stared at the long wooden pole in my hand then back at my instructor, my eyes as wide as hard-boiled eggs. "You want me to do what now?"

"I want you to try to attack her. You know, swing the staff like you mean to hit her with it."

Raine arched a perfectly shaped brow. "Just go ahead and try."

My clammy fingers tightened around the staff. *Here goes nothing.* Holding it like a baseball bat, I took a swing.

The sharp crack of wood against wood echoed around the vast gymnasium, the smack reverberating down my arm bones and making my teeth chatter. A pleased smile crossed the redhead's full lips as she held her staff out blocking my blow.

"Again," shouted Ryder.

I took a step back and swung again, approaching from the opposite side. Again, she deflected my blow, but this time she pushed back and sent me flailing backward. I hit the parquet floor with a thud, the pain shooting up my tailbone. I bit back a scream, clenching my jaw so hard I was lucky I didn't break any teeth.

Ryder sauntered over and extended his hand to help me up.

I narrowed my eyes at him and pushed myself off the ground. Too little, too late.

"One more time," he announced.

This time I took a running start, hoping to gain some momentum against my obviously more-skilled opponent. Instead of swinging with the top part of the staff like I'd done before, just before I reached her, I pivoted the pole, striking with the lower half. Instead of the crack of wood I'd expected, I hit flesh. Her upper shoulder to be exact.

Bright green eyes leveled on me for an instant before dark wood sailed by my head, and everything went black.

⁂

"LUNA, LUNA, WAKE UP." A SMOOTH VOICE CALLED TO ME from the darkness.

My head throbbed, and my thoughts were hazy. I floated around in a gloomy mist, and I had zero desire to fight my way out of it. Everything hurt.

"Luna, come on. Open your eyes." A light touch skimmed my cheek, and my brain synapses started firing again.

My eyes fluttered, bright light seeping its way through the cracks. It felt like a two-ton elephant was sitting on my head, and his massive legs pinned down the rest of me.

"There you are, come on back to me, kid."

My eyes snapped open as my hazy brain finally registered the voice. Ryder's anxious face hovered over me, a small smile tipping up his lips when my eyes focused on his.

"What the heck happened?" My hand flew to the tender spot on the side of my head. I winced as my fingers brushed the bruised area. I tried to sit up, but my head spun and Ryder gently pushed me back onto the small bed. Where was I? The little room was sterile and white and smelled of disinfectant.

"Well, you got a good hit on Raine, and she didn't take it so well."

Jumbled thoughts clamored around in my mind. Fire red hair, those evil eyes searing into me, then nothingness.

"That psycho whacked me on the head!" I cried.

He tried to suppress a chuckle, but his dark eyes sparkled like the brightest stars on a pitch night. "Yeah, I'm going to have to talk to her about that. We don't allow head hits without the appropriate gear."

"Ya think?"

He inched closer, and my breath hitched—the intense throbbing momentarily forgotten. I held my breath as he brushed a lock of hair behind my ear, my skin tingling at his touch. His dark brows knitted, and he frowned as he examined the massive bump on my temple. "The good news is, the healer doesn't think you have a concussion. She should be back in a second to fix you right up. She wanted to make sure you were awake first."

"Great," I mumbled.

"You should be proud of yourself, Luna. You did good out there. Raine's a tough opponent and getting a hit in on her is a pretty big accomplishment on your first day."

I snorted. "Then why do I feel like road kill?"

"Because you're human—or mostly anyway. You gotta remember all of these students have an edge on you. They're going to be stronger, faster, and heal more quickly than you but don't let that discourage you. On the contrary, use it to make you tougher."

"So that was supposed to be some sort of a lesson?" I arched a brow and winced, regretting it immediately.

He patted me on the shoulder and rose. "Take it for what you will. I'm going to let the healer know you're awake. We don't want you missing your next class."

Seriously?

He disappeared from the room leaving me to my messy thoughts. It was only my first day of classes, and I'd already landed in the supes' version of an infirmary. Also I was fairly certain I was now on Raine's bad side—a place Cinder warned me was not somewhere I wanted to be. And I'd caught the attention of The Seven. This did not bode well.

⚊⚊

A HALF AN HOUR LATER, I WAS SITTING NEXT TO CINDER IN the front row of Spellcraft. The bump on my forehead was completely gone; too bad the healer couldn't wipe away the memories of it too. Raine and Aeria sat a few rows behind us, and I'd been the lucky recipient of their dark glares when I'd walked into the class. Fortunately, Cinder had flagged me down with a big smile and an empty seat beside her.

I could still feel their hatred boring into the back of my head like heat-seeking missiles.

After an excruciating two hours of staring cross-eyed at the smart board filled with spells in languages I didn't understand, Professor Arcana finally dismissed the class. Unlike the jerk Ryder, the wizened old warlock had taken it easy on me and hadn't called on me once. Thank the stars.

The professor lifted a wrinkly finger as the students began to file out of the classroom. "Ms. Hallows, I'd like a word with you before you go."

"Okay, sure."

Cinder nudged me with her elbow. "I'll meet you outside so we can walk to lunch together, and you can tell me more about what happened."

I nodded and packed my tablet and new spellbook into my backpack. Two tall shadows loomed over me, and the hair on the back of my nape prickled. Lifting my gaze, I met a pair of familiar icy lilac eyes. Beside the Fae prince stood another one of The Seven, but I couldn't remember his name. He was tall like Drake, but whereas the faery was finely muscled, this guy was beefy with wide shoulders and bulging pecs.

My mouth went completely dry. What was it with all these supes being so dang gorgeous? And where were my beautiful genes?

"Well done today, human." The prince's piercing gaze roamed over me, and I resisted the urge to squirm.

"Yeah," added the dark-haired guy. "Raine's been crying about it all day." He chuckled.

"Um, thanks." I zipped up my backpack and threw it over my shoulder. "I'd probably still be crying if I hadn't gone to the healer."

"Yes, that is a shame about you being so fragile and human and all." Drake's nose twitched as if he'd smelled rotting garbage. "Maybe next time Ryder will let you wear some padding." His lips twisted into a sardonic grin as he brushed his hair behind his pointy ear.

"It's not that bad," I snapped. Something about the prince's snottiness just rubbed me the wrong way. "Humanity has its perks too—like you know, having actual feelings." I spun around and marched up to the professor's desk.

The sound of footsteps behind me made me want to turn around to see Drake's reaction, but I forced myself to still. I wouldn't give him the satisfaction. Plus I doubted the ice prince had any feelings anyway.

Once the classroom door closed behind them, the tension seeped out of my shoulders.

"How's your first day going, Ms. Hallows?" Professor Arcana's voice drew me from my inner thoughts.

"Not spectacular."

His gray eyes twinkled, and he twisted the end of his long, graying beard. "Stick with it, and you'll see things will get easier."

"Thanks." I didn't think I really had a choice. I had to be here as part of the president's—my father's—mandate about half-bloods.

"You have your spellbook?" he asked.

"Yup." I motioned to my backpack.

"I'd like you to start practicing during your spare time. You've got quite a bit to catch up on. We'll start slow, but I may pair you with one of the advanced students in the coming weeks for some private tutoring."

I gulped. "Okay."

He lowered his voice, leaning in. "I know your father well, Ms. Hallows. And there isn't one of his children that I've encountered that hasn't been incredibly gifted." He paused, his watery eyes skimming over me. "It's only a matter of time."

He meant for it to sound encouraging, but it only made the massive pit in my stomach double in size. Being Garrix's daughter was the only reason I'd been invited to this elite school, but what if they were all wrong and I didn't have what it takes?

CHAPTER 9

J ust one more class, and I would officially survive day one
at Darkhen. Luckily, lunch had gone by without a hitch—
no fights, insults or threatening voices. I still hadn't told
Cinder about that, and I wasn't sure if I ever would. It
could've just been my overactive imagination freaking out. And
with all the stress I'd been under, it totally made sense, right?

As Cinder and I walked down the hall to Flying and Shifting
101, a dark-haired demon bad boy caught my eye. He stood in
the doorway of the teacher's lounge with his arm against the
door, trapping a woman beneath him. The brunette Barbie
batted her sooty lashes at him, a huge smile spreading her
bright red lips.

A twinge of jealousy flared in my chest, and it was all I could
do to choke it down before it swallowed me whole. What the
heck was that about? I wanted to smack myself. Just because I'd
been in love with his persona on a TV show didn't mean I'd like
the real man. And Ryder probably flirted with all the girls
anyway. Plus he was totally off limits. Still, I couldn't help but
gawk at the gorgeous pair blatantly flirting.

"Luna, you're staring again," Cinder whispered.

I whipped my head toward her, shaking it out. "No, I wasn't."

She giggled. "It's okay, I get it. He's totally hot. But I haven't told you about rule number two at Darkhen: Never fall for the gorgeous, completely unattainable and off limits instructors."

"Got it." But somehow my raging hormones refused to listen. "So who is that with him—just out of curiosity?"

"Right." She shook her head. "That's Ms. Mikalson. She's the Demons and Fiends instructor. We'll probably have her next semester." Cinder lowered her voice as we neared. "She's a succubus—besides Ryder, she's the only other Underworlder on staff."

"Wait...what? Isn't a succubus a sex demon or something?" Nausea crawled up my throat.

"Yup, pretty much. They seduce men into sex and rip out their powers while they're at their most vulnerable." Her lips tipped into a wry grin. "Seems pretty cool to me."

I had to repress the urge to gag as visions of her and Ryder swam across my mind. Oh bleh!

We scurried by them, and I was surprised when Cinder led us past the classroom I thought we were going to. "Wasn't that it?"

"Today we're outside. The location of the class varies depending on what we're working on."

Goose bumps crawled all over my flesh at the idea of being outside in these frigid temps. "I don't even know why I'm in this class. I can't fly or shift. What's the point?"

A grin split her pink lips. "Everyone flies at Darkblood Academy." She winked before tugging me down the stairs. "You'll see."

After trudging across campus through the deep snow for what felt like forever, a large stone building came to view beneath the towering pines. The thatched roof seemed in no way capable of protecting whatever lived in there from the harsh climate. I pulled my crappy, fraying coat tighter around myself. Great, I was going to freeze for the entire class period.

"Come on, slow poke!" Cinder tugged me along, her long legs eating up the distance like nothing. Draeko, the dragon territory, was in the northernmost Azarian mountains. From what I'd heard, the temperature wasn't that different from Winter Court so she was used to the bountiful snow. No wonder she bounced through it like a gazelle, while I felt like a bumbling elephant. It never snowed this much in the outskirts of the city.

When we finally reached the building, Cinder swung the thick wooden doors open, and a blast of sultry air washed over me. It warmed my frozen nose, immediately spreading across my cheeks as we crossed the threshold. Once my nostrils thawed out, the odor of hay and manure swirled all around me.

I'd been so excited by the warmth, I hadn't even realized we were standing in the middle of a barn. At the far end, a group of students gathered around a middle-aged woman. When she saw us, she waved us over with a bright smile.

"Cinder, and you must be Luna," she said, checking her tablet.

"That's me."

"Welcome to Flying and Shifting 101. I'm Mrs. Thornberry, and I'll be your instructor for the semester." Though she looked no more than mid-forties, long silver hair trailed down her back, nearly reaching her butt.

I searched her back for wings, but no unearthly appendages protruded from her shoulder blades. She must've been a shifter of some sort.

Behind her, icy lilac eyes caught my attention. Damn, why was Drake in all of my classes? The moment our gazes met, I averted mine to search through my backpack. No, I wasn't avoiding him—I needed to find my tablet.

"As I was saying class, today you will be assigned to your unipeg."

A wave of excited murmurs rolled through the other students.

"Our whats?" I whispered to Cinder.

She ticked her head toward the stalls on either side of us. I could just make out the wide rear end of a white horse; the front half of his body was behind the thick stone wall. From the sounds of it, he was happily munching on some grains and had zero interest in us.

"You mean the horses?" I hitched my thumb over my shoulder.

"They're not horses. They're unipegs," she whispered. "Just wait, and you'll see."

"Ladies, hush now," said Mrs. Thornberry as she handed us each a slip of paper. I glanced down at the name Zeus, and the number eight penned in swirly writing. "Once you receive your assigned animal, you may go introduce yourselves. Get acquainted, as you will be spending the next few years at Darkhen with your unipeg. They're incredibly intelligent and loyal beasts, and it will behoove you to make nice. They can be quite temperamental and do require a firm hand."

Cinder tugged on my arm, pulling me toward the stalls. "What number did you get?"

Oh, so that's what that number was. "Eight. You?"

"I'm eleven. My unipeg's name is Bella. I hope she's sweet."

"I got Zeus."

Her eyes widened before she schooled her expression back to normal.

"What? Have you heard of him or something?"

"Um... nope. Just liked the name that's all." She quickened her pace toward the end of the row. Stopping in front of stall number eleven, Cinder leaned against the gate and clucked her tongue.

A dark gray horn popped out followed by the rest of the creature's pearly white head. My eyes bulged out as I stared at the horn protruding from the horse's forehead. "It's a freakin' unicorn!"

She laughed, patting the creature on the nose. "No, silly. It's a unipeg."

As if the animal had heard her, massive wings unfurled from its body, spreading to encompass the entire stall. She gave them a quick flap, revealing the feathery underside made up of a rainbow of colors.

"Flying unicorns!" The mythical creatures that had made an appearance on *Hitched* flashed through my mind's eye. Kimmie-Jayne had been just as blown away as I was when the bachelors rode up to the mansion on them.

She rolled her eyes at me. "It's a unipeg—a cross between a unicorn and Pegasus. That's why it can fly."

"It's incredible." I reached my hand out and slowly stroked the animal's soft nose. She nuzzled against my palm and whinnied. "She seems nice."

"Yeah, thank goodness. Ash told me some horror stories about—" She cut herself off, slapping her hand over her mouth.

"About what?"

"Nothing. Some of them are just a little harder to manage than others." She plastered on a smile, but even I could tell she was hiding something. "Come on, let's go find Zeus."

We followed the sound of furiously stomping hooves straight to the stall marked eight. A large black backside was pressed up against the gate, his long tail twitching agitatedly.

"Hey there, Zeus." I forced a soothing lilt into my tone even though my heart pounded against my ribs. I was a city girl; I never grew up around farm animals—let alone a massive supernatural beast like this.

The unipeg swung his head around and snorted, his wide nostrils expelling a spray of snot in our direction. Cinder ducked in time, but my human reflexes were no match for the supernatural boogers. *Ugh!* They splattered all over my shirt, leaving a trail of greenish goo dripping down my cream turtleneck.

Of course Drake and his friend decided to walk by at that exact moment. His lip curled in disgust while the dark-haired guy from earlier suppressed a laugh as they surveyed the damage. "Tough break, human," said Drake, "Zeus is a fiery fiend. Just hope you can manage him."

Cinder shot the ice prince a narrowed glare. "Don't listen to him, Luna. I'm sure you'll be fine. He just has to get to know you."

The dark-haired guy stepped forward, his brilliant blue eyes like the sky on a perfect summer day. He clucked at the animal, and Zeus cocked his head. "Easy, buddy. Come here and meet a new friend."

"It's no use, Raf," snapped Drake. "There's no way he's going to let a human be his master."

"Don't be bitter. Just because you couldn't tame the beast, doesn't mean that no one can."

I clapped my hand over my mouth to hide the huge smile on my face. I think Raf was my new favorite member of The Seven.

To my complete amazement, the ornery beast inched closer. After a few more soothing words, Zeus's massive head appeared over the gate. His obsidian eyes darted back and forth to each of us. Raf extended his hand slowly until he reached the unipeg's nose. Zeus sniffed him curiously before his ears lowered, and the whites of his eyes were no longer quite so wide.

"Good boy," Rafael murmured and brushed his fingers over the unipeg's muzzle. His palm lit up, bathing the space in a warm glow. Zeus whinnied and nuzzled into his hand.

"Hey, that's not fair." Drake crossed his arms over his chest.

"You can't use your soothing angel power on him. Of course he's going to like you."

"Relax, Drake. I'm only trying to calm him so Luna can try."

The Fae prince stomped off with a grunt, and I couldn't help the smile that crept across my face. I turned to the unipeg whisperer. "Thanks. Raf, right?"

He nodded and released his hold on Zeus. "It's Rafael, but Raf is fine too. Don't let the prince get to you; I never do. He's used to being the most interesting thing at Darkblood, but now that you're here, he's worried he'll be replaced."

"I'm sure my novelty will wear off soon. Especially if my powers never show up."

"I wouldn't be so sure about that." He gave me a tight smile and followed in the direction Drake had gone.

Once he was out of earshot, I turned to Cinder. "He doesn't seem that bad."

Her lips puckered as they trailed by him. "No, he's not. But he's part angel, he can't be a total dick all the time, right?"

We both laughed, and I stumbled back, hitting Zeus's stall door. He let out a sharp neigh and thrust his head forward. My eyes widened as a pointy horn came straight for me.

"Tempor parem!"

A scream stuck in my throat as the foreign words rang out from across the barn, and my eyes snapped shut. The air thickened, the sweet, smoky smell of magic coating the atmosphere. Slowly, I peeked through cracked lids. *Holy smokes!* I was alive and hadn't been gored by a wild unipeg.

Zeus's obsidian horn had stopped about an inch from the bridge of my nose. I spun to the left and the right, suddenly realizing the entire room had gone silent. Cinder stood beside me, her face frozen in a panicked expression. The other students were sprawled around the barn, oblivious to what had happened but also completely immobile.

Drake appeared from behind the stall door next to Zeus's,

his lilac eyes pulsing a frosty silver. Beads of sweat lined his brow, and his typically pallid complexion was a few shades lighter. "You might want to get out of the way. I don't know how much longer I can hold the spell."

It took a second for my brain to process what had happened. Everyone was frozen except for the prince and me. Somehow he'd saved me.

"Duck, now, Luna!" His shrill words kick started my brain, and I dropped to the ground as everything was once again set in motion.

Cinder screamed, and all the students spun toward us.

"I'm okay," I hissed at her from the ground.

Her mouth dropped, her dark brows knitting as she looked me over. "How'd you get down there?"

I pushed myself off the floor and searched the neighboring stall for Drake, but he was gone.

Brushing the dirt off my jeans, I loosed a breath. "I think I've had about enough for today."

Zeus pawed at the gate, his heavy hoof thumping on the wood.

"We'll continue this some other time, hellion." I grabbed my backpack off the ground and swung it over my shoulder. "I'll see you back in the dorm, Cinder. Tell Mrs. Thornberry I didn't feel well or something."

"But Luna!"

I practically sprinted out of the barn, ignoring Cinder's shouts. Invisible iron bands wrapped around my chest, and if I didn't get some fresh air I was fairly sure I'd explode. A chilly wind blasted my cheeks the moment I set foot outside. It was like tiny pinpricks on my skin, but it felt damned good.

As I trudged through the snow back to the dorms, the suffocating feeling relented, replaced by icy numbness. My first day was a complete disaster. How was I ever going to survive an entire semester? Or year?

CHAPTER 10

I t had been an entire freakin' month and not a tiny shred of magic had emerged. On the bright side, I was still alive and somehow successfully navigating life at Darkhen. Clutching my Defensive Magic book under my arm, I hurried to class. Since I couldn't actually perform any magic, I spent most of my time studying theories and memorizing spells I'd never get to use.

"Hey, Luna girl." An arm came around my shoulder, and Ash's burnt kindling scent closed in around me. "You ready for class?" He was the only one of The Seven who was friendly, and I was pretty sure it was because Cinder was his cousin and she made him.

"Nope."

"Just try to put up a little bit of a fight today, huh?"

I rolled my eyes at him and squirmed out from under his arm as we reached the classroom as he chuckled. I did kind of feel bad for him since he got stuck with me as his partner. I didn't know what Professor Malindra was thinking.

I wouldn't really call Ash and I great friends, but we did talk. There'd been a question on the tip of my tongue I'd been meaning to ask for a few days now. The other morning I'd been up early before class, and I'd seen him and the rest of The Seven led by Ryder skulk out into the forest. My curiosity piqued, I'd spied on them for the next few mornings noting the same pattern. I told myself it had nothing to do with stalking a certain dark-haired, off-limits instructor. *Lie.*

"So, Ash, where do you and the other Sev—and your friends go with Ryder in the mornings?"

The dragon shifter's emerald eyes flinched before returning to normal. "Special project we're working on with Ryder. You're not missing out on anything, trust me."

Something about his clipped tone told me I wasn't getting more info on the topic. So I held my tongue for now.

When we walked into the classroom, the space had been cleared of all the desks and a red circular mat sat in the center. Oh great, it was one of those days... The professor had already warned us we'd face each other one-on-one in a defensive magic test, but I didn't think it would be so soon.

She clapped her hands, and all the students lumbering around the circle went silent. "Today's the day, my dears. You'll finally be able to show us what you've learned so far in an epic display of your defensive talents."

Epic? More like disastrous.

The classroom door swung open, and Cillian and Ryder sauntered in. Ugh. I swung my hair forward, hoping I could hide behind the blonde curtain.

A rush of excitement swirled through the air as everyone murmured anxiously at the unexpected arrival of the headmaster. I was the exact opposite of excited—more like mortified for him to witness my impressive failure.

Professor Malindra motioned to Cillian and Ryder. "As you can see, we have a few special guests with us today."

Cillian gave a curt nod to the class and Ryder wiggled his fingers, which incited an eruption of giggles from the female population. His gaze slowly moved to mine, and when our eyes locked, a familiar tingle zipped up my spine. He mouthed "good luck," and I rewarded him with my most dramatic eye roll. He knew very well I was going to fail miserably. Combat, his class, was the only one out of the five I wasn't failing. And it was because it didn't rely purely on magical skill.

"All right then, shall we get started?"

A chorus of excited yeses rang out behind me. All I wanted to do was hide behind Ash, but he'd somehow managed to place us front and center.

A chill scurried up my spine, and I spun around to meet the cause of it nose-to-nose. Drake hovered right behind me, and I was forced to take a step back into Ash to avoid making out with him.

"Sorry," he muttered.

That was the extent of our conversations these days. We never spoke about him saving my life when my crazy unipeg, Zeus, tried to gore me. I attempted to thank him once, but he blew it off like it had never happened. So I did the same.

Professor Malindra cleared her throat, drawing my attention to the front of the class. Glancing down at her tablet, she marked something off. "Instead of battling your partners, today you will face someone new. We don't want you getting too comfortable now, do we?"

I groaned louder than intended, and a few of my classmates snickered. Great, with my luck I'd get Raine, and she'd accidentally maim me.

"Guess you're really going to have to step up your game today," whispered Ash, his emerald eyes twinkling.

"I hope you get your ass kicked," I hissed.

He chuckled, wrapping his arm around me again. "Remember what we practiced. You know all the spells, you just have to feel them."

Feel, shmeel. I didn't ever feel anything but a gaping emptiness inside me. I didn't have any magic, and I doubted I ever would. Maybe they'd send me home at the end of the semester when they realized I was a half-blood dud. At least I'd get to see Jay.

Professor Malindra called the first set of names—Raine and Aeria. That would be an interesting match; watching the uber-powerful besties battle it out should definitely provide some entertainment.

By the wicked twitch of Drake's lips on the other side of Ash, I guessed he felt the same.

"Aeria, you attack first and Raine you must defend yourself using only your powers. I'm not looking for physical displays of strength, ladies. And remember, if you step beyond the mat, you automatically fail the exercise." The professor stepped out of the red circle of death. "And begin."

Before Malindra's mouth was fully closed, an ethereal melody filled the air. Aeria's nostrils flared, her lips pressed in a tight line as her chest rose and fell with the tune. My head began to spin, a dense fog clouding my senses and I latched onto Ash before my knees buckled. Damn siren's song.

"Copertum!" Professor Malindra threw her hands up, and a golden bubble surrounded the two girls. The unearthly tune cut off, and the haze over my brain began to lift.

"You okay, kid?" Ryder was suddenly at my side, taking Ash's place to steady me.

I straightened, crossing my arms over my chest. "Yeah, I'm fine. I should've seen that one coming."

"Have you been working on your mental block?" Since I hadn't been able to spark any real abilities, Ryder had me practicing blocking out others' powers. It sounded good in theory, but the supes were just too strong.

"I've been trying, but even Cinder's measly powers can break through."

"Maybe we'll have to arrange some one-on-one training." He

shot me a wicked grin, and my insides clenched. Man, why did he still have that effect on me? I'd thought after a month of spending time with the real Ryder as opposed to the one I'd been crushing on from the TV show, I would've gotten over the lusty feelings by now. But no such luck. Every time I saw him with Ms. Sexy Succubus I wanted to vomit.

A bright flash of light yanked my attention back to the battling divas. I looked up in time to see Aeria and her neon blue hair fly through the air and crash into the far wall before crumpling to the floor. Ouch!

The golden bubble around Raine disappeared, and she stepped out of the circle with a triumphant smile.

"Well done," said Professor Malindra, patting her on the shoulder.

"That girl is an animal," whispered Ryder. "Were you watching? Did you see how she broke through Aeria's song?"

My head bobbed up and down. I couldn't tell him I was too distracted by him to pay attention. Even if I had, I'd never be able to replicate what she'd done.

A few of The Seven gathered around Aeria and helped her up. Raf snaked his arm around her waist and led her to a chair. His palms began to glow, and his soothing energy radiated all the way across the opposite side of the room.

"I'd love to have healing powers like angels and nephilim do." The words popped out even though I hadn't meant to utter them aloud.

Ryder grimaced. "Yeah, yeah. I guess they're kinda cool abilities if you want to expend all your energy curing others."

Having experienced Raf's healing powers myself, I couldn't help the twinge of anger that bubbled up inside. "As opposed to your cool powers of sucking human souls out?"

A flash of yellow eclipsed Ryder's onyx irises, and his dark brows slammed together. "Please, don't hold back, Luna. Tell me how you really feel."

"Ryder, that's not what I meant—"

He spun away, moving between the other students so quickly he was nothing more than a black blur. When my eyes were finally able to focus on him again, he was on the opposite side of the room, standing beside Cillian. His arms were crossed tightly against his chest, black swirling tattoos peeking out from beneath his taut shirt.

Ugh, why couldn't I think before I spoke? And who knew he'd be so touchy about the whole demon thing?

"Okay, next two in the circle—Luna and Drake," announced Professor Malindra.

"What?" My gaze bounced from Ash to Drake and back. "That has to be a mistake."

"Come forward, please."

As I walked to the center of the circle of death, I caught Ryder's eye. As mad as he'd been a second ago, now the only thing that reflected in those dark irises was worry. Worry I was about to get my butt kicked and end up in the infirmary for the rest of the week. Drake was the most powerful in our entire defensive magic class—heck, probably in the entire academy.

From the corner of my eye, I saw Ryder whisper something to Cillian, but the headmaster shook his head.

Drake took his spot across from me, his intense lilac eyes practically glowing. There was no way he was going to take it easy on me, not with Cillian and Ryder watching. If I'd been the religious kind, I would've been praying like mad right now. After my prayers went unanswered for so many years, I'd given up on believing anyone up there was listening. Which was kind of ironic since I was sitting in a room with an angel and a half-angel.

The professor's voice snapped me from my jumbled thoughts. "Luna, you attack first."

A roar of laughter burst from the rest of the class. To

Drake's credit, his lip only slightly curled before he schooled it back to his typical cool mask.

All the defensive spells I'd learned swirled through my mind —I knew the words by heart, but it didn't help when I couldn't wield any power behind them. A trickle of sweat snaked down my back as my blood pumped in double time.

"Whenever you're ready, Ms. Hallows..."

Come on, Luna. Again that feeling of needing to shed my skin came over me, my flesh prickled and I was sure if I didn't move or do something, my insides would burst. I squeezed my eyes shut and spat out the first words that came to mind. "Venite ignis fuoco!" I threw my hands out and stared hopelessly at my sprawled fingers.

Nothing. Not even a flicker or a flame.

A few people snickered, but the majority of the class seemed to feel bad for me. Poor little half-blood without magic. *You don't belong here.* The creepy words I'd heard in the hall on my first day swam through my mind. They were right. I didn't belong here.

"Try again, Ms. Hallows."

I glanced up at Drake and shrugged. Maybe fire was too advanced. I'd go for something easier this time. "Venite aris manifesto!" Again my hands shot out, but not an ounce of wind blew through the classroom as I'd intended.

"Do we really have to keep doing this?" Drake turned to Professor Malindra.

Heat swam across my cheeks, the burn rushing down my neck and all the way up my ears. It was a good thing my hair covered them.

"All right, Luna, let's try something else. Drake, you attack her, and you defend yourself, dear."

My jaw dropped, and a few muffled gasps bubbled across the classroom.

"Is that a good idea, Malindra?" Ryder's voice snapped my attention toward him and the headmaster.

Again, Cillian said a few words to his demon nephew. Ryder's lips twisted into a scowl, but he didn't say anything further.

I turned back to Drake whose icy gaze raked over me. Deep purple specks sparked to life as he drew on his magic. I was so dead.

"Come on, Luna, use your shield," Ash whisper-hissed from just outside the circle. He'd gotten himself a front row view of the showdown.

Oh right, the defensive shield I'd never once managed to summon.

"And begin!"

A wave of freezing air slammed into me, pushing me back to the edge of the circle. My arms shot out as I mumbled the shield spell over and over. My teeth chattered, but nothing happened.

"Point for Drake," said the professor. "Again."

The ice prince's light brows drew together as he regarded me. Was that pity? Regret? Whatever it was, it vanished. He lifted his hands and shards of ice ripped toward me. I threw my hands up to protect my face from the sharp glass-like projectiles as I continued to mutter the shielding encantation. "Protectum ad armorae, protectum ad armorae."

The ice cut my uniform shirt, digging into my flesh like tiny daggers. "Mother, father!" I screeched. I huddled at the edge of the circle, only a few inches away from safety—and failing the exercise.

The barrage of ice stopped, and I straightened, brushing the melting icicles off my clothes. At least with ice, I didn't have to worry about the missiles getting permanently stuck in my skin. It suddenly occurred to me that Drake *was* going easy on me.

It must have also occurred to our professor. "Last round,

Drake. I'd like you to step it up this time. No faery magic, I want spellcraft."

He nodded, his lips thinning.

A growl reverberated from across the room where Cillian and Ryder stood. I couldn't be certain, but it sure sounded like it came from my demon instructor. "Luna, concentrate!" he hissed.

I wanted to punch him. It wasn't like I wanted to fail. I didn't like being tortured and made fun of as the only human at the academy. At least if I had powers, I wouldn't feel like a complete waste of space. Anger rippled inside me. I hated being weak and defenseless. My entire life I'd been strong—I had to be to survive being bounced around foster care for a year after Mrs. Hallows died.

"Begin!"

Drake's eyes locked on mine, an unearthly glow lining his irises. This was it. "Volant pugione!"

It only took a second for the words to register in my mind. Daggers. That a-hole prince was going to impale me with knives! Four blades shot through the air, flying end over end as if in slow motion.

"Protectum ad armorae, protectum ad armorae." The crazed words tumbled from my lips over and over as the speeding projectiles neared, a bubble of fury expanding in my chest the closer they got. No one thought I belonged here—hell, I didn't think I belonged here, but that didn't mean they could use me as a human pincushion.

I slid to the ground at the last second, throwing my arms over my head. A sharp sting cut across my forearm, and I bit back a scream, squeezing my eyes shut. Then everything went silent.

Warmth surrounded me, and I slowly opened my eyes and pushed myself off the ground. A hazy blue bubble cocooned me in safety. My eyes widened as I took in all the blurry faces gawking at me from the other side.

"You did it!" Ryder's face coalesced just outside my glimmering orb.

I shook my head. No, it couldn't be. Someone else must have pitied me and summoned up a safety spell to save me from total mortification.

"Come on out." He extended his hand, but it went no further than the exterior of the bubble.

I stood up and the magical sphere burst, letting all the commotion around me in. Ryder's arms shot out to tug me into an embrace, but he pulled back right before reaching me. Instead, he patted me on the shoulder and rewarded me with a beaming smile. "Nicely done, kid. I knew you had it in you."

Ash appeared next, tugging me into a big hug. "It was about time, human!" A huge smile spread across my lips. Over his shoulder, Drake's tall form appeared.

A twinge of anger squirmed its way through the unrestrained glee. I popped my hands on my hips and shot him my nastiest glare. "Thanks for almost killing me, jerk."

He moved closer, a look in his eye I didn't think I'd live long enough to see. "You did well for a half-blood," he muttered, but it was too late, I'd already seen the shine of pride in his eyes.

I had to clench my jaw to keep it from dropping open. The ice prince wasn't completely emotionless after all. "Thanks. Who knew fearing for my life would scare the magic out of me?"

"I did." With a smirk, he sauntered off to join Raine and Aeria who sulked on the opposite side of the classroom.

For once, they were the only ones shooting me hateful glares. The rest of the students actually seemed happy for me.

Ryder appeared once again by my side. His dark gaze roamed over my arms and legs, and his lips twisted. In all the excitement, I'd completely forgotten about the bloody cuts.

Apparently, Ryder had not. Everything else fell away, the rest of the class fading into the background at his ever-nearing proximity. He took my hand, extending my arm and ran his finger over the length of it. Tiny electric shocks prickled my flesh at his gentle touch. "We have to get these looked at. The last thing we need is you getting some weird human infection."

I swallowed hard, unable to speak when he looked at me like that. Like he actually cared, like I could possibly be more than just his student.

Cillian cleared his throat, appearing over Ryder's shoulder. I'd forgotten how imposing the angel headmaster could be as he loomed over us. Ryder dropped my arm and turned to his uncle. "She did good, right?"

"Very good, Luna. I'm pleased the classes are finally paying off. Kimmie-Jayne will be happy to hear it."

"Thanks." I'd texted with my half-sister a few times in the past month. She usually checked in about once a week for an update on my training. She'd be thrilled to hear something finally clicked.

"Ryder, why don't you take Luna to the healer to get those cuts cured?"

He lifted his hand to his head and saluted. "Will do, boss."

CHAPTER 11

"**A**re you sure you don't want to come with us to the movie?" Cinder, Maxi and Alissa stood by our dorm door dressed in plain clothes. Well, plain wasn't exactly an accurate description. It was a Friday night, and they'd swapped out the traditional school uniforms for sexy dresses and sparkly mini-skirts. It seemed like a bit much for a movie night at the quad, but what did I know?

I tightened the tie of my fuzzy robe and stared at the book on spellcraft splayed across my bed. "Nah, I should really study." After my magic made a cameo in Defensive Magic class a week ago, it decided to go back in hiding.

Cinder waggled her finger at me. "Okay, but don't forget, you can't go out tonight."

"Yes, mom," I teased. "Rule number three: No going out in the Fae forest on a full moon."

She clapped her hands. "Very good, Luna. We'll make a model student out of you yet!"

"Have fun, girls." With a genuine smile on my face, I waved at the dragon shifters who'd adopted me. I never would've survived this long without them.

As soon as the door slammed shut, I hopped off my bed and shrugged out of my robe. Jeans and a comfy old sweatshirt were hidden beneath. I hadn't been lying to my friends, I really did need to study, but it wasn't spellcraft I needed to work on. I'd memorized those incantations a long time ago... it was another beast I needed to conquer.

Slipping on my boots, a beanie and my thick uniform coat, I dashed out of my room. The corridors were silent as I crept down the quiet floor. Luckily, all my dragon shifter floor mates had gone to movie night.

The first major unipeg race was coming up in under a week, and I still hadn't even been able to mount Zeus. The animal was more thickheaded than a mule and twice as ornery. Every time I got the chance, I snuck down to the stables to make nice with the jerk. We'd made progress at least—he didn't try to bite me when I fed him the elaria fruit he loved so much. I clutched the oval, pink-skinned fruit in my hand, which was now permanently stocked in my dorm room. I couldn't blame the guy; they were delicious and nothing like we had in the human world. Its pillowy, white flesh tasted like a cross between mango and cotton candy.

My mouth watered at the thought.

Swinging the backdoor open, a frosty blast of winter wind nearly dampened my resolve. Freakin' a, it was cold! I hiked up my coat collar and pulled my scarf over my nose. I just had to reach the barn, and then I'd be fine. Somehow the weird faery magic kept it nice and toasty for the unipegs.

Following the dimly lit path toward the stables, the icy air prickled my skin. The encroaching Fae forest loomed all around me, the towering pines caging me in. A full moon hovered over the treetops, bathing the dark green in a creepy ethereal glow.

An eerie howl shattered the stillness, echoing across the forest. What in all the realms was that? Another howl rang out from the opposite direction. My head whipped from side to side, searching the dark shadows. A chill skittered up my spine, and I hurried down the path. *Just keep moving.*

The dense foliage finally parted, and the gray stone stables appeared. Relief unfurled in my chest as I sprinted the last few yards. As I slammed the barn door shut behind me and leaned against the rough timber, I mentally cursed myself for not asking more questions about this full moon lockdown. Maybe I'd been stupid to think I'd be safe within the academy grounds.

A gruff snort drew me from my momentary meltdown, and I pushed myself off the door. Zeus's head poked over his stall gate. His nostrils flared as I neared.

"Hey buddy," I whispered, creeping closer.

He stomped his hoof, the clash of his metal shoe against the stone floor clanging across the quiet barn.

"Relax. I just brought you this." I held out the elaria fruit, and his obsidian eyes widened. He stretched out his neck, his lips elongating to reach for the treat I held out of reach. "You remember the drill, Zeus. A bite of fruit for a pat on the head."

I could've sworn the beast rolled his eyes at me. After a brief pause, he huffed and lowered his spiked horn. Slowly reaching forward, I ran my fingers over his soft nose and up to his shaggy mane.

He stepped back, pulling his head out of reach and stared at me expectantly. Man, this unipeg did not mess around. "Fine, here you go." I held out the elaria, and he bared his big white teeth before taking a huge bite. I snatched my hand back right before he took the whole fruit and my fingers with it.

Chomping away happily, his lips lifted into a grin. *I swear!* I snuck another quick pat in while he chewed, always marveled by how soft and silky his mane was. It was nothing like the short, brittle hair of the horses hitched up to the carriages around Central Park.

"Listen, Zeus, we've got less than a week till the opening race of the year, and if I can't even manage to mount you, I'm going to be the laughing stock of the school. I'm not saying we have to win or anything—you just need to let me get on." He stopped munching, his dark eyes scrutinizing me. "Please. Do this for me, and I promise to bring you special treats every night for the rest of my days here." Which might not be very long if I couldn't get a handle on my magic, but he didn't need to know that.

He snorted again, eyeing the remaining half of elaria fruit in my hand.

"Come on, what do you say?"

Zeus reached for the fruit, nuzzling my hand, which I took as a good sign. Usually he would've just tried to rip it out of my grasp. I handed it to him, and he continued to chew happily.

This was it. I had to try. I grabbed the halter from the hook and eased it over his head, making sure not to catch his unicorn in the straps. He tensed as I slid it over his ears, momentarily pausing his chomping. "Good boy," I muttered. "You just keep eating and pay no mind to what I'm doing over here."

With the halter securely fastened, I inched open the gate. The creak of the old hinges made my heart jump up my throat. A trickle of sweat dripped down my back as I pried it open the rest of the way.

Zeus eyed me curiously as he finished off the last bit of his treat. I managed to lead him out of the stall and hook him up to the crossties. He watched my every move, those intense irises boring into me with each step I took. When I approached him with the saddle pad, his eyes widened, the bright white brilliant against the velvety onyx hue. He swung his head back and forth, pawing at the ground.

"Come on, Zeus. Just one quick try. I promise I won't even take you outside."

He huffed but lowered his head so I quickly swung the pad and the saddle over his back, careful to avoid his majestic wings. I'd never even seen their rainbow underside yet. He always kept them tucked tight to his body as if purposely hiding their beauty from me.

Cinching up the girth, a wave of giddiness swam over me. This was the farthest I'd gotten so far with the wily creature. The last part was the bridle—the trickiest by far. There was always that half a second from slipping the halter off and the bridle on where he could bolt. Then I'd be spending my night chasing Zeus across the Fae forest—and I'd probably get eaten by whatever was out there.

Steeling my nerves, I slipped the leather bridle off the hook and crept toward the unipeg. He eyed it warily as I approached. "This is the last part, Zeus. We're almost done, and then I'll give you another elaria fruit. What do you think?" I pulled the succulent fruit out of my pocket, and he whinnied. Setting it down by his stall door, I held up the bridle. "Ready?"

He remained still, so I took that as a yes. Unsnapping the crossties, I drew in a breath. With one hand, I eased the halter off, the bridle firmly clutched in the other. One...two...three. I slipped the bridle over his horn and ears, slid the bit into his mouth and quickly latched the leather straps. *Yes!* He hadn't even tried to bite my fingers off like I'd expected.

Now I had to get on.

Moving to his side, I tugged the stirrup down and he backed up a few steps.

"Come on, Zeus. This is it. Let me get on for a few seconds and then you get your treat."

He stopped moving, but his neck was fully craned facing me as I attempted to get my foot in the iron. *Here goes nothing.* Hitching my right foot in the stirrup, I hauled myself up.

Zeus took off.

"No!" I screeched as he reared. I clutched onto the reins, hanging from one foot as he raced backward down the stable. "Stop, Zeus!" My shouts did nothing as the stubborn beast bucked, determined to get the poor dangling human off his back.

My foot was slipping, and my grip on the reins faltered. I couldn't hold on much longer. With Zeus bucking and rearing, I couldn't swing my other leg over his body. He backed up all the way to the stable doors, ramming his butt against the timber. Oh sh—shnap! This crazy animal was going to break the doors down.

I had no other choice but to let go. Releasing the reins, it felt like I was falling forever. Just my luck, I'd get assigned the absurdly tall beast who towered over all the other unipegs. I hit the ground with a thud, the sharp pain ricocheting up my spine and leaching through every single bone.

I bit down on my lower lip when I hit the stone floor and a briny, metallic taste filled my mouth. *Bleh.* Staring up at the black beast, I shot him a narrowed glare. "I hate you."

The moment I was off, his body relaxed, the crazy in his eyes dissipating. He huffed and trotted over to his stall without giving me a second look.

I pushed myself off the ground, brushing the dirt and hay off my butt. That was definitely going to leave a bruise. I limped over to Zeus's stall and considered removing the bridle and saddle. Nah. Let him suffer. If he were so smart, he'd figure out a way to get it off himself. Latching the gate, I trudged out, making sure to grab the remaining elaria fruit before I left. I took a big bite of it just to spite the obstinate beast.

He snorted as I walked away, flashing me his muscular backside.

My shoulders slumped as I shrugged into my coat. I was never going to tame that wild animal. I was destined to spend my days at Darkblood grounded, without ever experiencing the thrill of flying. Unless Cinder took pity on me one day and let me ride her dragon.

The chilly air seeped right through my coat the moment I

stepped outside. This night had been a total disaster. I should've gone with Cinder and the girls to the movie. A carefree night was just what I needed.

The snow crunched beneath my boots as I plodded up the pathway back to the dormitories. The full moon hung high in the air, seemingly at its pinnacle, illuminating the blanket of freshly fallen snow. Hugging myself to keep the cold from sneaking in, I hurried up the path as my frosty breath swirled at my nose. The trees thickened, dark green limbs reaching out to grab me as I passed. A jagged branch snagged the arm of my jacket, and I staggered back. A sharp rip had me cursing before I spun around to survey the damage on my new academy-issued coat. *Great, torn already.*

Breaking free from the stupid vindictive branch, I turned back toward the dormitory. Only it was gone. As was the clearly marked path I'd been following a second ago. I whipped my head back toward the stables. And the barn.

What the actual eff?

Towering pines boxed me in, the forest growing denser by the moment. I rubbed my eyes, convinced I was seeing things. The trees seemed to be multiplying right before me, sucking me deeper and deeper into the woods.

Darkness blossomed in every direction, the monstrous pines having grown so tall they blocked out the lustrous full moon visible only moments ago.

Panic seized my heart, her icy fingers wrapping around my frantically thundering organ. *Stay calm, Luna.* I couldn't possibly be lost. I'd been less than a hundred yards from the dormitory when I got turned around.

The snap of a nearby branch sent my pulse skyrocketing. I spun in the direction of the sound. "Is someone out here?"

Silence.

"Hello?"

The crunch of snow beneath heavy boots sent me spinning

in the opposite direction. Squinting, I stared at the break in the trees. The leaves began to shake, and my hands followed their lead.

A hooded creature emerged from the shadows, bright, neon-yellow eyes peeking out from under a dark cowl.

Good goblins!

Ice surged through my veins, running all the way up through my vocal chords. I wanted to scream, to run, to do anything, but I was frozen in place.

Unearthly irises pierced me, their intensity more fierce than the chill setting in my bones. "Mortal," he growled, the sound more animal than human. "You dare set foot in my dominion?"

"I, um... I'm sorry. I didn't mean to. I got turned around somehow and ended up here."

Another hooded figure emerged from behind a nearby tree, the same neon eyes glowing beneath the dark hood. I clasped my hands together to keep them from trembling. This was bad —really bad.

The second creature sniffed the air, his cowl sliding back an inch, revealing brown leathery skin beneath. "Blood, human blood," it hissed. "And something else too..."

My heart staggered as I glanced at the tear in my coat. A tiny trickle of blood seeped from the opening. *That damn tree cut me*!

They slunk closer, the pair moving as one. I took a step back, then another.

"Me want a taste," said one, lifting a clawed finger.

"She smells delicious," hissed the other.

Okay, now it was time to run. I spun around and sprinted through the darkness. Rogue branches tore at my coat as I ran. Pumping my arms back and forth, I wound through the thick copse of trees, no idea if I was going in the right direction or disappearing further into the twisted forest.

The crunch of heavy footfalls behind me quickened my

pace. I was suddenly very thankful for all the running Ryder made us do in combat class. Whatever those things were, they weren't giving up. I swung a quick left, hoping to lose them and dug my heels into the ground, throwing my hands up to keep my balance.

My heart leapt up my throat as six pairs of lupine eyes froze every ounce of blood running through my veins.

CHAPTER 12

Wolves—a whole pack of them. Only they were nothing like the ones I'd seen at Central Park Zoo. They looked like wolves on steroids, easily the size of small horses.

I backed up a step, and the giant gray one snarled. His huge amber eyes lit up as they scanned over me, his nose high in the air. He ticked his head to a smaller brown one, and the animal scampered off disappearing in the dark trees. Behind me, I could still make out the heavy footsteps of my attackers. They'd slowed from the sounds of it, but they were nearby.

Oh fudge, I was so dead. My only choice was which way I'd rather die—by wolf or whatever the hell those creepy hooded things were.

The leader of the pack moved forward, and the other four tightened the circle around him. A low rumble reverberated in the gray wolf's throat as he inched closer, his silvery gray fur glistening under the moonlight. If it weren't for the sharp teeth and menacing growls, the wild animal would've been beautiful.

Behind me, the scuffle of approaching footsteps drew my

attention and I spun around. The two dark figures emerged from the dense forest, their eyes aglow. *Dead, I'm so dead.*

The giant gray wolf let out a sharp howl and lunged.

I screamed and threw my arms up to cover my face as a blur of sharp white teeth and claws sprang at me. I waited for the pain, for the searing slash of teeth against flesh, but it never came. Instead a wave of warmth tingled my flesh. Prying my eyelids open, I took in the blue bubble radiating around me. I huffed out a breath of relief, my shoulders sagging.

The muffled sounds of fighting animals resonated beyond my orb of safety as the wolves and the hooded creatures battled it out.

My breath came in haggard pants as I pushed myself off the snowy ground. I had to get out of there while the monsters were distracted. My blue bubble moved with me as I crept toward the never-ending tree line.

Hidden within the safety of the shadows, I leaned up against a rough bark and sucked in a sharp breath. The protective sphere suddenly disappeared, shattering my hopes along with it. "Damn you, magic!" *Can't you just stick with me?*

A hand clamped over my mouth, and my heart stopped.

I gasped, trying to wriggle free from my captor's iron hold, but his arm encircled my waist from behind the tree. I was trapped.

"Don't scream. It's me, mini minx." The familiar raspy voice did things to my insides that no mere male voice should be capable of.

I slumped back against the tree and he released his hold, appearing in front of me. My knees quivered, and I was about a second from hitting the floor again when Ryder's steady arm shot out, pulling me into his chest.

"It's okay. I got you." His warm breath tickled my ear as he whispered softly.

With my nose pressed against his jacket, it was impossible

not to breathe in his musky, sandalwood scent. It was inviting yet mysterious, much like the man I was currently pressed up against. My fingers were splayed out across his washboard abs, and I had to suppress the urge to run them over every finely sculpted dip and hollow. *Bad, Luna!*

A sharp howl set the hairs on my neck bristling, and all lusty thoughts vanished.

"We have to get out of here now," said Ryder. Glancing down at me, his sexy lips curled into a smirk revealing that damn dimple. "Can you walk or do I have to carry you?"

I smacked him in the stomach, and it was like hitting a brick wall. I winced, gritting my teeth. That definitely hurt me more than it did him. "I'm fine. As long as you know how to get back. One minute I was on the path and the next everything went topsy-turvy."

He took my hand, tightly clenching his big fingers around my frozen ones and turned us down a footpath that hadn't been there a second ago. "That's exactly why you're not supposed to be out on a full moon. Didn't you hear the announcements? See the dozens of posted warning signs?"

I shrugged as he tugged me between the trees. "I didn't think it was such a big deal."

"What were you doing out here anyway?"

"I went to see Zeus. I never meant to leave the campus grounds."

"The full moon is the one night when the Fae have the run of their territory. All the nastiest creatures come out to play, and the faery magic roams free. Those damn Fae are tricky little fu—fiends. They can warp time and space, and you could've been lost circling the forest for days." He raked his hand through his hair and grunted.

"Okay, okay I got it. I'm sorry—no more outings on the full moon. What kind of Fae were they anyway?" They were nothing like the beautiful creatures that roamed the academy.

"Trolls."

I opened my mouth to ask more, but a sudden stab of pain in my arm turned my question into a squeal.

"What's wrong?" Ryder spun around, momentarily halting our frenzied pace.

"I don't know; my arm hurts." I tried to lift up the one he wasn't holding but it refused to comply. Come to think of it, it had been kind of numb and tingly.

His brows furrowed and he grabbed my other hand, lifting my arm to examine it. He let out a sharp hiss when he reached halfway up my bicep. "You're bleeding."

I'd completely forgotten about the branch that snagged my coat. "It's nothing. I got caught on a tree limb when I was running."

A dark storm brewed within his impossibly onyx irises as they lifted from my arm to meet my gaze. He cursed and swung me into his arms before I could open my mouth. The woods raced by us in a blur of dark greens and browns awash in white. I squeezed my eyes shut, scared I'd puke.

I didn't open them again until a wave of warm air hit me. We were back in the dorms, and Ryder was darting up the stairs like one of those trolls was still on our heels.

We reached my room, and he barreled through the door. Luckily, Cinder wasn't back yet or that would've been hella embarrassing.

"Ryder, what is going on?" I screeched as he dropped me on my bed. As if on cue, my arm began to throb. I probably hadn't felt it before because of the freezing temps outside.

"Take your coat off, now." The fire burning in his bottomless irises made my breath hitch. "Now, Luna!" he growled, a flash of yellow eclipsing the black.

I tugged my coat off, the pain in my arm crawling down to my fingers. Blood had soaked through my sweater, leaving a dark crimson stain on my new pullover.

"The sweater too, and shirt if it's long sleeved."

I shot him a glare. "Seriously?" He expected me to get naked in front of him?

"Luna, just do as I say, now!"

There was a tremble in his voice that froze my insides. Without another word, I slipped off my sweater and shirt, wrapping my good arm over my half-naked torso. Thank goodness I was wearing my only cute black bra.

His eyes widened, and a string of curses flew from his lips as he examined my arm. I was scared to look at the wound after his reaction.

"Shit, Luna! What were you thinking going out there by yourself?" He shook his head, his irises no longer black, completely replaced by an eerie translucent citrine.

"I already said I was sorry. What more can I say?" My arm felt like it had a pulse of its own, the erratic staccato intensifying with every breath I took. I steeled my nerves and took a peek.

Son of a biscuit! I gasped. Dark blue veins ran up and down my arm, a jagged wound spilling deep crimson liquid from my flesh. "Wh-what is this?"

He knelt down in front me, the panic I was feeling mirrored in his tense expression. "Poison. It travels fast. If we don't get it out of you..." His gaze moved from my shoulder toward my collarbone where the blue veins spiderwebbed across my skin.

"How about the healer?"

He shook his head. "It'll be too late. I have to get the poison out now."

My eyes widened. "How?"

He grimaced and swallowed hard, his Adam's apple bobbing. "Do you trust me?"

I nodded quickly. I did, even though I wasn't sure why.

Ryder took my arm and lifted it to his mouth, his lips about to close over the oozing wound.

I snatched my arm back, shaking my head. "You're going to suck it out of me?" The idea was both repulsive and strangely thrilling.

"I have to. It's the fastest way."

My heart jackhammered against my ribs. "But won't it poison you?"

"I'm a demon. I'm sure I'll be fine."

My head whipped back and forth, my insides roiling. I wasn't sure I was willing to take that risk. "What if something happens to you..."

He lifted his finger to my lips, halting the words on my tongue. "I promised to take care of you. If I don't do this, you *will* die. No more arguing—there's no time."

The dark veins spread as he spoke, coiling around my heart like a venomous snake and its frantic beating slowed. "Okay, do it."

I couldn't tear my eyes away as his lips closed around the festering wound. He sucked, and my insides clenched, his burning yellow gaze remaining locked on mine. My fingers curled around the soft comforter as heat blazed in my core. This was messed up on so many levels. How could I be turned on by this?

With every spine-tingling pull of his lips, the dark veins receded. Fire ripped through my veins, and I clenched my teeth through the bizarre sensations. The pressure from my chest relented almost immediately, and I drew in a deep breath. A tiny voice in the back of my mind told me this was what it felt like to get your soul ripped out. And I was *totally* okay with it.

Ryder's lips detached, and he raced to the bathroom. The gagging sounds seeped through the closed door, and my heart clenched. He had literally swallowed poison for me. A second later he was back, eyeing the vanishing navy veins. A trickle of black sludge dribbled down his chin, and nausea clawed at the back of my throat.

"Just a little more," he muttered, his voice all breathy and way too sexy considering what was going on.

I nodded, my throat too dry to utter a sound.

His lips closed over the wound once again, and my head fell back, the odd mixture of pleasure and pain spilling through my veins. Goose bumps prickled my skin, every single nerve ending lit up like live wire. When my gaze met his once again, his eyes were unreadable. His pupils had thinned to tiny slits, the irises completely consumed in vibrant yellow.

With one final slurp, he released his hold on my arm and sat back. His eyes were glossy, and a strange smirk pulled at his lips.

"Are you okay?" I mumbled.

He spat into a paper towel he pulled from his jeans pocket, a dark sludgy loogie coating the white. Shooting up to his feet, he swayed for a moment before righting himself.

I jumped up to help him, but he held his hand up, pushing me away. "I have to go. If you need anything call the healer, but you should be fine now."

"How about you?"

He shook his head, but the hazy expression lingered. The brilliant yellow pulsated in his irises. "I nee—need to go now." His words were a raspy growl, more beast than human.

Before I could even get the words "thank you" out, he spun around and darted from my room in a blur.

CHAPTER 13

I crept up the stairs to the administration wing, a swarm of bumblebee stingers jabbing at my insides. I'd been summoned to the headmaster's office, and after last night's fiasco it couldn't be good news. As tough as things had been here at Darkhen Academy, I didn't want to go home. *What home?* An annoying but sadly accurate voice whispered in my mind.

Cillian couldn't send me away now, right? Not when I was finally starting to show some hints of magical powers.

The small desk in front of the headmaster's office was empty—no Darby in sight. I didn't miss the creepy old man one bit. Cillian's door was ajar as I approached and hushed voices escaped through the crack.

My ears perked up at the familiar gruff one.

"You should've seen her last night, Cill," Ryder growled. "She shouldn't be here; she's not ready for any of this."

My heart plummeted... Was he talking about me?

"She's fine now, and that's what matters," said Cillian. "And she has to be here. There's no other option for her now. We promised Kimmie-Jayne we'd keep her safe, and we will."

The loud crack of what sounded like a fist hitting a desk made me jump back a foot. "That's easy for you to say. You're not the one out there with her."

Cillian's voice took on a soothing tone, his words lilting like a babbling brook and I leaned closer to the thick timber. "I have faith in you nephew. You'll do everything in your power to keep her safe."

"What if it's not good enough?"

Cillian grunted. "It has to be. For all our sakes." He paused, and it sounded like he was shuffling some papers on his desk. "You're not getting too close are you?"

"Of course not." Ryder blew out a breath. "Any news from Logan?"

The headmaster huffed. "Nothing good. The attacks are getting more frequent and more flagrant. Garrix won't be able to keep this out of the media much longer regardless of the efforts of the Gargoyle Guardian Council." He paused, and I could almost see the gears grinding in the angel's mind. "How's training going? Are they ready?"

"Not quite, but they're getting there. They're powerful, Cillian, really powerful, but still..."

"Still what?"

"They're young and naïve, and I'm not sure they're ready for what's to come."

"They're only a few years younger than you, nephew. Were you ready?"

Ryder snorted. "Touché."

The sound of his approaching footsteps sent me racing out of the foyer and down the steps toward the main hall. I'd have to find out what my punishment was for breaking the full moon rules later. Right now, I had to beat Ryder to class and try to make sense of what I'd overheard.

Hurtling through the gym doors five minutes later, I smacked right into a hard body. I glanced up knowing full well whom I'd run into. I'd already memorized every curve of his body and mouthwatering scent after last night. How'd he get back here so freakin' quickly?

Ryder stiffened, taking a step back and heat flushed my cheeks. The wound on my arm tingled as if recognizing the feel of his lips. "Glad to see you could join us, Ms. Hallows."

Ms. Hallows? What? No kid, mini minx or even Luna?

I wrapped my arms across my chest, and his gaze flickered to the bandage across my bicep.

He lowered his voice, his dark eyes back to normal, the craze I'd seen last night long gone. "Are you well enough for class?"

I nodded. "I feel fine." If he wanted to pretend like nothing happened then so could I. I wasn't the one being shady and keeping secrets.

"Fine." He ticked his head at Drake, and I groaned. "Mr. Wintersbee you'll be sparring with our newbie today."

Drake rolled his eyes as he approached, his gaze scanning the white bandage. "She's already injured. I don't want to be held responsible for what happens."

Raine and Aeria giggled from behind him, the two girls shooting nasty glares my way. Beside them stood the remaining Seven in a tight circle. A pair of amber eyes caught mine, and the image of the gray wolf in the forest darted across my mind. Triston. I didn't know him well, but the citrine pin on his polo shirt marked him a shifter. Could he have been the massive gray wolf I'd encountered last night?

"Luna? Luna, are you still with us?" Ryder's annoyed tone made it clear it hadn't been the first time he'd called my name.

"Yeah, sorry. What did you say?"

He handed me a pair of kickboxing gloves and matching head-gear. "Get going. You've got a lot of work to catch up on today."

Drake threw me a scowl as he led the way to the corner of

the gym. At least he'd save me the humiliation of being ridiculed front and center. When we reached our training mat, the ice prince strapped on his gloves and tossed the headgear to the floor. He didn't even think I could get one hit in... well, I'd show him. I made it my mission for the day to land at least one punch in the pretty boy's face.

Drake smirked and put his fists up. "Come at me."

I channeled all the fear and anger from last night's twisted events plus the turmoil building from what I'd overheard this morning and attacked. My fists flew at him like angry bumble-bees, but he swatted each hit away with ease. It only added more fuel to the fire.

I surprised him with a roundhouse kick, my foot connecting with his upper shoulder. "Yes!" I squealed.

A small smirk tugged his lip up. "Should I start fighting back now?"

"I'd like to see you try."

His lilac eyes twinkled, and his movements became a blur. Holding my gloved fists over my face was all I could do to keep myself from getting knocked out. A second later, I smacked into the mat with an earthshaking thud. Okay, maybe I'd been a little overconfident.

Drake held out his hand and helped me up, to my utter shock. "Not bad for a human. You lasted a full thirty seconds. I've put Scarlett down quicker than that."

Scarlett—the quiet vampire member of The Seven. I'd barely had any contact with her since the first day in the locker room. She mostly kept to herself, rarely even socializing with her elite squad.

"Do you guys practice on your own, outside of class hours?" The image of Ryder leading the group of them into the forest in the early morning danced across my mind.

He shrugged, sweeping his hair behind his pointed ear.

"Sometimes. It takes practice to be the best—I mean for the others, of course."

"Of course." I shook my head, suppressing a grin. I needed to get in on this after hours practice. Maybe I could convince Ash to let me join them... Doubtful.

Ryder strutted over, his dark eyes assessing me. "How's it going over here?"

"I haven't killed her yet so that's something."

Such an ass.

"The human was inquiring about getting in some extra practice," Drake went on. "Maybe you could hook her up with that, Ryder?"

The demon's eyes narrowed, and I could've sworn the mighty ice prince actually flinched.

"Or I guess someone else could," he muttered.

Ryder drew in a long breath then huffed it out. "No, you're right. I probably should work with Luna one-on-one."

My heart stuttered, and all the saliva evaporated from my mouth. "Huh?" I managed.

"I hope you don't have plans after class, Luna, because for the next few weeks, your ass is mine."

My core clenched, shooting heat all the way up my neck and spreading across my cheeks.

"And if you're lucky," he continued, "I'll talk to Cillian about letting that count toward your penance for that little stunt last night."

Drake quirked a brow. "What did the human do?"

"Nothing," Ryder and I hissed in unison.

Our instructor turned back to the rest of the class. "Continue as you were, and I'll see you this afternoon, Luna," he called over his shoulder.

"Thanks for that," I muttered to my sparring partner once the infuriating demon was out of earshot.

"You will be thanking me later when Ryder turns you into a

total badass." He ran his hand over his spikey hair. "You want Aeria and Raine to respect you? Prove to them and everyone at Darkblood that you really do belong here."

What was this? Was Drake Wintersbee actually giving me good advice? This guy's mood swings gave me whiplash.

"Well, it would help if I could get my magic under control or to even appear when I wanted it to," I whined.

He rolled his eyes, the mask of boredom he usually wore slipping back on. "You do know how it works here, right? Sure, I'm Fae, and I have Fae magic—control over the winter elements, but before I got here, I couldn't summon daggers, levitate or even conjure up a protective orb. I had to learn all that. As did everyone else here. So sure, you're human and you don't have any inherited magic, but suck it up and learn. Like we all did."

My jaw dropped, and I was utterly speechless. Sure, he'd been a dick about it, but he was right. Maybe it was time I stopped blaming my lack of magic on the universe and started taking control of my abilities myself.

CHAPTER 14

"Him?" I squeaked.

Drake stood beside Professor Malindra with his arms pressed against his chest, his lean muscular arms straining against the black uniform polo. The scowl etched across his lips making it clear he was less than thrilled with our instructor's suggestion.

"Why yes, dear. Drake is the obvious choice for a tutor. He's the strongest in our class, and you've already proven to work well together. Professor Arcana and I already discussed it, and he'll be tutoring you in both spellcraft and defensive magic."

"He shot daggers at me!"

"But he coaxed your magic out, didn't he?" She gave me a smug smile. *Crap on crackers.* This was so not what I was thinking when I asked her for help. I figured Ash would be the logical choice since he was my partner. And he didn't totally hate me unlike the ice prince.

"I can't commit to everyday," Drake finally said. "But I suppose I could do a few days a week, for an hour max."

Professor gave him a beaming smile and patted him on the

shoulder. "That's perfect, thank you, young prince. I'll leave you two to work out the details."

As soon as she walked away, I slumped down in my desk. "You don't have to do this," I said, staring up at him. "I know you'd just as soon kill me than help me."

He shrugged. "Maybe I've grown a heart in the past few weeks. Maybe I've decided you're not as bad as I thought. For a human anyway."

I arched a skeptical brow.

"Triston told me what happened on the full moon."

I knew that gray wolf was him!

"Surviving trolls, the Fae forest and a pack of wolves is pretty impressive for anyone." He cocked his head, those lilac eyes scrutinizing me. "But don't let it go to your head, human. I still don't think half-bloods belong at Darkhen Academy."

Those freaky words from my first day at the academy swam across my mind. "Was it you?"

His light brow arched. "Was what me?"

"My first day here someone said almost those exact words about me not belonging here. They were trying to freak me out or something when I was walking alone in the hall."

He shook his head. "I don't hide in the shadows and scare little girls. That's not my thing. If I had something to say to you, I'd say it right to your face."

Good point. Drake Wintersbee was nothing if not straight-forward.

"So are you ready to practice or what?"

I opened the defensive magic book on my desk and flipped through a few yellowing pages. "Where should we start, oh wise one?"

Drake cracked a smile before pulling up a desk next to mine. A few seconds later, he was all business as he began quizzing me on defensive maneuvers. From the corner of my eye, I couldn't help but trace the sharp line of his jaw and the flicker of light in his unique lilac irises.

Maybe this wouldn't be the worst thing ever.

ZEUS WAS THE WORST THING EVER. DESPITE MY CONTINUED attempts to tame the wild beast with my nightly elaria fruit visits, I still hadn't succeeded in mounting the stubborn brute.

The day of the big race had finally come, and the entire academy had shown up to witness my humiliation. I was the only student failing Flying and Shifting 101, and now I'd become the only first year not to compete in the biggest event of the semester.

"How's he looking today?" Cinder gave me a hopeful smile as she sauntered over. She looked perfect with her sleek onyx hair in a high ponytail and her slim-fitting riding pants tucked into shiny black boots.

I was a mess in an untucked polo and jeans. What did it matter what I looked like when I was going to be grounded anyway? "No progress," I muttered. Which wasn't exactly true. I had managed to get him bridled and saddled which was a feat in and of itself.

She patted my shoulder, eyeing the ornery stallion. "You should at least try."

"So the entire school can witness my mortification? Thanks, but no thanks." I slumped down on the trunk in front of Zeus's stall. "I'm destined to spend my short days at Darkhen magic-less and flightless."

"Don't count yourself out just yet." Raf appeared, a dark shock of hair tumbling over his forehead. The handsome nephilim never spoke much, but he wasn't as standoffish as some of the other Seven.

Cinder's golden eyes shone with excitement. "Are you going

to help her?"

"I don't know how much I can do, but I can shoot the old bastard with a little soothing angel light and see if it calms him down a bit."

Over his shoulder, I caught Drake's eyes fixed on us. His pinched expression was unreadable as usual. Had he sent Raf over or was he pissed he was helping me?

Raf's quiet murmurs coaxed Zeus's head over the stall gate. "Easy, easy, big guy." He extended his hand, allowing the mercurial unipeg to get a whiff. The animal huffed, and Raf ran his fingers over his muzzle. Hazy golden light emanated from his palm, the warmth bathing the space in soothing energy.

Man, I needed a shot of that stuff.

Raf backed away and smiled. "Good luck." Before spinning around, he threw Cinder a cute grin.

"Thanks," I called out behind him. I nudged my roomie in the arm. "Did you see that look?"

"What look?" Her cheeks flamed.

"Raf totally gave you a flirty grin. I thought you said The Seven never talk to anyone, they're too good for all of us, blah, blah, blah."

She shook her head laughing. "It must be because of you. Besides Ash, none of them had ever said a word to me before you showed up. If you haven't noticed, you seemed to have caught the interest of the male members of the exclusive squad."

A rebuttal was on my lips when Mrs. Thornberry appeared, drawing my attention away from our discussion. "Are you girls ready?"

"Yes, ma'am," answered Cinder, way too eagerly for my liking. I pressed my lips together and inclined my head.

"Let's go then. Everyone's waiting."

A swarm of butterflies took off in my belly, their wings battering my insides as I led Zeus out of the barn. I cautiously followed behind Cinder and Bella. Her beautiful white unipeg completed the dragon shifter's picture perfect image. If my roommate hadn't been such a sweetheart, I totally would've been jealous. She had it all—a loving family, a powerful position in the Azarian political world as the sister of the dragon alpha, and she was gorgeous and sweet.

I was lucky she'd adopted me without considering the social ramifications. I guessed I had my half-sister and brother-in-law to thank for that.

The roar of the crowd drew me from my inner musings as we stepped onto the field. Tilting my head up, I found the source of the ruckus. A gigantic floating stadium had been erected below the cloud line. They hadn't been kidding, it did seem like the entire academy had shown up for the spectacle. Thousands of bodies lined the bleachers—way more people than attended the school. Had the Fae locals come to watch too?

Kill. Me. Now.

It was enough to become the academy's laughing stock, but the entire Winter Court?

No sooner had the words popped into my mind... The Fae king, Elrian Wintersbee, and one of the hottest former bachelors from *Hitched* sauntered my way. His pale blue high-collared suit graced his slim lines, hugging his shoulders all the way down to his tapered waist. His platinum blonde hair was neatly tied behind the nape of his neck, his presence screaming royalty.

For a second, his icy lilac eyes met mine and my heart flip-flopped. They were exact replicas of his younger brother's. Then his gaze lifted over my shoulder, and a smile settled over his lips.

Following his eye line, I found Drake seated atop his elegant dapple unipeg. The animal seemed an extension of his limbs, unlike my wily beast who struggled against the bit in his mouth.

Drake trotted past me, meeting his brother with the most genuine smile I'd ever witnessed from the ice prince. He slid off his steed and wrapped Elrian in a hug. I quickly walked by with my head down, praying Zeus wouldn't buck or rear or do any of a number of terrible things to further my mortification.

Before I made it far, Drake called out my name, startling me. "Get over here, human. Someone wants to meet you."

I turned slowly, still half-certain he was messing with me. The king of the Fae wanted to meet *me*?

Elrian stepped forward, extending a hand, his lilac eyes twinkling. "Ms. Hallows, it's a pleasure." His gaze skimmed over me, his lip curled in amusement. "The resemblance is quite remarkable."

I attempted a lame curtsy, but ended up straightening at the last second to avoid ending up on my butt in front of the Winter Court king. "The pleasure is all mine, your Highness." At least I'd learned something from watching Kimmie-Jayne interacting with the royals on TV.

Elrian cocked his head at his brother. "You're right. She does have spunk—just like her sister." He whispered the last part.

Drake paled, and I couldn't help the twinge of glee that exploded in my chest. Drake had been talking to his brother about *me*?

"I look forward to seeing you out there." He tilted his head skyward.

The ice prince sneered. "Not likely. She still hasn't been able to mount good old Zeus."

"Oh no?" The king moved closer to the unipeg, and I nearly pulled him back scared he'd try to gore the royal. Then I'd really be screwed.

To my surprise, Zeus leaned into Elrian's touch and whinnied.

My eyes snapped open. "How'd you do that?"

Elrian chuckled, running his hand up and down the animal's muzzle. "Zeus used to be mine when I was a bit younger than you. We donated him to the academy a few years back." He ticked his head at Drake. "He never took a liking to my brother either."

Drake frowned, crossing his arms against his chest. "He's a stubborn beast."

"Come on, Ms. Hallows. I'll help you on." Elrian took hold of Zeus's reins as I stared dumbly at the surprising king.

"Come on, Luna. We don't have all day," muttered Drake, as he leapt onto his unipeg.

My blood started pumping again, and I urged my legs forward. This was it—it was now or never. The king gave me a leg up, and a moment later I was on. After two months of fighting with the obstinate animal, I was on!

"Thank you," I mumbled breathlessly. My heart was dancing in my chest, and I was afraid it might break out at any moment.

"Good luck, you two." With a smile, Elrian turned toward the unipeg-hitched chariots that were ferrying the guests to the floating stadium.

Glancing around, I scanned the field for Cinder, but she and Bella were nowhere in sight. They'd probably already headed up. I gulped as I stared upward at the ever-growing crowd. It was a good thing I couldn't make out much detail from this distance because the Fae struck me as a rather intimidating bunch.

Beside me, Drake nudged his steed forward and its magnificent wings unfurled, revealing a colorful rainbow beneath. Over his shoulder he called out, "You do know how to fly these things, right?"

"Right!" I shouted behind him. *Lie.* I knew the theory, but I had yet to put it in practice.

Here goes nothing!

CHAPTER 15

Digging my heels into the irreverent beast, I urged him onward with a cluck of my tongue. He actually moved forward a few steps. My heart soared as I ran through the commands I'd been memorizing for weeks.

Zeus's head swung about, his hooves anxiously pawing the ground. He eyed the sky above where his barn-mates already circled. Nervous energy fluttered around us, and if I didn't know better, I'd think the blasted unipeg was actually excited.

The crowd above our heads continued to chant and clap as some of the students put on a preshow, the magnificent unipegs soaring with their brightly tinted wings painting a rainbow of colors across the serene blue sky.

Even the air seemed warmer than normal, the typical arctic blast absent for once. Must've been faery magic.

I patted Zeus's neck, and he craned his head around to look at me. Those obsidian eyes scorched over me as he waited expectantly. *Bossy little unipeg.* "You ready?"

He snorted in response.

"Ad litem!" I called out, and I could've sworn the animal smiled at me. He unfurled his sleek black wings, and my heart took off with his hooves. With a powerful flap, my stomach dropped as we lurched into the air.

The snow-coated ground fell away, and my pulse skyrocketed. "Holy flying unicorns! It worked!" I squeezed my thighs and calves around Zeus's midsection as we flew higher up. The closer we got to the stadium, the warmer the air got. I'd expected an icy blast, but instead a series of flickering torches lining the stands caught my eye. Their heat radiated across the floating arena, warming the surrounding air and actually making the high altitudes bearable.

Zeus led the way, my hands loose on his reins. He joined his fellow unipegs prancing around the ring. There was no doubt about it, he was happy. And showing off. His magnificent wings overshadowed all the others, the rainbow of colors beneath a striking contrast to his deep onyx hue.

Cinder and Bella flew over as soon as she caught sight of me. "You did it!" She clapped her hands, a huge grin spreading across her face.

"It was all thanks to King Elrian." I patted Zeus again, hoping his old master's name would make him happy.

My roommate arched a dark brow. "King Elrian? How did that happen?"

I shook my head, keeping a tight grip on my reins. "I'll tell you about it later. Don't we have a race to start?"

She ticked her head toward two posts floating in the middle of the stadium. A banner was stretched across the poles, the crests of each of the seven houses emblazoned on the fabric. I guessed I'd be on team dragon shifters since the humans didn't exactly have any formal representation. "Come on, let's get to the starting line. It looks like we're about to begin."

A huge clock appeared over the stadium flashing red neon numbers. It was counting down, and there was less than a minute remaining. Zeus followed behind Bella without me having to utter a word. It was like the crazy unipeg was on autopilot. It was obvious he'd done this before and was loving every minute of it.

We sidled up to the starting line, Cinder taking the spot beside Ash. He leaned over, and his eyes widened when he recognized me. "Damn, Luna girl. I didn't think I'd see you up here."

"Neither did I."

Drake appeared flanking me, his dapple-gray unipeg pawing the air. He patted his steed and turned to me. "Don't get too excited, human, the Fae have held the winning title for the past eight semesters."

"Maybe that's because they'd never raced against Zeus." I'm not sure where the false bravado came from, but I went with it.

"You remember the rules?" asked Cinder, turning my attention back to my friend.

"Yup. Three laps around the stadium and no crossing over the blue line." A neon cerulean ring floated around the circumference of the arena, illuminating a clear path.

"And no playing dirty," added Ash with a veiled look at Drake.

I gulped as I glanced down at the ground below. Falling from this height would hurt like a mother, even with the magical safety net positioned below the stadium.

The crowd began to count down from ten, and my heart raged wildly against my ribs. In the front row, I caught a glimpse of Cillian and Ryder. My instructor's dark gaze was heavy on me. He was probably as surprised as I was to see me up here.

As the clock winded down, Ryder mouthed, "Good luck."

I shot him a smile and focused my attention on the sprawling blue before me.

"Three... two... one!" The buzzer sounded and Zeus leapt forward, jerking me with him. Strands of blonde hair whipped across my face as we zipped by Cinder and Bella, then Ash and his mount, Phoenix, then almost all the other students in my class.

Holy unipegs, this guy could fly! My heart thundered in my ribcage as excitement hemorrhaged through my veins. The adrenaline coursing through my system was a completely new high. Just a few lengths in front of us was Drake. Apollo's massive dapple-gray hindquarters pounded the air in front of us, his wings sending a blast of wind in our direction.

I ducked just in time, grabbing onto Zeus's mane to avoid getting tossed off. "Good boy, Zeus," I mumbled. "Please don't drop me. It's a really long way down for a mortal like me." He threw his head back and snorted. I hoped that meant, "No, of course I won't drop you, dear Luna," in unipeg speak.

As we rounded the stadium for the second time, I hazarded a quick glance behind me. All the other riders had fallen back. Only Drake and I remained at the head of the pack, and Zeus was gaining on Apollo.

I slackened my hold on his mouth, giving him free reins and he sprinted forward. The roar of the crowd reverberated across my eardrums, drowning out the mad thumping of my heart.

Were they actually cheering for me?

Then Drake's earlier words came to mind: the Fae had won this race the past eight times. That's probably why the king was here. Sinking my heels into Zeus's midsection, I urged him forward. King Elrian never should've helped me on this wild beast. His loss—or Drake's to be more exact.

With a mighty flap, we inched forward, now nose-to-nose with Drake and Apollo. The ice prince shot me a sidelong glance, his typical cocky expression nowhere to be seen.

"Velocem!" he snarled at his steed.

The unipeg panted and huffed, a string of saliva dribbling down his mouth, but he surged forward. Glancing up, the brightly colored flags at the finish line flapped in the breeze. Only a quarter of a lap left.

"Velocem!" I echoed Drake's command to speed up and Zeus sailed ahead, eating up the air below us. The wind smacked against my face, tugging my cheeks back and I ducked down to reduce the air resistance. I wondered how fast we were going.

We turned the final bend with Apollo less than one unipeg-length in front of us. I dug my heels into Zeus's sides pleading with him to go a little faster. After what a disaster I'd been the entire semester, I finally had a chance to prove to everyone I belonged here.

Zeus lunged forward as we approached the final few yards. The red and white floating finish line was just within our reach. Apollo and Zeus continued neck and neck, neither giving the other the advantage for more than a second. Beads of sweat accumulated on my brow as I clenched my jaw to the finish line.

A gust of wind came from nowhere, forcing my eyes to squeeze shut. I felt Zeus's head snap back too as if the wind had slapped him. What the heck? My eyes reopened in time to see Apollo crossing the finish line, winning by a nose.

The crowd went wild, clapping and chanting in a language I didn't recognize. But I did catch the name being repeated—Prince Drake. My shoulders slumped forward as Zeus slowed, the tremors of his labored breath and thundering heart vibrating beneath the saddle. Beyond the finish line, a vast lush field had appeared floating in the middle of the stadium. I made Zeus trot around in a circle to slow his heart rate, his beautiful wings flapping leisurely at his sides.

As the rest of my class crossed the finish line, they gathered around Drake to congratulate him. I chewed on my lower lip as I neared. I was being a sore loser, and I knew it. But I'd been so close. If it hadn't been for that random gust of wind, we would've won. I was sure of it. A dark voice in the back of my mind whispered traitorously, *maybe it hadn't been so random*.

"Luna! Oh my gods! You almost won." Cinder and Bella

trotted up, a huge smile engraved in my roomie's face. She looked as fresh as a daisy, every single hair perfectly in place.

I hadn't even been able to run my hand through the wicked knots tangling my locks. "Yeah, almost," I muttered.

She sidled up next to me and smacked me on the shoulder. "That was the first time you've ever ridden Zeus, and you got second place! That's incredible. Imagine what will happen next time after you've had some time to practice."

A big smile parted my lips. I hadn't even thought of that. "Thanks, Cinder. You're right as usual. How'd you guys do?"

She shrugged. "I don't know, about half way down the pack, but Ash and Phoenix did really well. They came in a little after you."

I scanned the dense mass of students, which had now mixed with the crowd spilling down from the bleachers. Drake and Ash were in the center with the remaining Seven huddling around them. I hadn't even seen how Raine or Aeria had done, but by the sour expressions puckering their faces, I'd guess not great.

Raine caught me staring and wiggled her fingers at me, scowling. A puff of air flew at my face, making me blink. What the heck? An evil grin split her perfect lips before she turned away and began pawing at Drake.

Had Raine been the reason I lost? Did she twirl her little fingers and whip up that gust of wind making Zeus falter?

"What's wrong?" asked Cinder. "The vein on your forehead looks like it's about to explode."

I slapped my hand over my brow and frowned. "I think Raine sabotaged the race. Right before we got to the finish line, this freak wind blew by. It distracted Zeus and I closed my eyes. When I reopened them, Drake had won."

She glanced over at The Seven, her dark brows tightly knitted. "It wouldn't surprise me. Raine always gets what she wants.

And if she wanted Drake to win, she definitely could've made it happen."

I couldn't tear my eyes away from Raine who was now all over Drake, cooing and gushing. Anger bubbled up in my veins. "That little bi—witch!"

"Hey, hey, potty mouth, we don't use that language here at Darkhen." Ryder appeared from amid the masses, wearing his trademark smirk. Cinder shot me a wink and waggled her brows at me before turning away to join the rest of our class.

I bit my tongue holding back the flurry of curses I wanted to throw at the conniving little witch who'd cost me the win.

"What's wrong? You should be celebrating your near victory."

I wanted to shout about Raine's sabotage, but I had zero proof. The last thing I needed was for Ryder to think I was a sore loser. So I slapped a smile on my face and hoped it looked convincing. "Nothing. Everything's fine."

He held his hand out, and I slid off Zeus, my legs a little wobbly when they hit the ground. His hands shot up to my shoulders to steady me, and the unexpected contact sent little sparks up and down my arms. A delicious tremor raced up my spine, and I shuddered.

Why did he always have that weird effect on me? And more importantly, did he feel it too?

My eyes lifted to his, but the impenetrable darkness was unreadable.

"You good?"

"Great. I should be celebrating, right?" I grabbed Zeus's reins, a part of me wondering if I'd ever be able to mount the beast again without King Elrian's help. "I should probably get him back to the barn and hose him down. He worked his butt off today."

"You two looked incredible out there. You certainly got everyone's attention—especially the Winter Court attendees."

Somehow, I wasn't sure that was necessarily a good thing. I dropped Zeus's reins and let him munch on some grass.

"You won't be Darkhen Academy's little human secret for long, not the way news travels in the Fae realm." The crease between his brows deepened as if he wasn't pleased about that.

My thoughts turned to the conversation with Cillian I'd overheard. I had so many questions that I couldn't ask without divulging I'd been eavesdropping. What was going on with these attacks in the human world and what did I have to do with any of it?

"By the way," he added, "Kimmie-Jayne wanted to surprise you today by coming, but something came up in Draeko and she and Fenix couldn't make it."

"Thanks. I didn't realize you two still kept in touch." I tried to squash down the twinge of jealousy bubbling up to the surface. So they'd dated? So he'd practically admitted to being in love with her? She was married now and... And this whole thing was stupid anyway. I could never be with him—not while I attended Darkblood and he was a teacher here.

"We have been speaking more since you arrived." His voice yanked me away from my inner rambling. "She likes to be kept up to date on your advancements." He raked a hand through his dark hair, mussing it up in the most unbelievably sexy way. I bit my lower lip to keep from saying something stupid, and his gaze dropped to my lips. They remained locked there for a never-ending moment, and heat pooled in my lower half. A low growl reverberated in Ryder's chest, and vivid yellow flashed across his irises.

I swallowed hard, and he cleared his throat as he ran his hand over his face. When he blinked, his eyes were back to normal once again. "Anyway, speaking of your training, I'll give you a pass for this evening. We can pick back up tomorrow since from the looks of it, you guys have some celebrating to do."

Right on cue, Cinder approached with Alissa and Maxi on either side of her. "Big party at the Fae dorm tonight." Her voice dripped with excitement. "And our whole class is invited. Drake specifically asked to make sure you'd be there."

My cheeks heated, the feel of Ryder's eyes boring into the side of my face more intense than the scorching summer sun. "Whatever, he just wants to make sure I'm there so he can gloat about beating me."

"Well, I don't care what the reason is," said Maxi. "I just know I'm going to be there."

"So are you coming or what?" Cinder asked, slipping her arm through mine. "It's going to be your first Darkhen party!"

I laughed, her effervescing excitement contagious. "Well then, how can I say no to that?"

Ryder stepped forward, his muscley arms stretched across his chest, the swirling tattoos poking out from beneath his t-shirt. "I'll let you ladies get to the partying. Don't forget to take care of your unipegs first." With a heart-stopping smile, he sauntered away. I couldn't keep my gaze from trailing after him —his broad shoulders beneath that tight black t-shirt slimming down to a tapered waist, and that butt... I could watch it walking away from me all day.

"Come on, lover girl." Cinder tugged on my arm with a mischievous grin I decided to ignore. Grabbing Zeus's reins, I followed her and Bella back toward the stables.

CHAPTER 16

The raging beats vibrated the entire hallway of the seventh floor—the Fae floor. I followed closely behind Cinder, tugging down my leather skirt. It rode farther up my butt with every step. I should've known better than to let my roommate pick out my clothes for the evening, but she'd insisted. Getting invited to a Fae party was a huge deal, and according to her, it was necessary we played the part.

It was my one and only party skirt. I'd worn it to a club with Jay one night in Brooklyn and had been too scared to drink or even move for fear of spilling something on it. It had taken me an entire summer of working at Dunkin' Donuts to afford it.

And now, here I was wearing it to my first supernatural dorm party. It had disaster written all over it.

The corridor opened up into a large common area, about twice the size of the one on the dragon floor. Two humongous flat screen TVs sat on either end of the space with plush leather couches lining the center. I'd heard the Fae got preferential treatment, but this was the first time I'd seen it. A sprawling bar had been set up in the corner, and I recognized the dark-haired Fae male playing bartender from my Potions and Poisons class. I'd been so focused on passing my classes since I'd arrived at Darkhen that I'd completely forgotten there was no legal drinking age in Azar. I was planning on remedying that situation tonight. I didn't think I could hang with a bunch of stuck up faeries without a little liquid courage.

We passed under a pale blue banner hung across the archway with the faery crest emblazoned in the corners, and *Champions* written in big bold letters.

Ugh. I rolled my eyes as I followed Cinder, Alissa and Maxi toward the nearest vacant couch. Hundreds of twinkling stars were strung up from the dark rafters, bathing the spacious room in soft, lustrous light. I stared up at them as we sat, their shimmering light calling to me. My eyes widened as they focused in closer. *What?* Tiny iridescent flapping wings caught my eye—hundreds of teeny pixies flew over our heads.

"Pretty cool, huh?" Drake appeared with Ash, Raf and Triston in tow.

Allisa and Maxi's jaws dropped in unison as their wide eyes traveled over the notorious males of The Seven. Out of their academy uniforms and in dark jeans and fitted shirts, they were pretty hot. Especially all standing together like that, exuding dark power. It pooled around them like their very presence demanded it. I'd never felt it as strongly before—maybe it was because they were all together or maybe it was my magic starting to pick up on others' energy.

"Oh yeah," said Maxi.

"Super cool," added Alissa.

"So are they like your Fae servants or something?" I ticked my head toward the ceiling. I'd heard that the Fae royals and high lords and ladies treated the rest of the lower realm dwellers like trash.

Cinder's elbow jabbed me in the gut, but I didn't back down, fixing my gaze on the ice prince. I was feeling feisty tonight. I'd seen how they'd been treated on *Hitched*.

"Not exactly," Drake growled. "The pixies are more like hired help."

A moment of heavy silence ensued, and I could almost see the hate rolling off my girlfriends aimed in my direction. They were thrilled to have been invited, and I was ruining their fun. Why was I being so hostile? Maybe I *was* being a sore loser.

I opened my mouth to say something clever, but Ash cut me off. "Can I get anyone a drink? I know I could use one." He ran his hand through his dirty-blonde hair, a cute twinkle lighting up his green irises. He was decidedly my favorite of The Seven.

"I'm right behind you, cuz," said Cinder. Maxi and Alissa popped up right behind her. Before following the guys, my roomie turned back around, and whispered over her shoulder, "Play nice, Luna."

I shrugged. "I can't make any promises."

Raf and Triston followed after the girls, leaving me alone with the mercurial Drake. I never knew what to expect from the guy. One minute he was a complete jerk and the other he was attempting polite conversation and hanging out with me at a party I felt I had no place at.

He folded onto the couch beside me, sipping from a fancy goblet. The deep lavender liquid shimmered through the glass, catching my eye. The swanky crystal flute was nothing like what drinks were served in at college parties back home.

"What is that stuff anyway?" I asked. A floral scent swirled in the air, seeming to emanate from the mysterious beverage.

"Faery wine." His brow perked up into a mischievous arch. "You want a taste?"

A blur of rumors twirled through my mind about not drinking or eating anything faery-related. But were those true or only a part of the fairy tales?

I squashed the errant thoughts, remembering Cinder's parting words. I could play nice. This was a party after all, and I was supposed to be having fun, right? "Sure," I finally answered.

He handed me the ornate goblet, an uncharacteristic smile pulling at his lips. I lifted the cool glass to my mouth, and the fragrant scent wafted up my nose. "Only take a little, I'm not sure of the effects it'll have on a half-blood."

And there he went calling me names. Just for that I chugged down a big swallow.

"Whoa, whoa, take it easy there." He snatched the glass away from me as the sweet, chilly liquid slid down my throat.

"Wow, that's incredible." I licked my lips cherishing every last drop. "What's it made of?"

"It's a fruit that only grows in the Winter realm, kind of like one of your human berries but it's lavender in color and much sweeter. It's said to have some mind-altering properties but not in small doses."

My eyes bulged out of my head. "Like hallucinogenic as in drugs? Are you trying to drug me, your Highness?" I hiccupped the last word out and giggled.

"You'll be fine. Even with that big gulp you took." He shook his head. "Do you like to do things just to spite me?"

"Maybe." My voice took on an unexpected sing-song tone. Sh—shnickers this stuff worked fast.

Drake's gaze lifted over my shoulder, and the momentary giddiness vanished when I followed his sightline. Raine and Aeria sauntered over, their resident mean girl sneers darkening their beautiful faces.

Raine slid onto the couch beside Drake, and Aeria dropped down next to me. "Oh, Drakey, you better watch out. Your exclusive Fae parties won't stay that way for long if you keep inviting all the riffraff." The witch's electric green irises pierced my flesh, a wave of heat rising up my neck.

Aeria tittered on the other side of me, her giggle like musical notes. I turned to her to avoid Raine's scathing glare, and my eyes were caught by the neon blue of her cascading hair. It was the most unique hue I'd ever seen, and I was fairly certain it didn't come out of a bottle. If she weren't such a B, I would've loved to ask her my million questions about sirens and the ocean realm.

Raine continued to whisper with Drake, an annoying cackle bursting free every few moments. Ugh. I didn't think I could sit here and watch this for much longer. Drake's goblet on the table caught my eye. It called to me, the shimmering purple liquid begging to be consumed.

I reached for it, but Aeria's delicate hand smacked my arm. "Hey, what the hell?"

"It's not a good idea, human," she warned, taking a sip from her own fancy glass. "That Fae wine is powerful. I don't even touch the stuff."

"Drake said I could." Man, I sounded like an annoying child.

Her slender shoulders lifted, bouncing her soft waves of curls. "Do whatever you want, but you'll be the one paying for it in the morning."

Why would Aeria be nice to me? My paranoid mind considered the implications. She probably didn't want me to have fun. That wine was the most delicious beverage I'd ever tasted. I glanced over at Raine and Drake. She was practically sitting on his lap, her tongue down his ear as she continued to whisper.

What in the realms were they talking about? And were they like a thing? I'd never noticed them acting overly friendly before. Raine's eyes found mine over Drake's shoulder, and she nibbled on his ear.

Oh, vomit. I shot up to my feet and grabbed the goblet before anyone noticed. I needed to find Cinder or I was so out of there. Taking another big gulp, I searched the room for my friends. Judging by the beautiful, lithe forms littering the space, it really was an almost all-Fae party. Why did Drake invite me anyway?

The thumping beats of the bass vibrated my eardrums as I moved through the crowd. I recognized a few Fae here and there from my classes, but none I wanted to talk to. I sucked down another delicious sip, the elaborate goblet in my hand starting to get heavy. Bodies writhed around me, dancing to the DJ's electrifying beats. My body longed to move too, the exotic rhythms taking over my hips. I swayed to the music as I moved through a group of beautiful Fae males, and a hand landed on my waist. Spinning around ready to slap someone, I found a pair of familiar green eyes.

"Ash!" I threw my arms around his neck. Not sure where the overly exuberant gesture came from.

"Hey, Luna girl. Did you get lost?"

"Yeah, sort of. Where are Cinder and the others?"

He scanned the crowd, biting his lower lip. "Not sure. They're around here somewhere. Want to dance?"

I already had my arms wrapped around his neck, so why not? Finishing off my drink, I dropped it off on the nearest table. Man, that stuff was way too good. Licking my lips, I let my body take over as I moved to the intoxicating beats. Ash's arms snaked around my waist and drew me closer. Then he released me, spinning me around in a circle. I threw my arms in the air and laughed as the room twirled around me.

I hadn't expected the dragon shifter to be such a good dancer. At the next spin, I landed in someone else's arms. Arms I never thought would be around me. Drake's icy lilac eyes bored into me as he pulled me into his chest. "You stole my drink, didn't you?" His lip curled into a smirk.

"Nope. I have no idea what you're talking about."

He leaned close, his frosty breath skimming my ear. "Liar. I can smell it on your breath."

Spinning me out once again, I landed back in Ash's embrace. My head felt like it was on the tilt-a-whirl. I leaned into the big dragon to keep my knees from buckling. Over his shoulder, Raine and Drake danced, their bodies pressed so close together I couldn't tell where one began and the other ended. I placed my hand on Ash's chest to steady myself as a wave of nausea crashed over me.

"You okay, Luna?"

I cupped my head, hoping to keep it from spinning right off. "Um, yeah. I just need to sit down for a second."

"You want me to come with you?"

I shook my head. Bad idea. Sprinting across the dance floor, I frantically searched for the nearest bathroom. Oh please don't let me puke in front of everyone, oh please!

Barreling through the dark oak doors of the common area, the music began to die down. If the Fae floor was anything like ours, the bathrooms should be at the end of the hall. The familiar golden plaque above a door made me squeal with delight. I rushed in and headed straight for the toilet. Sliding to the cold tile floor, I positioned my head over the ceramic bowl.

But I was fine.

The urge to puke vanished entirely, replaced by a warm giddiness. Hmm... well that was weird. Pushing myself off the floor and splashing a little cold water on my face, I stared at my reflection in the mirror. I looked good—damned good. My makeup was still perfectly intact, and my long golden locks fell in silky waves over my bare shoulders.

A flier pinned up to the mirror caught my eye—it was a reminder that Ryder's combat class was moved an hour back tomorrow morning. The demon bad boy's face filled my vision, and warmth spread from my core. My heart beat wildly in my chest. I needed to see him. Like right now.

I rushed out of the bathroom and darted down the hall to the stairs. A part of my mind was screaming that this was a terrible idea, but the hazy drunk part told it to shut up. I just wanted to run my fingers through his dark hair, feel his abs stirring under my touch, trace his tattoos with my fingertips.

Damn, what was wrong with me?

I shoved the logical thoughts aside as I made my way

toward the faculty's living quarters. Their building was attached to the student dormitories through an enclosed walkway much like the gym was. Finally reaching the second level, I hurried across the corridor, my heartbeats thumping in time with the slap of my heeled-boots on the hardwood floors.

I swung the door to the walkway open, and the hair on the back of my neck rose. I froze as a wave of goose bumps prickled my skin. At the opposite end of the corridor, something moved in the shadows.

"Hello? Who's there?"

A dark blob peeled its way out of the darkness and coalesced into a shapeless black mass. Glowing red eyes honed in on me, and the smoke monster surged forward.

Aw, hell no! My heart leapt into my throat, ice crystallizing across my veins, but my limbs failed to cooperate. I tried to turn and run, but my body refused to obey. Squeezing my eyes shut, I rubbed them desperately. This must be a hallucination, a side effect from that crazy Fae wine. There's no way a figment of my imagination was about to kill me.

The creature's crimson-eyed gaze consumed me; no matter what I tried, I couldn't break free from its hold. All the defensive spells I'd learned dribbled out of my mind like a leaky tire.

"Get out while you can, Luna. You shouldn't be here." A raspy voice hissed the words, but the monster's lips never moved. Heck, it didn't even have a mouth. I stood paralyzed, backed against the wall as tendrils of smoke reached for me. Icy fingers pierced my chest, and my lungs constricted as the dark cloud rolled over me.

My lids grew heavy, every limb in my body suddenly weighing a ton. I wanted to scream, but even my vocal chords were paralyzed. The dense black thickened around me until I could no longer breathe. My knees buckled, and the darkness consumed me.

CHAPTER 17

"Luna. Luna, wake up!"

A warm hand cupped my cheek, the familiar voice melting the ice and heating the blood in my veins. I fought the thick black cloud holding me down, and my eyes snapped open.

Piercing dark irises hovered over me, full lips pulled into an irresistible pout. My arms moved of their own accord, wrapping themselves around the neck belonging to the face that starred in most of my dreams.

I pressed my lips against his. They were soft and warm and tasted like the sweetest candy. When I didn't meet any resistance, I knew it had to be a dream or another faery wine hallucination—a damned good one.

Ryder's mouth moved over mine with an urgency that rivaled my own. I pulled him closer so his firm chest rested against mine as my tongue explored his delicious full lips. His hand curled behind my neck, drawing our mouths closer so that his heady scent consumed me.

Holy best dream ever!

A growl reverberated in his throat, and he lurched back, his eyes wild. Bright yellow consumed his irises.

Reality smacked into me like a two-by-four. It wasn't a dream. I'd kissed Ryder, and he'd kissed me back. Warmth surged through my chest as unbridled giddiness threatened to burst free from its skeletal confines.

"Luna, we can't." He raked his hand through his hair, pacing like a mad man in front of my bed.

Somehow, I was back in my room. I tried to focus on the comforter curled between my fingers instead of his words and the dark expression on his face.

"I never should've done that. That was a huge mistake."

I sat up, pulling my knees into my chest. *Ouch.*

His black gaze was fixed on me, the depth of emotions swirling inside too muddled up to read. His lips said one thing, but his eyes divulged another story.

I chewed on my lower lip as he regarded me—with terror or maybe something else? It was hidden too deep to decipher. "Why was it such a mistake?" I finally muttered, the tremble in my voice betraying the hardened shell I was going for.

"You know the rules..."

I stood, reaching for him, but he took a step back. Hot tears pricked at my eyelids. "But you kissed me back."

"I shouldn't have. I really, really shouldn't have. You've been drinking and—" He began pacing like a caged lion once again. The muscles in his arms quivered as he swung them back and forth.

"Then why did you?" I knew I felt something. Whatever this thing between us was, it wasn't only one sided. After months of denying it, I couldn't anymore.

He raked a hand through his wild locks, tugging at the ends. "Christ, Luna, for a horrible moment, I thought you were dead. I found you on the floor—you were so cold. I-I thought I'd lost you."

"So you *do* care about me?" I hated how pathetic I sounded.

"Of course I care about you." He paused and bit back whatever else he was going to say. "I'm supposed to be protecting you. I promised Kimmie-Jayne..."

My eyes widened as cold certainty slapped me in the face. All the pieces of the puzzle slid into place, and I sucked in a breath. "You're still in love with her—with my half-sister." I wrapped my arms tight around myself, hoping to keep the fragments from crumbling. That's why he'd kissed me back. That's why he'd been so flirty from the start. "Do I remind you of her or something?" I choked out.

He didn't respond, but he didn't need to. The answer was written across his face. He was still in love with her, and I was nothing more than the consolation prize—the conveniently forbidden student he couldn't have.

"That's not—"

"Please leave."

His lips pulled down, his expression darkening. "You shouldn't be alone right now. Not after what happened with that thing..."

I shot him my best glare, all the happiness from a second ago morphing into billowing rage. "I said leave! I can't look at you, and I really don't want to be anywhere near you right now." I slumped down on the bed as my temples began to throb. "I'd rather take my chances with the smoke monster," I mumbled under my breath.

His dark brows furrowed, the vibrant yellow in his eyes vanishing. "Fine. I'll leave you for now, but we need to talk about what happened tomorrow—with that demon, I mean. And I'll be right outside your door if you need me. I'm not leaving you, no matter what you say."

"I won't need you," I growled. I turned my back to him and curled into a ball before the door slammed behind him. As soon as it did, the waterfall of tears came.

How could I have been so stupid? How could I have thought he actually liked me? Just because he flirted with me a little didn't mean anything. He was a flirt!

My chest heaved as sobs poured out onto the pillow. I'd been so consumed with Ryder's kiss I hadn't even had a second to process what happened with that demon. A chill skittered up my back. I could've died.

And yet somehow, Ryder's rejection stung a thousand times more.

The click of the doorknob sent my heart into overdrive, and I yanked the comforter up over my head. "I said I wanted to be alone!"

Light footsteps drifted over the plush carpeting, much too dainty to belong to Ryder. "It's me, Cinder." She rushed over to the side of my bed and sank down beside me. "Are you okay? I looked everywhere for you at the party and when I found Ryder outside our room, I freaked. Did you see him? He doesn't look so good. Anyway, he told me what happened, and I can't believe you were attacked."

I drew the covers back and sat up. When my friend's eyes landed on mine, her lips turned into a pout. I must've looked like total crapola. "Was that all he told you?"

"All? You were attacked by a relix demon on campus, Luna. That's pretty huge."

I swept away the dark mascara, which I could practically feel ringing my eyes like a deranged raccoon and tucked my hair behind my ears. I didn't want her looking at me with those pitiful doe eyes anymore.

She reached her hand out, stroking my arm. "Did something *else* happen?"

I snagged my lower lip between my teeth as I considered telling her about the kiss. I didn't want to relive the embarrassment, but another part of me needed to tell someone to make it real. Otherwise it could've just been a terrible, incredible dream.

"Luna, you can tell me anything." Her warm golden eyes were like honey. I'd really lucked out on my roommate. "Did something happen with Drake?"

I shook my head and huffed. "Ryder. I...um... sort of kissed him."

"What?" she cried.

I slapped my hand over her mouth and eyed the door where he presumably still stood guard. "Shh!"

A huge smile split her lips as I removed my palm. "How did that happen?"

"The demon knocked me out or something, and the next thing I knew, I woke up here in our room. Ryder was hovering over me, and I was still pretty out of it. FYI, never drink the faery wine." I rubbed my temples, which pounded with the intensity of a runaway freight train. "Or maybe it was the weird thing the demon did to me. Anyway, I really thought I was dreaming, especially when he kissed me back."

"He what?" she whisper-hissed.

A grin pulled at my lips, but I suppressed it reminding myself what a jerk he'd been about it afterward. "But then he said it was a big mistake and blah, blah, blah."

Cinder reached out and patted my shoulder. "I'm sorry, Luna. I know you liked him, but even if he did have feelings for you, he couldn't act on them. He'd be fired."

"Yeah, well I don't think that's the problem anyway." She quirked a dark brow as I considered telling her my suspicions. "I'm pretty sure he's still in love with Kimmie-Jayne."

She shook her head, her lips puckering. "That doesn't make any sense. It's been over a year since *Hitched* aired; there's no way he'd still be pining over her. Plus I've seen him with other women—" She cut herself off when I scowled. "And anyway,

Kimmie-Jayne's married to Fenix. There's no hope for them. Ever. Did he actually say that he still loved her?"

"No, but he didn't have to. I could just tell."

Cinder wrapped her slender arms around me and pulled me into a hug, patting my back. "I'm sorry, Luna. I really am. But maybe it's for the best. You and Ryder could never really be together—not while he's a teacher and you're a student, regardless of how either of you felt."

"I know," I huffed into her shoulder.

She released me and sat back, a worried mom-look still in her eyes. "You should probably get some rest. You've had a rough night. We'll talk more in the morning."

I nodded and settled back down under the covers. "Thanks, Cinder. You're the best roommate I ever could've wished for."

"I know." She winked and headed for the bathroom.

"How was the rest of the party by the way?"

Stopping midstride, she turned back with a huge smile lighting up her heart-shaped face. "It was good, really good. You were right, some of The Seven guys aren't that bad."

"Are we talking about a certain dark-haired nephilim?"

"Maybe... He disappeared right after I lost you along with Drake and the others. But it was fun until then." With a shrug, she twirled around and disappeared into the bathroom.

As I snuggled under the soft comforter, I was happy for my friend. At least someone's love life was heading in the right direction. I was closer to getting attacked by another demon or poisoned by a vicious tree than having a real relationship.

CHAPTER 18

Of course Ryder's class had to be the first one of the day the next morning. And of course, I practically tripped over him when I stepped out of my room still half asleep.

"You're still here?" I hissed as I steadied myself against the opposite wall.

"I told you I would be, didn't I?" For once, I wasn't the only one that looked like crapola. I didn't even think it was possible for the gorgeous demon. Dark circles rimmed his eyes and his button-down shirt was all crumpled from spending the night on the floor.

A tiny twinge of happiness swirled in my heart that he'd stayed, but I shoved it down, reminding myself he wanted nothing to do with me. And he was most likely in love with my gorgeous half-sister.

His eyes raked over me, and I resisted the urge to squirm beneath his intense stare. "Did you shower today?" he finally asked, breaking the awkward silence.

My jaw dropped. What kind of a question was that? "Of course I did, but it's really none of your business."

A smirk tugged at his lips as he shook his head. "Sorry, that came out wrong. Did you notice anything unusual when you changed? Um, when you were undressed?" His cheeks reddened. And I had been sure that nothing made the demon bad boy blush.

"Not that I noticed," I choked out. "Why?"

He glanced at his watch. "Walk with me. We need to talk."

"I don't think so." Talking with him was the last thing I wanted to do.

"I'm not asking, Luna." I opened my mouth to object further, but there was something about the hollow look in his eye that stopped me.

I stomped behind him as he led the way back toward the faculty quarters. My body stiffened as we neared the walkway where I'd been attacked. He held the door open, and I froze.

"Don't worry. Security already made a sweep of the campus. The demon's gone." He reached for my shoulder, but I recoiled, hitting the wall and shot him a good glare. "Luna..."

I threw my hand up, shaking my head. "No." I wasn't getting into this again. Not when I'd finally quit crying. "So what did you want to talk about?"

He released a breath and led me through the walkway, sticking close beside me. "Relix demons—the kind that attacked you—serve a very particular purpose. They're lower level demons that usually work for someone higher up the food chain. They're typically sent out to mark their prey."

"Excuse me?"

"I wanted to tell you last night, but—"

I threw my hand up again cutting him off. "I remember; I was there. So what does that mean?"

We stopped in front of a door with his name stamped across a golden nameplate. "It means that if he succeeded, any demon will be able to sniff you out because of the mark."

G.K. DEROSA

"Great. So it's like some sort of supernatural homing device?"

He nodded as he ushered me inside his room. "That's why I'd asked if you'd noticed anything. It's a rather distinctive mark, but sometimes it doesn't show up right away."

I tugged at the collar of my uniform blouse and peeked down my shirt. Nope, nothing unusual. "You're a demon, so shouldn't you be able to tell if I've been marked?"

"Technically, I'm only half demon, but yes, I still should be able to sense it."

He eyed my blouse again, and I crossed my arms over my chest, his penetrating gaze sending unwelcome heated ripples over my skin. "So maybe it didn't work?"

I glanced around the room, the fact that I was standing inside Ryder's bedroom only now clicking. It looked a lot like ours with dark mahogany wood and fancy embellishments. Only instead of two double beds, a huge king-sized one took up the majority of the chamber. A decent-sized sofa sat across from a fireplace, and a small kitchenette in the corner rounded out the cozy space.

"Maybe," he said before disappearing into what I assumed was his bathroom. My mind couldn't help but wander to naughty thoughts—Ryder undressing just a few feet away from me. His swirling tattoos inked over his rippling abs, his broad chest and shoulders rubbing against his trademark tight tees.

I clenched my teeth as heat swam up my neck. *Stop it!*

A second later, he reappeared wearing a new shirt and jeans. His hair was slicked back, and he was back to his normal hot self. Even the five o'clock shadow darkening his jaw only magnified his bad boy good looks.

Ugh. I hated him.

"So what do I do if this mysterious mark shows up?"

He looked up from tying his shoes. "Tell me immediately."

"Yes, sir."

Standing, he slowly sauntered over. My heart rate doubled at his proximity, and all the saliva evaporated from my mouth. "Luna, this is serious." He tipped my chin up, forcing my eyes to his. "What happened last night, we can't let it come between us, okay?"

I clenched my jaw to keep from saying something stupid.

"Your safety is my number one priority. You can't shut me out—ever. No matter what happens. Promise?"

I swallowed hard, a knot of emotions clogging my throat. I nodded and he released his hold on my chin, moving his hands to my shoulders instead.

"I need you to say it."

Damn those beautiful dark eyes piercing into me. "I promise," I muttered.

"Good. Now let's get to class before you're late." He spun away and darted toward the door.

My body deflated without his touch. Yup, hate him. I ran after him, lengthening my stride to keep up with his. It looked like my grand tradition of falling for the wrong guys was destined to continue.

We reached the gym only a few minutes late thanks to Ryder's breakneck demon speed. I'd practically sprinted to keep up. A few of the girls threw me side-eye when they saw me walk in with our hot instructor. And one guy—Drake.

Weird. Maybe forsaking all men for a while was the best move. These supe guys were ten times more confusing than the human ones. And hotter...

A nauseating thought crept through my mind as a wave of angry glares shot in my direction. How many of these girls had Ryder kissed and then rejected? From the evil stare downs I was getting, I couldn't have been the only one.

I shook the depressing thought off and headed for the locker room to change. Scarlett, the quiet vampire member of The Seven, stood beside my locker pulling her shirt over her head. Apparently, I wasn't the only one frequently late to this class.

She sniffed the air as I approached, her crimson-stained lips twisting into a pout. "You smell different today," she announced as I stuffed my uniform in my locker.

They were the first words the girl had ever spoken to me. Of course they had to be weird. "Um, sorry?"

Her nostrils flared as her ruby-rimmed irises scanned over me. "I don't know. I'll let you know if I figure it out." She shut her locker and walked out.

Well, that was super bizarre.

The rest of the class flew by, thankfully. Maybe all I'd needed was a good one-on-one smack down to start to feel normal again. Luckily, Raine was more than happy to oblige.

As I limped from gym class, Drake ran up beside me. "Hey. Are you okay? Ryder told us—me what happened."

"He did? That's funny, I thought the administration would want to keep a demon attack on campus under wraps."

"They do. I'm special." He smirked, and I knew he really believed what he was saying. "Anyway, the demon's gone so you don't have to worry about him anymore."

"Thanks." And how did he know he was gone? More importantly, did he know about the mark?

"So did you want to practice today after class?"

"I can't today. I have my one-on-one session with Ryder." I groaned internally. "How about tomorrow before Defensive Magic class?"

"Sounds good."

The click-clack of approaching heels alerted me to Raine's arrival before she opened her mouth. "Hey, Drakey." Wrapping her arm around the prince's waist, she nuzzled his neck.

Now they were together?

He stiffened beside me, pulling away from Raine's hold. She pouted but didn't give him more than an inch of extra space.

Turning to me, she flashed her big white teeth. "Glad to see you're alive, human. Those relix demons don't mess around."

Drake snarled. "Give it a rest, Raine. After the faery wine and the demon, the fact that she's still standing means a lot."

Wow, was that a compliment from the ice prince himself?

"Later, Luna." Drake strode off with Raine following behind like a lost puppy. Of all the girls in the school, he had to pick her to date?

I glanced up at the clock overhead. Ugh. The day had only just begun, and I already couldn't wait for it to be over. If I'd been back at home, I would've dragged Jay out of class and skipped the rest of the day.

I missed my friend. Since I'd been at Darkhen, we'd texted a few times, but neither of us was very good at keeping in touch.

The rest of the day passed in a blur, and before I knew it, it was time to meet Ryder in the gym. My stomach roiled at the thought. The last thing I needed right now was some sweaty alone time with my hot instructor.

Pulling my hair into a high ponytail, I crept in, hoping he'd somehow forgotten about our session. My eyes focused in on the most perfect male form hanging from the pull up bar. Sweat glistened off his bare chest, the black tattoos curling around his pecs and abs even more incredible than I'd imagined. A pair of loose black sweatpants hung from his hips, accentuating the V muscle disappearing beneath his waistband.

I wiped the drool from my chin and marched forward. His eyes caught mine and he dropped down to the mat, grabbing his tank from the floor. "You're early, mini minx, that's what I like to see."

I shot him a narrowed glare, but a tiny part of me smiled at the hated nickname.

He rubbed the shirt over his glistening chest and abs before tugging it over his head. "You ready?"

I dropped my backpack on the floor and joined him on the mat. "I guess."

"Now more than ever, it's important we get you well-trained. Until your magic fully surfaces, you'll have to rely on your physical prowess to defend yourself."

"Right." The only physical prowess I could focus on right now was his. His broad bare shoulders and massive biceps were still on full display.

He stepped closer, handing me the bright red gloves and helped strap them on. His salty, musky scent enveloped me, and I was finding it hard to breathe without breathing him in.

When he finished, I took a step back and my heart rate decelerated with the much-needed space between us.

"Now, most of your opponents will be bigger, stronger and faster than you. Like me." He smirked. "So I'm not going to take it easy on you."

I bounced from foot to foot. "That's encouraging."

"Come at me. Nothing's off limits this time. Got it?"

My brow arched of its own accord. Maybe this was going to be more fun than I thought. After he stomped all over my heart, at least I could get some good retaliatory punches in.

I let out a battle cry and charged, my fists flying. He let me get exactly one good punch into his gut before he started to defend himself. No matter how fast I thought I was moving, he was faster.

I threw an upper cut, and he dodged it. I gave him my best roundhouse, and he ducked well before my foot made contact.

I kicked, I punched, and I'm not embarrassed to admit, I even tried biting when I tackled him to the floor. But he was so fast and strong, the only hits I landed were those he allowed.

I straddled him on the mat, my breaths coming hard and fast, and he was as fresh as a daisy. He hitched his hand under my thigh and spun me upside down so fast my head whirled. I smacked the mat, and all the wind siphoned from my lungs. He hovered over me, his big arms caging me in.

"What are you going to do now?" he taunted.

I squirmed beneath him, but the full length of his body pinned me to the floor. If I weren't so frustrated, this would've been way hot. I shoved against his rock-hard chest, but he wouldn't budge. My chest rose and fell rapidly, each inhale coming closer to brushing against his.

"Come on, kid. If I were an actual attacker, I could've had you by now. Your soul would've been mine." He pressed harder against me, and a flicker of yellow flashed across his dark irises. A low growl vibrated his throat, and my eyes flew to his bobbing Adam's apple. "Do you know how easy it would be for me to..." He inched closer, his lips millimeters away from mine. The minute air between us crackled with intensity. I sucked in a breath as my heart wreaked havoc against my ribs.

Roughly shaking his head, Ryder squeezed his eyes shut and sat up.

My muscles ached from the past half hour, but most of all I missed the feel of his body pressed against mine.

When his eyelids reopened, the yellow was gone, only the bottomless black remaining. "I think that's good enough for today." He extended his hand and pulled me up, but my legs wobbled beneath me and I barreled right into him.

Whoa, head rush.

His arms encircled me for a second before he righted us both, slowly releasing me. "You okay?"

"Yeah, I'm fine. Thanks."

His gaze ran over me again, the laser sharp focus heating my skin. The crease between his brows deepened as he focused on a spot right below my collarbone.

"What?" I slapped my hand over my chest.

He leaned in, craning his neck. "Do you have a birthmark or something above your right brea—below your collarbone?"

"No..."

Ryder peeled my hand off my chest, and he hissed. "Shit, Luna. You've been marked." A slew of more colorful curses flew from his clenched teeth as he ran his fingers over the sensitive spot. It tingled under his touch.

"I need to see it." I raced to the locker room with Ryder on my heels. Bursting through the door, I darted to the mirror. Just above my right breast, an angry red mark puckered my flesh. Rising to my tiptoes, I leaned closer to make out the details. Three sixes arranged in a circle so that their bases all touched were emblazoned into my skin. "What the hell is that?"

Ryder's teeth ground together. "It's the devil's mark," he hissed, "the symbol of the Underworld."

I traced the enflamed carving and winced. "So what does this mean? I'm an official demon target now?"

"It means you and I are going to be spending a lot more time together."

Yippee.

CHAPTER 19

Ryder paced the length of Cillian's expansive office, that caged-lion look glimmering in his bottomless irises. The headmaster bent over me as he scrutinized the devil's mark. For the third time, he placed his palm over my chest and warm light emanated from his fingertips. The soothing sensation penetrated my skin, filling my insides with a divine sense of peace and tranquility.

And for the third time, he tore his hand away muttering curses in some language I couldn't understand.

"It's not going to work," Ryder hissed from the other side of the room.

The crackling flames in the grand fireplace did nothing to lessen the frostiness in his voice. I kept my eyes glued to the deep orange and yellow dancing flares because looking at either of the angry men was starting to stress me out. The more worried they got, the worse the anxiety building in my gut became.

Cillian sank down into the leather chair across from me. "I just don't understand why they'd come all this way for her," he mumbled to himself. "Getting into Darkhen Academy is no easy feat. And to risk that simply to mark a half-blood?"

His gaze lifted to mine, and his lips pressed together. "I'm sorry, that came out wrong."

"Whatever. It is what I am after all, right?" My fingers twitched with the need to touch the eerie symbol, but I clasped my hands together on my lap. "Why would the Underworld be interested in me?"

Cillian's gaze swiveled to the still-pacing demon. "Ryder, any thoughts? That is your area of expertise."

Clenching his fists at his sides he stalked closer. "I have no idea, but I know someone who will."

Cillian nodded, but I was still lost.

"Who?"

"Dear old dad. The devil himself."

I wanted to smack myself—duh. How could I forget that Ryder's father was Lucifer, the actual prince of hell?

Ryder's heavy gaze bored into me before swerving to the headmaster. "Cillian, change of plans, you'll have to be on mini minx's guard duty until I get back. It shouldn't take me long, but you never know with father."

The angel headmaster stood and moved closer to Ryder, lowering his voice he whispered, "I was thinking this could be a good test for *the team*."

My ears perked up. I may not have had supe hearing, but even I heard that one.

Ryder shook his head, his dark brows furrowing. "Absolutely not. Not when it's her life on the line."

"But how will they ever be ready if they're not tested?" Cillian argued. "I'll supervise."

"Um, guys, I'm right here." I shot up to my feet, waving. "Shouldn't I get to have a say in whatever you're talking about? And if you're trying to be sneaky about it, learn how to whisper."

A smirk pulled at Ryder's lips before it hardened to its bad boy mask. Cillian approached me and laid his hand on my shoulder. "I'm very sorry this is happening to you. Darkhen Academy was supposed to be a home for you, somewhere you'd feel safe. And you're right, you deserve to know the truth and be involved in these decisions."

"Cillian," Ryder growled. "She's not ready."

"Luna's in all their classes, she's been studying alongside them from day one. It was why she was brought here to begin with."

I slapped my hands on my hips and narrowed my eyes at Cillian then Ryder. "Someone better start spilling now."

The two men exchanged a covert glance, and Ryder threw his hands in the air. "Fine. What do I know?"

Cillian's big hand settled over my shoulder and he led me to the couch, sitting down beside me. "Everything I'm about to tell you must remain between us. You are familiar with 'The Seven' I'm sure." I nodded, and he continued. "The rumors about them are varied, but there is one thing that very few students in this school know. The children of the seven houses were brought together for a very specific purpose—to fight the creatures of the Underworld. With their unique powers combined, we'd hoped we could train them into an elite fighting force." He glanced up at his nephew. "And with Ryder's instruction and knowledge of the Underworld, we're succeeding. They've only been training so far—"

"Until the relix demon showed up," Ryder interjected. "You can thank them for ridding the school of that nasty beast."

"You see, they've proven themselves quite capable. I would like for them to guard you in Ryder's absence until we find a way to remove the mark."

My head spun at the thought of Drake, Raine, Ash and the others as some sort of supernatural slayer squad. That's insane... Sure, they seemed powerful, but they were all so young, like me.

But I'd seen what they could do; I'd felt the power swirling around them when they were together.

There was only one piece of the puzzle that still didn't fit—me. Clenching my fingers into tight little balls, I spat out my question. "You said they were the reason I was brought to Darkhen. What did that mean?"

Ryder and Cillian exchanged another veiled look. "You might as well tell her now," Ryder muttered.

"Each of the members of The Seven comes from one of the houses of Azar, along with Ryder as their trainer who represents the Underworld, that's eight. Now with the merging of the supernatural and human worlds, there is only one group not represented."

"The humans," I mumbled.

Ryder shot Cillian a glare. "I told you she'd figure it out."

"And not just any human," the headmaster continued. "One of Garrix's offspring. The dark warlock is extremely powerful as I'm sure you've heard. Most of his children have inherited his many gifts. We believe it's only a matter of time until you do as well."

"So that's why I was brought here. As a test? To see if I was good enough to join this slayer squad?"

Cillian nodded. "A warlock's powers are different than those of its wiccan counterparts. Contrary to popular belief, a warlock isn't just a male witch. In eons past, they were considered evil. Unlike witches, they have a small percentage of demon blood running through their veins. Their power is darker, more seductive. But for some reason, warlocks are always male, never female. Therefore we categorize you as half-witch, even though you are technically more than that. We were going to tell you everything eventually. We simply were waiting for your powers to emerge. Coming to Darkhen was a lot to process to begin with, and we didn't want to overload you with too much too fast."

Ryder refused to meet my gaze, his eyes pinned to the floor. They'd both been lying to me all along.

"Does Kimmie-Jayne know the real reason I was brought here?"

"Yes. But it wasn't the only reason she wanted to find you, Luna." Cillian reached for my shoulder, but I shrugged him off. "She wanted to get to know you, to become a part of your life. She found out late in hers about Garrix and her powers, and she didn't want that for you."

Ryder bent down in front of me kneeling. His hand reached for mine, but he snatched it back at the last moment. I hated how much that hurt. "There will always be a place for you here, Luna, whether you have powers or not. We'd never force you to do anything, just like we didn't force the others. They wanted to fight—to protect both of our worlds against the Underworld. If your magic decides to show up and play, great. If not, the academy is still your home. You belong here with us."

My throat tightened, a huge lump of emotion clogging my airways. I swallowed hard, but it didn't help. Hot tears pricked my eyes, and I blinked rapidly to keep them from spilling over. After losing Mrs. Hallows, my life had pretty much sucked bouncing around the foster care system for a year before I ended up at Astor Home, which had never been a real home. This was the first time that I'd felt at home anywhere. Sure, there were monsters and mean girls and unrequited love, but I'd discovered a part of me that had been missing all along.

Was I pissed they'd lied to me? Hells, yes. But did I kind of get it? Sure. If they'd brought me here and told me I was supposed to join some sort of supe slayer squad I would've run away screaming and/or laughing.

Ryder rose, his intense gaze still weighing on me. "I have to go, but I don't want to leave until I'm sure you're okay."

Cillian's watchful eyes moved from Ryder to me and back again.

"I'll be fine." I couldn't handle him looking at me like that anymore. "If you guys think I'll be safe with The Seven then I'm sure I will be. Besides, I've got a super cool magical blue safety bubble, right?"

"Right." Ryder smirked. "I'll be back as soon as I can." This time he didn't stop himself. His fingers closed around mine, and my heart flip-flopped. Turning to Cillian, he lifted his hand to his forehead, saluting. "See you soon, boss. Watch over the kid, huh?"

The imposing angel rolled his eyes, but a slight smile parted his perfect lips. "Of course. Good luck."

As soon as the door behind Ryder closed, Cillian turned to me, a knowing look in his sky blue eyes. "So is my demon nephew taking good care of you?"

I still found it weird when Cillian called Ryder his nephew. The guardian angel only looked a few years older than him. "Umhmm. He's a great instructor."

"Good." He stood up and motioned for me to follow him as he typed a quick message on his tablet. "I apologize for not being truthful with you from the beginning, but I didn't want to assert undo pressure. The move from the human world to this one had to be life-altering enough."

I trailed beside him as we descended the stairs of administration and headed toward the main hall. "It was. But I've been lucky to have Cinder to show me the way and even some of the other students have surprised me."

"I'm glad to hear that. Your sister was worried about how you'd acclimate, but I'm pleased her concerns were unfounded. She really does care about you, you know?"

I nodded. I knew she and Cillian were still tight, and if anyone still loved her, he would be on the top of my list. Kimmie-Jayne had been texting on occasion, but she hadn't been back to visit since she dropped me off. It stung a little.

Glancing up, the double doors of the gym drew me away from my thoughts.

"Are you ready to meet the team?" Cillian asked as he swung the heavy doors open.

"As ready as I'll ever be." I didn't have the heart to tell him that half of the team—the female half—would rather see me dead than protect me. True to form, Raine's flirty smile morphed into a scowl as she glanced over Drake's shoulder at my approach.

Cillian lifted his hands, and everyone quieted. "Thank you for gathering so quickly. I'm sorry about the late hour, but Ryder was forced to leave and I have a new mission for the seven of you."

Drake's eyes caught mine, something unreadable in his expression—as usual. Ash, Triston and Raf stood beside him, and they each gave me warmish smiles. Scarlett looked bored, and Aeria twirled a lock of blue hair around her finger. Maybe this wouldn't be as bad as I thought. Only Raine seemed intent on handing me over to the nearest demon.

"As you all know, Luna has been marked. As such, she's been informed as to the team's real purpose here at the academy. You all did a wonderful job killing the relix demon and now you've been tasked to protect her from what's to come." His voice lowered, taking on a dangerous edge. "And more will come."

"Why can't Ryder do this?" asked Raine. "Isn't she his responsibility?"

"She is all of our responsibilities, Raine. As is the safety of all the students at the academy." I swore he suppressed an eye roll, and I liked our headmaster just a little bit more because of it. "In any case, Ryder has gone to the Underworld to speak to his father. Until we can find a way of removing the mark, no one at Darkhen is safe."

A chill skittered up my back at his ominous words.

Drake lifted his hand, waggling his fingers. "I can take the first shift."

"Thank you, Drake. While that's very generous of you, the first shift will be an overnight one and as such, I feel it would be more appropriate for Luna to stay with the ladies."

My stomach plummeted. A whole night with Raine? She would definitely murder me in my sleep.

"She has to stay with us?" Aeria complained.

"Since the three of you ladies are suite mates it would make the most sense. There's no reason to put Luna's roommate, Cinder, in danger unnecessarily."

The idea suddenly didn't sound so bad. The last thing I wanted was for Cinder to get caught up in this mess.

"She can stay in my room," offered Scarlett. "I have an extra bed."

"Perfect, thank you, Scarlett." Cillian turned to the other girls. "I need one of you on guard at all times. You can alternate sleeping. If anything happens, call me immediately. I don't want you taking any unnecessary risks." Then he pivoted toward Drake. "You can pick up Luna from the girls' dorm in the morning and escort her to class. I'll leave it up to you boys to coordinate a schedule. Everyone understand?"

A mumble of yeses echoed across the empty gymnasium.

"I'll be on guard myself tonight, patrolling the campus along with our regular security team. Call me for anything." Cillian squeezed my shoulders, bending down to my eyelevel. "You'll be safe with them. I promise. And Ryder will be back with answers very soon."

"Thanks, Cillian."

As soon as the angel left, Drake sauntered over. His gaze narrowed in on the mark on my chest. "Ooh, that looks brutal. Does it sting?"

"A little." I rubbed at the raised symbol. Mostly it just creeped me out.

"Let's get this sleepover on the road. Shall we?" Raine swaggered by, motioning for me to follow.

Oh boy, was this going to be fun.

CHAPTER 20

After picking up a few necessities from my dorm and vaguely explaining what was going on to Cinder, the girls escorted me to their rooms. I had to promise my roommate I'd tell her exactly what was going on tomorrow. And I would. Regardless of what I'd promised Cillian about keeping his elite team a secret. Cinder was my roomie and best friend, and if I asked her to, she'd keep their secret too.

All of The Seven lived on the seventh floor—the Fae level of the dormitory. Apparently, training and living together were essential to bonding.

After spending only about twenty minutes with the girls, it was clear Scarlett wasn't too fond of the arrangement. I couldn't blame her. Raine and Aeria blatantly ignored the vampire the entire time we trudged through the dormitories.

Finally reaching the seventh floor, Raine stopped in front of a door with two golden nameplates on it. "This is our room, and Scarlett's is right next door. We share the bathroom so you can get in that way. If you need to."

"Got it."

Raine turned to Scarlett, her cute pixie nose in the air and pointed. "You take the first shift since she's staying in your room anyway. You can wake Aeria up at two, and I'll take the last shift at four." She glanced at her watch and sighed. "At least I'll get six hours of sleep."

"Thanks," I muttered as Aeria and Raine disappeared into their room, and I followed Scarlett down the hall. I wasn't so sure about sleeping with a vampire, but of the three female options, Scarlett seemed the best bet.

"Sorry, Raine can be a real bitch sometimes." She unlocked her door and ushered me in. I couldn't help but laugh as I walked into the dark room.

"I'm sorry for you. You're the one that has to deal with her all the time."

Scarlett turned on a light and pointed at the bare bed. "There should be extra sheets in the closet so make yourself comfortable."

"Thanks." I scanned the unfamiliar room, taking in all the posters of rock bands hung on Scarlett's side. These dorms were definitely bigger than ours—instead of twin beds, they had queens, their closets were twice the size of ours, and there was a fireplace. The Fae really did get the royal treatment at this school.

I grabbed some sheets from the closet and began to make my bed. "What happened to your old roommate?"

"Never had one. Since there are only three females on the team, I lucked out." Scarlett stretched out on her bed, her long black hair splaying out across the pillow.

"So how long have you been on the supe slayer squad?" I sat down, the cushy mattress bouncing beneath me.

She giggled, a weird girly sound coming from the quiet goth. "I like that. I'll have to tell Ryder to make the name official. The team has been around for a little less than a year. This is my second year at the academy, but everything changed when Cillian took over as headmaster. The focus suddenly shifted and bam, the supe slayer squad was born. Ash is the newest addition to the team and the school, while Drake's been here the longest. It's his third year. Darkblood isn't exactly structured like human universities. Most students only stay three years before graduating and others even less than that. The curriculum is pretty fluid."

"So how'd you get sucked into fighting the baddies?" From what I learned from my classes, vampires were demons too, so I didn't want to insult her.

A smile tipped up the corners of her lips. "I've just always been a badass."

"Now that I could see."

She flicked at her tongue ring, and the little black ball danced around the loop. "No, but seriously my sire is the queen of the Royal Vampires so she expects a lot from her progeny which is why she sent me here right after I was turned."

I remembered hearing about the Royal Vampires from *Hitched*. One of the queen's offspring, Lucíano was one of the bachelors. Gorgeous, of course. "Wait, so how old are you?"

"Nineteen. Although I'll spend the rest of my immortal life looking like I'm seventeen." She shrugged. "Could be worse I guess. I could be dead."

"What happened?" I snapped my jaw shut as soon as the words were out, but it was too late. "Unless you don't want to talk about it," I quickly added.

"Nah, I'm over it. I was a half-blood like you actually, living in Azar before the big revelation. My dad's human, and my mom's a sprite. She's one of the Fae queen mother's personal slaves—er, I mean assistants. Anyway, I was running an errand for the queen in the vampire realm, Nocturnis, when I was attacked."

"By a vamp?"

She shook her head, biting her lip and her fangs slipped out.

I clenched my jaw to keep from gasping. I'd never seen her sharp incisors before, and I couldn't help the squeal of surprise.

"No, it was a demon," she finally responded once her fangs retracted. "Carmen Rosa saved my life—or gave me a new one, anyway. The Fae wouldn't let me stay at Winter Court since I was now a vampire." She rolled her eyes and huffed. "And it takes a while to get your impulses under control, so Carmen Rosa took me in, then eventually sent me here. When I became particularly adept at my learned power, Ryder recruited me to the team."

"What's your extra ability?" I'd already seen her in combat and she was freakishly fast and strong, not to mention deadly with weapons, but I'd never seen her use magic.

"Necromancy."

I couldn't stop my jaw from dropping that time. "What?"

"It sounds worse than it is. Basically I can control dead things, and I dabble in some of the darker arts. But we don't like to talk about that stuff here at Darkhen. Ironic, right?"

"Wow, that's nuts. So that means you can control all vampires, since you're all technically dead, right?"

She nodded. "Yup."

There had to have been a couple hundred vampires here at the academy, not to mention all the ones living in Azar. Her ability was crazy powerful—no wonder they wanted her on the team.

Scarlett glanced up at the guitar-shaped clock over the entryway and grimaced. "You should probably get some sleep. I'll keep watch for the next few hours then I'll pass you on to Aeria."

I must have made a face because she chuckled. "Don't worry she's not as bad as Raine. Especially when her bestie's not around. Sometimes I think Raine has more shifter in her than witch. She's so territorial, if she had a dick, I'm pretty sure she'd pee on us to mark her territory."

G.K. DEROSA

Now I was laughing hysterically. The image of Raine with man parts was too funny—and creepy. Turning the light by my bed off, I pulled the blanket up to my chin and settled in under the warm comforter. "Thanks for this, Scarlett."

"No problem, half-blood." She winked and pulled a book out from her nightstand drawer. "Goodnight."

⚜

"LUNA, RUN!" A SHARP CRY SNAPPED MY EYELIDS OPEN. MY arms shot out to my sides as I fumbled in the darkness, my pupils still adjusting to the unfamiliar surroundings.

Glass cracked, hundreds of shards tinkling to the floor. A cold sweat rippled down my spine as my gaze finally focused on the creature hovering outside Scarlett's shattered bedroom window. Massive black wings beat the air as it poked its elongated crocodile snout through the glass, sharp claws ripping at the remaining splintered wood.

Scarlett slashed at the sleek black demon with a silver blade, her feet dancing beneath her with every strike. She whipped her head over her shoulder and caught my panicked gaze. "Luna, go!"

But I couldn't. My feet were planted to the ground, ancient roots holding them in place. The angry red mark on my chest pulsated.

Scarlett growled and lashed at the beast again, who'd managed to get two claws latched onto the interior wall. His thick hind legs struggled against the small opening, but he'd be in before long.

I had to do something. If I couldn't move, I could at least scream. She was probably the last person I ever thought I'd ask for help, but desperate times... "Raine, help! Aeria!"

The monster howled, an unearthly lament echoing across the entire chamber, which perked every hair on my body to

164

attention. With a swipe of its massive talons, it sent Scarlett hurtling across the room. She smacked into the far wall, and her neck twisted at an odd angle as she crumpled to the ground.

A muffled curse escaped my lips as the demon locked its glowing crimson eyes on me. Where were those two? "Raine, Aeria, I could use a little help in here!" The monster stalked closer, and my heart jackhammered against my ribs as all the useless defensive magic spells I'd committed to memory swirled in my head. "Protectum ad armorae," I spat, praying my blue bubble would appear.

No such luck.

The demon snarled, showcasing three rows of dagger-sharp teeth. "You're mine, little human." Its raspy reptilian voice sucked all the air from my lungs.

Breathe, Luna. *You can do this.* Okay so my magic was on the fritz—nothing shocking there. I couldn't just stand here and become this guy's midnight snack. My mind raced back to all my training sessions with Ryder. I eyed my opponent and as his elongated neck lashed out, I ducked and cut under his legs.

Spinning back around to face him, an open trunk against the wall caught my attention. An entire arsenal of sharp weapons glimmered from within. The demon lunged, but I dodged his attack, sliding toward the old chest. My fingers closed on the first metal object they encountered. Whipping the sword free, my eyes widened as I held out the golden blade.

Behind me, loud pounding on the door made my head spin. Muffled shouts seeped through the cracks, but I didn't have time to focus on what they were saying.

The demon's slick, tar-like skin glistened beneath the moonlight darting in through the cracked window. It stalked closer, every movement precise and measured. Sinewy muscles bunched and coiled beneath its taut flesh. "It's time for me to collect my reward. The dark lord will be very pleased," it hissed.

The symbol on my chest flared, a ruby glow emanating from

the hellish design. I tightened my hold on the sword's hilt to keep my fingers from trembling. "I don't think so, buddy." Jerking my arm back, I thrust the sword as the beast stretched out its neck leaving the vulnerable area exposed. The blade sank into its scaled hide. It let out a hideous screech as it pawed at the dangling sword.

I didn't wait around to see what happened next. Scrambling across the room, I reached the adjoining door and whipped it open. Raine and Aeria stood in the entryway with matching shocked expressions.

"What happened?" Raine shouted. "The room was spelled shut."

I hitched my thumb over my shoulder at the squealing demon. "It's still happening. And Scarlett's passed out in there with it."

"Cillian's on his way," said Aeria as she stood on her tiptoes to see over my head. She ticked her head at Raine. "Let's do this."

Redheaded and blue-haired Barbies darted into Scarlett's room, and I unwillingly trailed behind. The clatter of the sword hitting the ground jerked my attention to the wounded hell creature. Dark liquid oozed from the gash on its neck, but now that the blade was out, it no longer slowed it down.

Scarlett's crumpled form caught my eye, and I dashed over to her broken body. My breath hitched when my gaze landed on the sickening twist of her neck. Oh God, she's dead. No. No. No.

Wait a second. Nope, she's a vampire! I dragged her body toward the door and away from the fighting and propped her against the thick oak. "I'm so sorry I got you into this," I whispered.

"Watch out!" someone screamed.

I glanced up right in time to see a scorching ball of fire zipping toward me. Without thinking, I threw my hands out, squeezing my eyes shut. And waited. Waited for the searing pain to burn my flesh—but it never came. Instead, something bounced off my palms like a basketball rebounding off the backboard. Peering through the slits in my eyelids, I could just make out two flaming blue orbs soaring toward the demon.

My eyes snapped open, bulging out of my head. One fiery projectile smacked straight into its chest and the second right in its eye. The beast shrieked and staggered back, its massive hindquarters crashing into Scarlett's desk.

"Now, Aeria," Raine shouted.

The beautiful melody I'd heard in class a few weeks ago swirled through the air. I clamped my hands over my ears as my head began to spin. The creature teetered back, his crimson eyes growing hazy.

Raine ripped my hand from my ear and clasped it tightly in hers, then she grabbed Aeria's. "Repeat after me! Toree fuocum celis demoniom!"

"Toree fuocum celis demoniom, toree fuocum celis demoniom!" we all shouted in unison. Sparks flickered between our palms and searing heat scorched my hand. I gritted my teeth to keep from crying out as fire hemorrhaged through my veins. And then it burst from our palms in a wave of electric blue and brilliant orange.

The surge of power smacked into the demon, consuming him in a fiery flare that sent shockwaves across the room. My eyes bugged out as the creature's dark flesh was consumed from the inside out.

Cillian burst through the door clutching his angel blade. The timber smashed against the wall tearing my attention from the disintegrating demon to the striking angel. Brilliant alabaster wings lit up the dark room as he dashed toward us, blue flames dancing across his sword.

"You're late," said Raine, arching a perfectly plucked brow at our headmaster.

After assessing us each for damage, his eyes pivoted to the pile of sooty ash on the dorm room floor. "You girls did it? You vanquished the demon yourselves?"

We released our linked hands, and I shoved mine in my pockets, suddenly feeling awkward. That was like nothing I'd ever experienced. The surge of power that had flowed through us had been all consuming, mind-blowing.

"I told you we could handle ourselves," said Raine.

I glanced up at Cillian whose jaw was still slightly unhinged. "What took you so long?" I'd waited and waited for the badass angel to swoop in and save us like he'd done so many times on *Hitched*.

"I'm sorry. I couldn't get inside the building. Something very powerful conjured a warding spell that even I couldn't get around."

"We had the same issue," said Aeria, twirling a lock of azure hair around her finger. "Luna did a pretty good job of handling the demon on her own after vamp girl got herself killed." She pointed to Scarlett who still leaned lifeless against the other door.

Cillian's stormy blue eyes found mine. "You faced off against this Underworlder on your own?"

I shrugged, eyeing the golden sword covered in black demon goo. "Yeah, I guess so. For a few seconds anyway."

His big hand closed around my shoulder, and he smiled. "Well done, Luna. Ryder will be very proud of you. I guess I wasn't needed here after all." His angel sword blinked out of existence, and a sheepish grin crossed the handsome headmaster's face. "I'll call for cleanup."

"What about Scarlett?" I asked.

Raine crinkled her nose. "She'll be fine in a few hours. We can move the party into our room so security can handle the mess." She motioned to the mound of dark ash, and then turned to Cillian. "Do you think we'll have more visitors tonight?"

"Doubtful." He glanced through the broken glass, the first rays of sunlight peeking over the dark forest below. "Attacking during the day wouldn't be smart."

"I didn't think lower demons were smart." Raine crossed her arms over her chest.

"They're not, but whoever is sending them might be."

Cillian's words stirred a memory in my mind—something the creature had said. "Oh! Before it attacked me it said something like 'the dark lord will be pleased'."

"Ooh, creepy." Aeria twisted her hair into a messy bun on the top of her head. "Lucifer, maybe?"

Cillian shook his head. "No. Underworlders refer to him as king. The title lord would be beneath him, but it could refer to one of the six demon warlords who rule the subterranean levels of hell."

Great...

He rubbed at his chin, his light brows scrunched together. "I'll have to see what I can find out. Try to get a few hours of sleep, ladies. Security will be nearby." He spun toward the door, and I almost stopped him. Neither Raine nor Aeria had mentioned the magical light show we'd created when we'd held hands. In all the classes I'd attended in the past few months, I'd never seen anything like it. It felt like something worth mentioning.

I opened my mouth to say something, but Raine's elbow jabbed me in the gut. "Keep quiet," she hissed.

As soon as the door closed behind Cillian, I rubbed my bruised rib and snapped, "What the hell, Raine?"

She spun on me, her brilliant green eyes aglow. "You were going to tell him about the spell, right?"

I snagged my lip between my teeth and nodded. "Yeah, so?"

"We don't talk to Cillian about that sort of thing—only Ryder."

Aeria's head bobbed up and down.

"Why not?"

She ran her hand through her luxurious red mane and blew out a breath. "Let's just say that Cillian and Ryder have differing opinions on the use of darker magic."

"Dark magic?"

Aeria waggled her finger at me. "Dark*er* magic. The one that comes from darkbloods like us."

"Us?" I arched a brow.

Raine and Aeria exchanged a look. "Oh sweetie, you're so adorably clueless," said the blue-haired beauty. "You're part warlock, right? I can practically smell it on you. When Raine joined our hands, that surge of power came from *you*."

CHAPTER 21

It had been two days since Ryder left, and I missed him more than I cared to admit. Every time I closed my eyes my mind filled with images of the demon bad boy—his bottomless onyx irises, his tattoo-covered rippling abs and those full, kissable lips. I'd hoped some separation would quell the burgeoning feelings for my off-limits instructor, but if anything, his absence had only increased my infatuation.

I thought about him constantly—was he okay? Did he find the demon that marked me? Was he hanging out with daddy Lucifer?

"Hello, are you even listening to me?" Scarlett's annoyed voice snapped me out of my head.

"Sorry. I didn't sleep well last night so I'm kinda out of it," I said with a big yawn. *Lame, I know.*

We walked into the banquet hall, and all eyes turned on me as I strode in with Scarlett. Then their stares turned into all out gawking when Drake motioned for me to sit at *their* table. I could practically feel hundreds of eyes glued to my back as I crossed the hall to stand beside the Fae prince.

"I think I'm going to sit with Cinder today," I said to Drake.

Triston and Ash sat beside him, chowing down on burgers. "I doubt some demon's going to strike in the middle of a crowded lunch room."

"Fine." But he didn't sound fine.

"What?"

"You're not doing it because everyone's staring at you, right?"

My brows knitted together. "No. I don't care what everyone else thinks. I just want to sit with my friend and roommate who I haven't seen in days since I've been sequestered on the seventh floor."

Raine and Aeria sauntered up to the table, each giving me tight smiles. Coming from them, it was a huge improvement. I'd still been too scared to ask Aeria how she knew I was part warlock. I wasn't really, I was a witch from the way Cillian had explained it. And I really wanted to know what she meant about me having dark magic. I wished I could confide in Cinder about it, but I didn't want to freak her out. More than anyone, I wanted to talk to Ryder, but he wasn't here.

"Don't forget about training after lunch," said Drake as I turned to leave.

"Right. Where are we meeting?"

"My room."

A vein in Raine's forehead twitched, but she didn't say anything as she sank into the seat beside Drake.

"Okay, see you then." Again, the burn of a million eyeballs followed me all the way to the dragon-shifters' table. I folded myself into the seat, waiting for the watchful eyes to go back to their normally scheduled activities before opening my mouth.

"Glad you could join us," said Maxi, her snippety tone impossible to miss.

"Geez, I didn't think you'd mind one less person to share the bathroom with." I unwrapped the sandwich I'd grabbed on the way over and dug in.

Cinder's hand landed on my forearm, her warm golden eyes on me. "We're just worried about you, that's all."

"It's like you've been kidnapped by The Seven," added Alissa. Her gaze pivoted to their table before settling back on me.

I hated lying to my friends—especially Cinder. I vowed I'd tell her everything as soon as we were alone. The problem was, I didn't see that happening any time soon. Not with a horde of intimidating security guards attached to me twenty-four-seven.

"I promise I haven't been kidnapped. Cillian wanted me to spend more time training with Raine and Drake because of my witchiness. Some of our sessions go really late so it's been easier for me to stay the night."

"In Drake's room or Raine's?" Cinder's dark brows waggled, and I couldn't help the flush that crept up my cheeks.

"Scarlett's actually."

All three girls crinkled their noses in unison.

"She's actually really nice, you guys"—I lowered my voice —"way better than Raine or Aeria. Although, to be honest, they've been acting nicer than expected. I'm pretty sure Cillian's paying them off or something."

"So is the training working at least?" asked Cinder.

The explosion of power that wracked my core when we killed the demon still crackled over my skin, its memory forever etched in my mind. "I'm definitely making some progress." After what Aeria said about my dark magic, I wasn't ready to share the news with my friends. At least not until I found out more about it. From what I'd learned, shifters were on the lighter end of the magic spectrum, and I didn't want to freak them out.

The thirty-minute lunch break flew by as we caught up on all things dragon. I'd missed my best friend over the past few days.

From the corner of my eye, I caught a platinum blonde head

cocked in my direction. Turning toward the ice prince, our gazes met and he crooked a beckoning finger at me.

I grunted and shoved the remains of my sandwich in my mouth.

"Bossy, isn't he?" Cinder's lips curled into a smirk.

"You don't know the half of it," I mumbled around a mouthful of bread. "Sorry, but I have to go practice."

"I'll see you in Flying and Shifting?" asked Cinder. "It's unipeg day."

I rolled my eyes, worried about the welcome I'd receive from my mercurial steed. "Yup, see you there." Grabbing my backpack, I waved at the girls and rushed over to meet Drake at the banquet hall exit.

He glanced up at the clock over the door and huffed. "We only have an hour before our next class so you better be bringing your A-game."

"Geez, no pressure." I followed him through the walkways and up the stairs to the seventh floor in a semi-comfortable silence. I couldn't say Drake and I were friends, but I'd seen sides of the Fae prince I was fairly certain not many had.

Now including his private bedroom.

A massive four-poster bed sat in the center of the lavishly appointed room. Everything was dark wood and gold accents, plus the occasional splattering of pale blue—the official color of the Winter Court. Not a single item was out of place, no dirty clothes or books on the floor like you'd find in a typical guy's dorm room. A picture frame sat on his bedside table, but it was too far away to make out any details. A few landscapes in gilded frames lined the walls, but no other personal items. It was nothing like Scarlett's room with all the posters plastered across the walls.

"You live by yourself?" I finally asked when I'd finished ogling.

"Senior privilege."

"Oh, I figured it was a Fae prince privilege."

He shrugged. "That too." Dropping his backpack on the bed, he turned to me donning his characteristic expressionless mask. "So what do you want to work on today?"

I chewed on my lower lip. What I wanted were answers about my dark magic, and for some reason, I thought he could give them to me. Steeling my nerves, I spat it out. "Did Raine and Aeria tell you what happened with that demon?"

"Of course, they did." He didn't even bat an eye. Had they told him everything or left out the details like with Cillian? His brows furrowed as he scrutinized me. "What are you trying to say, Luna?"

"I want to practice whatever it was we did that day, but I don't know how to access it again." There, perfectly vague.

"Okay..." He picked up his spellcraft book and flipped through a few pages. "I think you guys used the banishing spell." He held the book out to me, his finger pressed against a passage.

It looked similar but wasn't quite the words we'd used. Those powerful words would be permanently emblazoned in my mind. "No it was: toree fuocum celis demoniom."

His eyes widened, and he snapped the book shut. "I see."

Crossing my arms over my chest, my foot tapped out a nervous beat on the plush carpeting. Did he really see?

"That would explain the ash," he mumbled to himself. He took another step toward me, his lilac eyes pulsating a deeper lavender as they seared into me. His lips twisted, and I could almost see the gears grinding in his head. "Raine told me you girls had vanquished the marai demon, but she'd been a bit hazy on the details. Now I can guess why." He moved closer still, his icy breath almost mingling with mine. I repressed the urge to step back, forcing my shaky legs to hold their ground. He sniffed the air around me, and his pointy ears twitched. "What did you say your non-human half was?"

"I didn't."

His lips pursed together, his heavy gaze still boring into me. "Warlock," he muttered, and then his light brows slammed together. "You're a darkblood like we are."

Crapcicle. He was the second person to say that.

"What the heck does that even mean?"

"They don't call it Darkblood Academy for nothing. Don't Cillian and Ryder tell you anything?"

"Apparently not enough." I did vaguely recall a conversation about darkbloods the day I arrived, but most of it was a blur.

"Come on, let's sit." He motioned toward his monstrous bed, and I arched a skeptical brow. "Or we could sit over here?" He pointed at the small leather sofa and chairs gathered around the fireplace.

"That works."

"So very untrusting, Luna. Believe me, if I wanted to get you into bed, I'd be much more charming about it."

My jaw fell open. Did the ice prince just flirt with me?

He dropped onto the couch, and I took the chair across from him. "First, a little supe 101 refresher course. All supernaturals have light and dark swirling inside them—none of the houses are inherently good or evil, but some have darker tendencies while others have lighter ones. Our sources of power differ, that's all. Shifters, like your dragon roommate, come from light magic, while the Coven Council—witches, warlocks, sorcerers and other magic users—like you, and the Fae like me, tend to live in the gray. We're the midpoint of the spectrum and can lean either way. Our headmaster, Cillian and my friend, Raf, along with all the other Sons of Heaven come from pure white light. They're the most 'good' of us all. Now, the Royal Vampires, like dear little Scarlett and the Underworlders, like our fearless leader, Ryder, are descendants of dark magic. It runs through their veins, and from what I understand, it's a constant battle for them to overcome their darker urges."

I couldn't imagine living like that. It was hard enough to harness your magic, but to have to keep it restrained? I'd seen the demon side of Ryder try to rise to the surface on a few occasions. A chill skirted up my spine at the memory of his elongated pupils and pulsing citrine irises.

"If your father is a warlock and based on what happened with the demon, I'd say there's a good chance you're leaning toward the dark side, little witch." An evil grin stretched his lips. "I must say, human, you're surprising me more and more each day."

I wasn't sure if that was a compliment or an insult so I ignored the comment and pushed on. "So let's say I do have this darker magic? What does that mean?"

"It means you could be more powerful than some of your full-blooded counterparts. If your power combined with Raine's and Aeria's was enough to decompose a marai demon, it means that the eight of us together could be unstoppable."

My chest tightened, the weight of his words crushing my lungs. Dark magic, demons, unstoppable? I didn't think I was ready for any of that.

He leaned forward, stretching across the table between us and tipped my chin up. "There's nothing to be scared of, Luna. Dark magic isn't bad or evil. All seven of us have it coursing through our veins, including our nephilim friend, and we're not so bad, right?" His lip slanted up, and he winked.

Right... Only the entire student body feared them.

"You ready to get to work?"

I nodded, but a pit of dread knotted my insides. What was I getting into?

CHAPTER 22

Another uneventful night passed and I was starting to think word of our badassery had spread to the Underworld, striking fear in the hearts of the demons that were supposed to come for me.

I'd even convinced Aeria and Raine to take the night off from guard duty so I could get some quality time with my roommate. They hadn't even put up much of a fight. Cinder and I huddled on her bed, scooping huge spoonfuls of ice cream into our mouths straight from the containers we'd snatched from the kitchen.

"So are you finally going to tell me what's going on?" she asked around a mouthful of chocolate ice cream.

I dropped the spoon into the half-empty tub. "Yes. But you have to swear to keep it a secret." Tugging down at my shirt collar, I showed her my puckered red skin bearing the devil's mark.

Her golden eyes blazed as she stared, her hand flying to her mouth to cover the gasp. "I swear," she mumbled.

I told her everything, from the mark to the real purpose of The Seven and all the way up to smiting the marai demon. As soon as the words were out, the two-ton elephant I'd been carrying around on my shoulders for the past few days vanished.

To her credit, Cinder hadn't even cringed when I told her my conversation with Drake and his assumptions that I was a darkblood.

"That's crazy." She shook her head, taking another bite of ice cream before snapping the lid back on. "And you haven't heard anything from Ryder?"

"Nope." A sharp pang jabbed at my heart. I'd even gone to check with Cillian earlier that day, but he'd said it had been radio silence since his departure. He assured me not to worry, but I couldn't help it. I hated how much I cared for the demon jerk.

Cinder glanced up at the clock on the wall, and a smile lit up her face. "You know what you need?"

"An exorcism?" To get the demon off my mind and out of my heart.

She laughed. "No. A fun night out to forget about all the other stuff going on." She dragged me off the bed and twirled me around in a circle. "Lucky for you I happen to know of a little get together going on tonight."

"I don't know if that's such a good idea." I curled my arms around my cozy sweatshirt. I was pretty ready to call it a night.

"It's just a couple dragons. They have a bonfire going at the edge of campus—a small party with s'mores and alcohol."

My eyebrows rose, nearly touching my hairline at the mention of the Fae forest. Though she hadn't said the actual words, it was their omission that struck a nerve. Even though we were only banned from the woods on the full moon, after what happened last time I wasn't sure I was ready to brave the creepy shadows yet.

Three quick knocks on our door drew my attention away from my dark musings. Cinder darted to the entryway with a mischievous look. Alissa and Maxi peeked their heads in a second later.

"You girls aren't ready yet?" Maxi whined.

Cinder shot me a come-on-let's-go look. "I'm still working on her."

"I don't know, you guys." I tugged on my tattered sweatshirt. "I'm practically in my pajamas."

"So hurry up and put some clothes on," said Alissa.

"Or just put your coat on over that," suggested Cinder. "No one's going to see what's underneath anyway."

Maxi readjusted the bag hanging from her shoulder, and the tinkle of glass clanging together caught my attention. "I have a beer with your name on it—it's a human kind and everything." She threw me a sneaky smile. "Besides, you've been hanging out with The Seven non-stop. Are you officially ditching team dragon or what?"

"No, of course not." I couldn't tell them what was going on. Spilling to Cinder was bad enough. The others would kill me if they knew I'd leaked the big secret of The Seven. "Okay, okay, I'll come."

Three girly squeals echoed across our room as I darted into the bathroom to freshen up. Maybe Cinder was right. A fun night out was exactly what I needed to get my mind away from the doom and gloom.

Without the light of the full moon, the Fae forest was even creepier than I remembered. Gargantuan evergreens loomed over us, their thick branches reaching out from the shadowy depths. My breaths rasped out a haggard pattern as I followed the girls along the path. Cinder assured me I wouldn't be poisoned if I brushed by a tree again—that had only been due to the magical effects of the full moon, but I still kept my distance from the green monsters.

The tinkling sounds of giddy chatter and boisterous laughter ahead quickened my pace. The path opened up into a small clearing where thirty or forty of our dorm mates huddled around a roaring bonfire.

"Made it!" Cinder grabbed my hand and tugged me toward the center of the party. Two metal kegs sat on a table to the right of the bonfire, and Cinder led us straight toward them. She handed me a cup and began to fill hers with the frosty amber liquid.

"This isn't some sort of magical dragon beer is it?"

She shook her head. "It's made here in Azar and it's called malta, but it's pretty much the same as your human beer. No strange side effects, I promise."

I sniffed the tawny beverage, and the scent of orange blossoms and hops wafted up my nose. "It smells good."

"Just drink it," said Alissa, pouring herself a big cup. "If you don't like it, I'll give you the human stuff."

Maxi held her beverage up to the three of us and clinked it against ours. "Cheers, girls! To another awesome semester at Darkblood Academy."

I took a sip, and the bubbly liquid slid down my throat. "Yum." It was slightly sweeter than beer and more effervescent. Tipping the cup back, I processed Maxi's words. The semester was almost over. With everything else going on, I'd completely lost track of the days. That meant final exams were coming up soon. Anxiety gurgled in my belly, and I swallowed it down with another gulp of malta.

"What happens if you don't pass the exams?" I asked the girls.

"You don't get to move up with the rest of the class," answered Alissa. She and Maxi had been here for a year so I assumed they'd already passed a good number of exams.

"Are they hard?"

"As hard as the class, I guess," answered Maxi.

They'd been dragon shifters all their lives so honing their skills had come naturally. Unlike mine.

Cinder wrapped an arm around my shoulders and squeezed. "You'll be fine, Luna."

"Besides Cillian and Ryder love you," added Maxi. "They'd never let you flunk out of the academy. You're their special little human pet." She smirked.

"Hey, I thought that was you." Ash appeared from behind the kegs, his lips twisted into a pout. "Where are Raine and Aeria?"

"Ha!" exclaimed Alissa. "Like those two would be caught dead at a dragon party."

"Excuse us for a minute." Ash wrapped his fingers around my forearm and tugged me away from the girls. "You know you're not supposed to be out alone."

"I'm not alone. I'm surrounded by thirty-some dragon shifters, and no one's tried to kill me for three whole days now."

He shook his head. "It's not the same. None of them are trained like we are. I don't like it."

I gave him my best smile. "But you're here now, and I'm safe with you, right?"

His green eyes sparkled and though he tried to fight it, his lips curved into a grin. "Stick with me like glue, Luna, girl. You got it?"

"Got it," I hissed. "Now can we go back to the party?" I glanced over my shoulder to find Maxi, Alissa and Cinder's eyes locked on us.

"All right, but don't make me regret this."

I glanced down at his empty hands and led him back toward the kegs. "Looks like you could use a drink. Then maybe you won't be so grumpy."

The next hour passed quickly in a blur of malta and a game similar to the human beer pong—only the cups floated in mid-air and you had to use magic to sink the small white ball into the cups. As the time ticked by, I convinced myself this was a great way to hone my magical skills.

And I was getting pretty awesome at it.

"Nice!" shouted Ash as my ball sank into the last malta-filled cup. He picked me up and spun me in a circle.

When he released me, I downed its contents and threw my hands up in victory. That was the third dragon team we'd beaten. I wasn't sure what it was, but my magic came to me more easily when I was around one of The Seven. The sweet, smoky smell always surrounded them, and it was almost like I could siphon its power and use it for myself.

Two male dragon-shifters I recognized from my Flying and Shifting class sauntered over. "You two up for another match?" said the dark-haired one.

I scanned the crowd around the bonfire, searching for Cinder. I hadn't really spent much time with her, and it had been the whole reason for coming out tonight. "Maybe next time," I said. "I gotta find my friend."

I turned to Ash as I rose to my tiptoes to search the mass of students. "Have you seen her?"

"Nope. I was too busy kicking those guys' asses. You're getting pretty good by the way."

"Thanks." I weaved my way through the crowd, and Ash trailed behind me. "Practicing with Drake has actually been better than expected."

He snorted. "Prince Drake helping anyone is monumental. You must have really impressed him."

A slight blush heated my cheeks. "He's only doing it because the professors are making him."

"Nah. Drake doesn't do anything he doesn't want to." He chuckled. "Unless he's doing it just to spite Raine."

I stopped as we reached the outer edge of the crowd and spun back to face him. "What's going on with the two of them?"

"I think they're hooking up again. From what Triston and Raf said they've been on and off again for a while now."

A twinge of jealousy bubbled up in my gut, but I squashed it down. I didn't have feelings for the ice prince so why would it matter to me? Those two were meant for each other.

Ash rubbed at the back of his neck, his gaze flitting around. "Speaking of hooking up, are you going to the end of the semester dance?"

My head snapped back, completely thrown off by his question. "I hadn't really thought about it, honestly. Until about an hour ago, I'd completely forgotten the end of the semester was practically here."

His gaze lingered over my face, an uncharacteristic shyness lighting up his emerald eyes. Oh no... was he trying to ask me to the dance?

A muffled cry rang out in the distance, dispelling the awkward moment. My head spun in its general direction as an icy chill skimmed up my spine. "What was that?"

Ash's pupils elongated, his irises glowing. "That was Cinder," he growled. "Stay here!" He sniffed the air and took off through the thick copse of pines. I raced behind him, pushing myself to keep up with his long strides.

"Wait up, Ash!" I panted.

"Go back!" he shouted over his shoulder.

But I couldn't. Not when my best friend could be in danger. Ash became nothing more than a shadow weaving between the trees, but his heavy footfalls left deep boot prints to follow in the blanket of snow.

Another scream ripped through the silence, and my heart leapt to my throat. That was definitely Cinder. I slowed as a growl reverberated through the pines ahead and tiptoed the remaining distance. Craning my neck around a thick trunk, all the air squeezed out of my lungs.

A dagger-like claw was pressed against Cinder's neck, a towering beast holding her captive against his monstrous chest. Two alabaster horns snaked from his massive head, glistening beneath the sliver of a moon above. Blood-red orbs flickered toward me for a moment before returning to its prey. A few yards in front of them stood a snarling, partially-shifted Ash.

Talons replaced my friend's fingers, and a long barbed tail twitched behind him. His face had elongated into an olive green snout, and razor sharp fangs filled his gaping maw.

"Don't even think about it, shifter," hissed the demon. "If you change, I'll slit her throat."

"Not if I burn you to a crisp first." Ash's gruff voice was barely human.

"And risk hurting this pretty little thing?"

"I won't, trust me." He stalked closer.

The demon ran his finger across Cinder's throat, and a thin line of blood trailed behind his sharp claw. She screamed and thrashed against him to no avail.

"Stop!" I shrieked, darting out from my hiding place.

Ash froze, his emerald irises bouncing back and forth between his cousin and me. "Dammit, Luna. I told you to stay back there."

The monster's eyes locked on mine, and the symbol on my chest pulsed red-hot and angry. I slapped my hand over the puckered skin as if somehow that would help.

"I was hoping you'd come out to play, half-blood."

I took a step closer, steeling my nerves. "Let her go. I know you're here for me."

"No, Luna," Cinder whimpered.

"You're not leaving with either of them," snarled Ash.

"Very brave words for a young dragon." His hand shot out, and a slick black substance burst out. Ash leapt out of the way, but the dark goo darted after him wrapping itself around his legs. He skidded across the snow and smacked into a thick trunk as the oily substance climbed up his body.

"What are you doing to him?" I yelled.

The demon huffed, and dark smoke shot out of his nostrils.

"I was sent for the human, but if I kill a few others along the way, the dark lord will only be that much more pleased."

Cinder began to cough as the smoke filled the air. She choked and spluttered, her hands desperately reaching for her throat, but the monster held them down. The dense smoke poured out of his mouth and nose clouding the air until Cinder went limp in his arms.

"Please, stop!"

He released his hold, and she crumpled to the ground. "As you wish." An evil smile showcased a row of gleaming fangs. "Come with me, human, and your other shifter friend won't suffer the same fate."

Ash whipped his head back and forth as he tried to push himself off the ground. "Don't do it, Luna."

I stepped closer, my breath stuck in my throat. If Cinder died, I'd never forgive myself. She was my best friend—pretty much the only one I'd ever had.

"That's right, little one, come right this way." He crooked a clawed finger at me.

"If you killed her, I'm not going anywhere with you," I spat.

He glanced down at my friend's drooping form. "She's still alive for now."

"I need to confirm that."

He motioned to Cinder with his palm up. "Come see for yourself."

"Don't, Luna!" Ash wriggled on the floor but whatever the monster spewed had him trapped. It climbed further up his body with every squirm.

I knelt down beside Cinder and released the breath I'd been holding once I saw the gentle rise and fall of her chest. She was still alive.

"You see," the creature hissed, "perfectly fine. Now it's time for us to go." His hairy hand closed around my shoulder, his claws digging into my flesh as he yanked me to my feet.

I squeezed my eyes shut, wincing from the pain as I found my footing. The demon dragged me a few yards as Ash's shouts grew more distant with every wobbly step.

A sharp screech tore through the air, and a dark shadow whizzed by. The hold on my arm released, and I tumbled face first into soft snow.

Oof! The fall smacked all the air from my lungs and stars danced across my vision. Blinking rapidly to refocus, I pushed myself off the ground as another howl rang out.

A few yards away, a dark figure pinned the demon to the ground, thick, corded arms pummeling into the creature. The smash of bone against flesh echoed through the quiet forest, sending goose bumps rippling over my skin. *Smack. Smack. Smack.*

Ryder?

I crept closer, my boots sinking into the soft snow. The moonbeams leaking through the thick canopy of trees high-lighted the broad shoulders and tapered waist of the man I'd recognize anywhere. Dark swirling tattoos snaked out from beneath his collar and shirtsleeves. The inky black practically glowed beneath the moonlight, coming to life on his skin.

The pounding of flesh drowned out the roar of my own heartbeats as I neared. Dark crimson splotches stained the pure snow. The demon lay motionless, eyes swollen shut, beneath Ryder's muscled thighs but still his fists relentlessly thrashed its dark flesh.

"Ryder?" My hand reached out for him, but I froze as he spun around. An ominous growl vibrated the air between us.

An unearthly citrine eclipsed his irises, his dark pupils a bottomless abyss of fury. His face was his own, and yet it wasn't. The darkness consuming his features distorted his appearance until I could barely recognize him.

"Ryder?" My breath hitched, but I somehow managed to squash the tremor building in my throat.

"Luna..." he rasped.

"Be careful," shouted Ash from a few yards back, still immobilized by the creature's black goop.

I steeled my nerves and shook my head as I extended my hand to him. Ryder would never hurt me. I believed it with every ounce of my being. His jaw softened, and the darkness twisting his features slid back beneath the surface. He pushed himself off the ground and accepted my hand. Icy fingers wrapped around mine, sending a chill straight up my veins.

Ryder tugged me into his arms, his chest heaving beneath mine. His heart jackhammered against my body, the erratic thrum so violent I could feel it through my thick coat.

He ran his hand through my hair and pressed my head into his firm chest. His musky scent enveloped me, cocooning me in safety. "You're okay," he muttered.

"I'm okay." I glanced up at him and the blinding yellow had receded, leaving only the dark onyx pools I'd come to love. I wished I could read the truth behind those stormy irises, the turbulent emotions that lingered just below the surface.

"Uh, guys, I could use a little help here." Ash's voice tore me away from the spell of his dark gaze.

With a grunt, Ryder released me and stomped over to Ash, and I ran to check on Cinder. Her breaths were shallow, but her eyelids fluttered when I spoke. "You're okay, Cinder. We're going to get you back, safe and sound."

Ryder somehow extricated Ash from the web of black goo and hauled Cinder into his arms. As the guys turned back toward the path, I scanned the white snow, marred by bloody splotches and my heart stopped.

"The demon's gone!"

CHAPTER 23

The radiant glow of Cillian's healing power bathed our entire dorm room in soothing warmth. The angel's big frame hunched over Cinder's still body, the heavenly light swirling around her. Even from a distance, its calming effect seeped into my skin, quelling some of the panic from earlier.

I stood by the foot of her bed with Ryder and Ash on either side of me. No one spoke as we waited with baited breaths. After a few more agonizing minutes, Cinder's eyelids fluttered. Slowly, her eyes opened, the golden hue dimmer than they'd been an hour ago when we'd been celebrating around the bonfire.

I'd been so stupid to put her life at risk. To put all their lives at risk.

I clenched my teeth as my best friend glanced up at me. "I'm so sorry, Cinder. It was all my fault you were attacked."

She shook her head and winced. Cillian's healing power may have mended the slash across her neck, but the pain remained in the tight set of her jaw and the deep crinkles around her eyes. "I'm the one that dragged you out there. If there's anyone to blame, it's me."

Cillian's blue eyes seared into mine. For an angel, he sure could be intimidating as hell. "You were both irresponsible going out there. You knew very well what could happen." Then he turned to Ash. "And you, you should have alerted the others as soon as you found her."

"It's not Ash's fault," I interjected. "He's not my keeper; none of you are. The longer I stay here, the more I'm putting you all at risk." I wrapped my arms around myself, letting the wretchedness consume me. "Maybe I should leave. As long as I have this thing on my chest, everyone around me is a target."

"This is a non-argument." Ryder's thick forearms squeezed against his chest as he peered down at me. "There's nowhere safer for you than here with us. Now that I'm back, I won't leave your side. No one else will be at risk."

The depth of emotion blazing from those impossibly black orbs resounded in his words. My heart staggered from its intensity. I rubbed at my chest, forcing it to continue beating.

Cinder laid her head back, her eyes closing once again.

"Come," said Cillian ushering us out of the room. "She needs to rest." He ticked his head at Ash. "Will you stay with her?"

He nodded quickly.

The hallway was quiet as we moved toward the fifth floor common area. It was well past curfew, and apparently most of my dorm mates had skedaddled from the woods and gone to bed before the demon showed up to break up the fiesta.

Cillian folded his big frame into the chair, and Ryder and I filled up the small sofa. His thigh grazed mine as he sat beside me, and tiny pops of electricity puckered the flesh beneath my jeans.

Ugh. I'd missed him way too much in the past few days.

"So what did you discover?" Cillian sat forward in his seat, his elbows propped on his knees.

"Dear old dad swears he has nothing to do with the mark. And for some reason, I believe him. He admitted there have been some rumblings among the six warlords of the Underworld. They're not pleased with their people being banned from the human realm."

"As predicted," Cillian muttered.

"Father believes someone's caught wind of what we're doing here and wants to put a stop to it."

"But how? Even within the walls of the academy, only a handful of staff knows what we're trying to accomplish with the team."

My mind flickered back to the marai demon and what Raine, Aeria and I *had* actually accomplished. I almost spilled the beans, but I ground my teeth together to keep the truth from slipping out. I'd have to tell Ryder when we were alone. My heart flip-flopped at the thought. Alone—with Ryder after so many days.

"There must be a traitor within our hallowed halls." A glimmer of humor sparked in his dark eyes.

Cillian huffed and clasped his hands together. "What else did you find out?"

Ryder rocked back and forth, and the couch squeaked beneath his weight.

"Well?"

He loosed a breath before continuing. "Father is well versed in the dark arts, as I'm sure you know. He thinks we're onto something with the seven of them—or actually eight." He tipped his head toward me, and my eyes widened. "He believes that harnessing their combined powers could truly create an unstoppable force. And he's not the only one to share in that belief."

Cillian frowned, his light brows pulling together. "So that's why she was marked?"

"It makes sense. She *is* the easiest target."

I jabbed my elbow into Ryder's side. "Hey! *She* is right here." Ryder's words plus the incident with the marai demon twirled around in my mind. "So they think by eliminating me, they'd destroy the team? But I barely have any powers. I have no idea what I'm doing."

"Which is how they want to keep it," said Ryder. "The stronger the eight of you become, the more you'll be feared." He pivoted toward Cillian, fixing his gaze on the headmaster. "Lucifer can't control the demons slipping through the wards much longer. Once the team is ready, we will have to take them to the human world. If they prove they can handle themselves, we can train more teams. We'll have a whole new generation of supernatural slayers. Some Underworlder must have figured this out, and they don't want anything wrecking their fun."

So it was true. The demons were getting into the human world like Jay's dad thought. They were killing humans. My fingers curled into tight little fists. "So how do we get rid of this mark? They're going to keep coming for me until we do."

"I'm still working on that, mini minx. Since the demon who placed it on you has been vanquished and the mark didn't disappear, it's a bit trickier than I'd hoped." He turned his body toward me and squeezed both my hands. "But don't worry, I promise to keep you safe in the mean time." His piercing eyes raked over me, heat trailing in their wake. The intensity of his gaze made my breath hitch, and I swallowed hard to stave off the relentless clawing in my throat.

From the corner of my eye, I caught Cillian's watchful baby blues on us. He cleared his throat, and Ryder dropped his gaze along with my hands. "We still have the abacor demon to deal with. We can't have him running around the academy grounds."

"Agreed. Unlike the two before him, abacors are higher-level demons. They're smart and won't be easy to track and kill."

I stifled a yawn and leaned back against the couch. Now that the adrenaline had worn off, my limbs were aching. I knew I should care about the missing demon, but I was exhausted.

"I'll have the team get on it first thing in the morning," said Ryder. "It'll be good practice for them—their first-upper level bad guy."

"Very well," said Cillian rising. His gaze settled on me before pivoting to Ryder. "You're on guard tonight?"

"Yup. I'll take her to my room now."

Cillian's bright blue eyes widened to the size of vast oceans, and I was fairly sure I mirrored his expression. "Excuse me?" he choked out. "You know students are strictly forbidden in faculty dorms."

They were? I'd already been to my instructor's room once before.

Ryder didn't flinch. "Cinder is safe with Ash. Bringing Luna to her room will only put the girl in the line of fire once again. I, for one, do not want to have to explain to Fenix and Flare that we got their little sister killed."

Cillian grunted.

"It's late. Scarlett and the girls are surely already asleep. Let them have one night off from babysitting. Luna can permanently move in with them tomorrow. If anyone comes tonight, I'll handle it."

The word babysitting had my nerves bristling, but I kept my mouth shut. For now.

"Fine," breathed Cillian, running a hand through his hair. "This is a one time exception." Dark shadows lined the handsome angel's eyes, and for once, he looked tired. Maybe healing Cinder had drained his angelic powers. "But Ryder—"

The demon raised his hand, cutting him off. "I know,

Cillian." The crease between his brows deepened, and his lips pressed together.

My gaze bounced back and forth between the two gorgeous men. Something unspoken passed between them, and Cillian turned to leave. "Sleep well, Luna."

"Thanks, you too, Cillian."

CHAPTER 24

Tension prickled my skin as we made the silent trudge to Ryder's room. My mentor was unusually quiet—no silly nicknames, no sarcastic quips, not even a flirty wink as we traversed the still hallways.

After his extended absence, it irked me how much I longed to hear any one of those stupid things from his lips. Man, I needed to get over him. Nothing good would ever come of this.

When we finally reached his room, he held the door open and ushered me in. A small duffel bag sat atop his ginormous bed with a few shirts spilling out. In all the commotion, I hadn't even asked when he'd gotten back from the Underworld or how he'd found us in the woods.

A crackling fire hissed and sputtered in the grand hearth, and I instinctively moved closer. The traumatic events of the evening had left a lingering chill in my bones. I sank into the sofa, my limbs heavy and lids heavier still.

I could feel Ryder's presence behind me before a soft blanket dropped across my lap. "You cold?" His breath tickled the back of my neck.

"A little." My lips trembled, but it wasn't from the lack of warmth.

He hopped over the back of the couch and scooted close beside me. Laying his arm across the cushion behind my head, his warmth encompassed me. His fingers danced a few inches from my shoulder—the near touch setting my nerve endings on edge. The proximity to his body did more to fuel the heat growing inside me than a dozen roaring bonfires.

"You shouldn't have gone out there tonight by yourself." He kept his gaze trained on the fireplace as he spoke, the reflected flames dancing across the pitch backdrop of his irises. "You could have gotten yourself killed." He ground his jaw, a tendon twitching just below the scruffy surface, and he finally turned to face me. "I was supposed to be keeping you safe, and I failed—again. I thought I'd found something I was good at, that I was finally doing something worthwhile. Maybe my father was right, and I have no business being here at the academy."

My neck snapped back. I was expecting a lecture, not a confession. I peered up at his dark eyes and shook my head. "You're the best instructor at Darkhen, Ryder. The way you've trained The Seven, they're going to be a crazy supernatural force because of you. And if you weren't here, I'd be dead at least a few times over. So don't worry, you've kept your word to Kimmie-Jayne. I know you'll keep me safe."

The corners of his eyes crinkled at the mention of my sister. "It's not *just* about my promise to her..." I felt a slight tug on my hair as his fingers closed around a few blonde locks. He twirled them between his thumb and forefinger slowly, and my heartbeat ratcheted up a few notches. "Gods, Luna, when I saw you in the middle of the forest with that demon, I lost it. The way his hands were on you, dragging you away and... All the walls I spend so much time building around my demon side crumbled in an instant. I wanted to rip him to shreds, gouge his eyes out with my nails, shove my fist down his throat and yank out his spine."

My breath hitched at the graphic picture he painted. A hint of yellow flashed across his irises, but it vanished a moment later. My mind flickered back to the dark shadow in the woods, pummeling the crap out of the demon. He *had* seemed like a different person, and I couldn't deny that a tiny part of me had been scared.

He drew in a deep breath, running his hand over his thigh. "For someone like me, control is everything, Luna. Without it, I'm nothing more than those monsters that have been coming after you. Hell, I used to be just like them." He paused and glanced down at the lock of hair twisted between his fingers. "I've been having a hard time maintaining my control around you, and I'll be damned if I know why."

I gulped, all these unexpected confessions squeezing my lungs. I wanted to tell him about what happened with the marai demon and Drake's guess about me being a darkblood, but I was scared to open my mouth. If I did, would he ever open up to me again?

"I wasn't always this productive member of Azarian society." His eyes flickered to the fire once more. "I spent a long time being angry—at my father for abandoning my mom and me, at my mom for still loving a man who'd ruined her life, and mostly at myself for not being able to control my darker tendencies. It took a lot for me to claw my way out of that doomed spiral. But I did it. And I can't go back." He exhaled a breath and pivoted toward me. "That's why I can't lose control, Luna. I just can't. Do you get it?"

I nodded, the raw emotion in his voice stabbing my insides. My mind whirled to the episode of *Hitched* when he revealed that his mother had been a human who fell in love with the devil. She'd almost died while pregnant and instead of losing her, Lucifer turned her into a demon—a soul-sucking one.

Things between his parents fell apart quickly after that. My heart constricted at the pain in his voice, knowing what was behind it.

He shook his head, running a hand through his mussed up hair. A dark lock tumbled over his forehead, and my fingers itched to brush it back into place. I held still, his intense gaze locked on mine as if my irises held the answers to some great mystery.

"Anyway, it's really late. We should probably get to bed."

My brows nearly reached my hairline, and heat flushed my cheeks.

He chuckled, squeezing my shoulder, a devious smile sparkling his eyes and revealing his sexy dimple. "Get your mind out of the gutter, mini minx. You get my bed, and I'll crash here on the couch."

And just like that, the old Ryder was back.

I grabbed a throw pillow and smacked him across the face. He laughed and chucked one right back at me. The next thing I knew, pillows were flying and I was ducking behind the couch, crawling on all fours to scramble for safety. Somehow the overwhelming sleepiness had vanished. I slid down behind a leather chair, nervous giggles fluttering in my chest. He'd amassed all the cushions on his side, and I was left without ammo.

"Come on out, mini minx. I've got you surrounded," he teased.

I peeked over the edge of the chair, and Ryder stood on the opposite side of the coffee table armed with a pillow in each hand.

"Surrender now, and I'll let you walk out of here alive."

"Not a chance!" I ducked down as mystical words filled my mind. The pages of my spellcraft book came to life and danced across my vision. "Venite ad miem," I whispered, and the pillows shot out from Ryder's clutches and landed in my hands.

His eyes widened as I sent them flying back in his direction guided only by my magic. He sat there wide-eyed as they smacked him right on the forehead. They slid to the ground and he growled, "Impressive; looks like someone's been practicing while I was gone." He shoved them aside and an evil smirk tugged his lips up. "But you're in big trouble now." Leaping across the room, he pummeled straight into me. His big body pressed me to the floor, and all the air squeezed right out of my lungs. "What are you going to do now?"

His corded arms caged me in as he hovered a few inches above me. My arms were trapped at my sides, useless. His chest rose and fell quickly, nearly touching mine with each inhale. I struggled beneath him for a minute or two before my body relaxed, giving up the fight. He glanced down at me with a pleased expression across his handsome face. "You surrender?"

"Never!" I squirmed again, this time able to wiggle a few trapped fingers. I grazed his upper thigh, then my fingers moved higher and... *oh!* My fingertips brushed a hard part of his anatomy.

A raspy growl vibrated his throat, and his eyes jolted wide open. His entire body tensed, and I took advantage of the momentary distraction, refusing to focus on the burn of my cheeks. Wrapping my leg around his torso, I pushed myself up and twirled us around so I was now on top of him.

Triumphantly sitting across his hips, I threw my hands in the air. "Winner!" All my combat lessons had finally paid off.

"Well done, mini minx." He laughed, pushing himself up to a sitting position and something hard poked against my short shorts.

Ryder froze, the easy laugh dying out in his throat. I gulped. The feel of his body beneath mine made my insides clench, and fire rushed my core. His eyes flashed a brilliant citrine, and his arms snaked around my waist. My breaths came in shallow pants as his lips inched closer.

My tongue darted out, wetting my bottom lip, and he let

out another sexy growl, his eyes locked on my mouth. I blinked. He closed the remaining distance between us, and his lips crashed into mine.

Heat swirled in my belly as his tongue engaged mine in a fevered dance. His kisses were frenzied, demanding, and out of control. It was all I could do to keep up. He cupped the back of my neck, angling it to deepen the kiss, and I moaned against his lips. A blazing fire ignited in my chest intensified by every touch, every heated caress. His hands moved to my lower back, skimming the hem of my shirt, and I arched into him.

He kissed me like the world was ending, and each second was precious and finite. And it was... because as much as I tried to bury the niggling thought, I knew what was coming after this. After the lusty haze fell away. He'd basically just warned me in his emotion-fueled confession.

My heart tripped over itself, and I pulled back. Ryder's obsidian irises glowed above me, a brilliant gold outlining the darkness. He clenched his jaw and pressed his kissable lips into a tight line. I wanted nothing more than for him to capture my mouth once more, but he didn't.

He huffed out a shaky breath and splayed his hands on my hips. A second later, I was no longer straddling his lap. Instead, I sat on the plush carpeting, my eyes glued to the creamy beige color. I refused to look up at him because I knew what would happen once I did.

We remained in silence for a few interminable moments longer, neither meeting the other's gaze. Finally, Ryder loosed a breath and slid his arms around my shoulders and beneath my knees. Hauling me into his chest, he zipped to his bed and lay me down.

For the briefest moment, his eyes met mine, a dark storm brewing beneath the obsidian surface. His lips brushed my forehead, and he whispered, "I'm sorry." He spun away in a dark blur, disappearing into the bathroom, and my heart broke into a million pieces.

He didn't need to say more because I already knew. He said it all with those two words. I rolled over and curled into a ball. Hot tears pricked my eyes, but I refused to let them spill over. Not here, not in his bed, surrounded by his musky, sandalwood scent.

So I squeezed my eyes shut and willed myself to sleep, ignoring the stabbing pains in my heart as deep fissures tore across the surface.

CHAPTER 25

Ryder woke me before the sun was up, and then disappeared into his bathroom to shower. I yanked the covers over my head, not ready to face the day— or him. How could I have gotten my hopes up again? Stupid, stupid, stupid. Even if Ryder did feel something for me, which I was now pretty sure he did, he could never fully act on it. Not when he needed to keep his dark urges under such tight control. Not while he was my teacher, and I was his student.

I was fairly certain Cillian would kill him. And what about Kimmie-Jayne? What would she think about me lusting after her former bachelor?

I shook my head, pushing the pointless thoughts aside. It didn't matter. Ryder and I could never be together. My chest constricted, and I couldn't suck enough air in. Throwing the comforter off, I raced to the window and jerked it open. The chilly morning air was like a smack in the face. And exactly what I needed.

Ryder sauntered out of the bathroom, a gray towel hung loose around his hips. Sleek black tattoos covered his chest and abs, climbing and dipping over every perfect indentation.

I tore my gaze away from his sculpted torso and bit my lower lip. Holy demon babies, was he doing it on purpose? Or did he really have no idea what effect he had over me?

"You okay?" he asked, moving nearer.

My hand shot up before he got too close. I couldn't think when he got in my personal space. "I'm fine. I just needed some air." *Can't he put some clothes on?*

His full lips twisted into an irresistible pout. "We need to talk about—"

"No!" I hissed. "I don't need you to rehash all the reasons why kissing me was a mistake or how it can never happen again or that you're still in love with my half-sister. Let's just pretend like it never happened. That worked so well for us last time."

"Luna..." He stepped toward me, holding out his hand.

Anger surged in my gut. I opened my mouth to shout no again, but a blue bubble appeared around me. Ryder's figure blurred through the swirling translucent azure. It was hard to make out the details of his face, but his expression darkened before he spun away.

A few minutes later he emerged from his closet fully dressed. My safety bubble had disappeared, and I sat huddled on his bed. The sun still hadn't quite come up yet; faint rays of light peeked through the dense forest below. "Why are we up so early anyway?"

"I have to meet the team, and I wanted to show you where we train."

My brows pulled together. "I thought you trained in the gym."

"That's just for class, but we generally meet in the mornings at a more private location."

"Okay... Can I go back to my room to get changed?"

He nodded. "I'll take you there now."

I hopped off the bed and waited by the door as he slipped on his boots. Without lifting his gaze to me, he whispered, "I know you're mad, and you have every right to be. There's no excuse for my behavior, and all I can say is I'm sorry for hurting you. I don't know why I can't control myself around you. No matter what, I'm sticking by your side though, and I will see you through this. Even if you hate me for it."

My throat tightened, a knot of emotion making it hard to breathe. I didn't look at him as he stood up and walked toward me. Or the rest of the way to my dorm room.

I refused to play along with his mood swings. I was done lusting over the unattainable Ryder Strong.

༺༻

AFTER A TRUDGE THROUGH THE BITTER COLD TO A SMALL stone building at the edge of the academy grounds, meeting Drake's judgmental, icy glare was the last thing I needed this morning. He and the other Seven stood in the center of the training room, each decked out in workout attire. So the moment he walked up to me, I infused my voice with as much venom as possible and narrowed my eyes at him. "I know I effed up big time last night. I've already heard it from Cillian and Ryder; I don't need a scolding from you too."

Raine quirked a brow, a shadow of a smile tilting her perfect lips up. "I'm starting to like this new side of the snarky little half-blood."

Aeria chuckled beside her as they watched our exchange.

"I wasn't going to scold you," said the prince, crossing his arms against his chest. "I was simply going to reprimand you for not letting us in on the fun."

Ash sauntered over, dark shadows rimming his sunken eyes. "Dude, it wasn't that fun."

Drake squeezed his friend's shoulder and smirked. "Maybe not for you, little dragon. When you get a bit more powerful, you'll see the fun will really begin."

With a grunt, Ash shook the Fae's arm off. "Whatever."

"All right, kids." Ryder clapped his hands, drawing our attention toward him. "As I'm sure you've all heard by now, our little Luna was attacked on campus *again*. Until we can get that mark off her chest, we can expect these attempts to continue. The good news is, it gives you guys more of a chance to practice demon killing."

A chorus of whoops shot out around me.

I scanned the training room while Ryder spoke to distract myself from ogling his body in that tight t-shirt and those loose hanging sweatpants. A dazzling array of metal weapons lined the walls—from nun chucks to crossbows to gleaming swords. I didn't think there was a single weapon in existence that wasn't in this hidden arsenal. Beside the weapons, tall bookshelves climbed the walls filled to the brim with ancient texts and small glass containers, beakers and bottles. Ingredients for potions? Most likely.

The dip in Ryder's voice drew my attention back to his speech. "The abacor demon that crashed the party in the woods last night won't be an easy kill. Unlike the other two demons who've come, this guy is more than just vile goo and brawn as Ash can attest to."

"We heard you almost tore it to shreds," said Triston, his lips spreading into a wolfish grin.

Ryder nodded, but his jaw tightened. "Almost. But as you can see, it still managed to get away. Abacors are smart, upper-level demons and more than anything, they're powerful. I need you all on high alert today when you're on the hunt. It's doubtful he'll come out in broad daylight, but you've all been excused from your classes for the day. I want this beast caught before bedtime. You guys got it?"

"Yes, sir," they all shouted in unison.

"I need you guys to break up into two groups, and I want a nice balance of power. You're going to need to work together to vanquish this guy. It won't be like the marai demon. Drake, Scarlett and Triston: you're team one and Raine, Ash, Aeria and Raf: you'll be team two."

Raine twitched beside me, and I knew exactly what she was thinking because the same thought was racing through my mind. Ryder still didn't know how we'd defeated that demon.

I nudged her in the arm. It was time to come clean. Everyone in here was a darkblood like me—possibly—so there was no reason to keep it a secret any longer.

Raine waggled her fingers at Ryder when I made no move to interrupt him. The less I had to talk to him, the better.

"Yes, Raine?"

"There's something we left out of our marai demon debrief with Cillian."

His dark brow lifted. "Okay. So what happened?"

"I whipped up a little alternative magic spell and used Aeria and Luna as energy magnifiers to vanquish it. That little half-blood's power packs a pretty big punch. I've never felt anything like it."

Aeria's head bounced up and down, confirming the story. Heat rushed to my cheeks as a shadow of what I'd felt that night tingled through my veins. It was strangely satisfying to hear Raine speak so highly of my power and confirm what I'd thought had been mind blowing.

Ryder scratched at his chin, the rasp of his nails against his day old scruff magnified in the tense silence. I could feel the others' heavy gaze burning into the side of my face, only intensifying the heat creeping across my cheeks.

"That's pretty big news, Raine. Thanks for enlightening me on this newest development." His dark eyes shot to me for a second before settling back on the rest of the team.

Whatever. Maybe I would've told him if he hadn't been such a jerk after kissing me. Again.

"Can you go over all the details, please?"

She recounted exactly what happened, from the surge of power that exploded through us when our hands joined to the full incineration of the nasty winged-monster.

"So Luna's a darkblood like one of us?" asked Ash, sparks lighting up his emerald eyes.

"Seems possible," Ryder answered.

"Who *is* your father anyway, Luna?" Drake leaned forward, craning his head around the others to drill me with his frosty gaze.

My eyes jumped to Ryder's, unbidden. Cillian had thought it best to keep my father's identity a secret, but maybe it was time for the truth to come out. At least within this secret circle anyway.

Ryder cleared his throat, releasing a breath. "Her father is a high warlock. His name isn't important right now, but suffice it to say that Luna's inheritable magical abilities are numerous due to her parentage."

"That's pretty freakin' cool," said Scarlett, shooting me a smile.

"So which team do I get to be on?" I finally asked.

Ryder tsked. "Sorry mini minx, but you're benched for this mission. You'll be spending the day with Cillian."

"What?" I drilled my stubborn instructor with my most hateful glare. "But Raine and Aeria just told you that I have real powers. I should be out there helping."

He shook his head adamantly. "Absolutely not. If you're out there, I'll just be worried about you." He snapped his jaw shut and raked a hand over his face. "I'd be concerned with your safety. The others have been training for almost a year now. You've just been thrown into this whole new world. The best place for you is safely tucked away in the headmaster's office."

"This is BS," I growled under my breath. "You can't make me stay there in some misguided attempt to protect me."

Ryder erased the distance between us, his massive body

looming over me. Darkness twisted his expression. "Oh yes, I can. I can ground your ass for the rest of the semester if I want to. I'm your instructor."

I glared up at him, fury uncoiling in my chest like a venomous serpent. Man, I loathed him right now. "It's not fair." I hated how whiney I sounded, but it was all I could come up with without spilling my real feelings in an avalanche of spiteful words.

After another heated moment, he stepped back and I could breathe again. From my periphery, I caught all eyes on us, and it was all I could do to keep the heat from spreading across my cheeks and tinting them fifty shades of red.

"I can take her to Cillian's," offered Drake.

"No," Ryder barked. "I'll take her, and we'll meet up in the main hall. Team one you've got the exterior grounds first and team two you're inside. I'll patrol on my own, covering both areas. Security is aware of the threat, but they've been ordered to inform me immediately if they spot the abacor."

The Seven nodded, their expressions grim, like soldiers ready for battle.

"Pick your weapon of choice while I'm gone. Nothing flashy, remember we're trying to keep this low key. There's no reason to cause a panic at the school. The rest of the students have no idea what's going on, and we'd like to keep it that way."

Ryder stepped beside me, his hand making a move toward my lower back. I squirmed away before he made contact and marched toward the door. From the corner of my eye, I swore Drake smirked, having caught the awkward exchange. But I couldn't be sure.

"Good luck, you guys," I called over my shoulder as anger ate away at me for not being included. For now. The moment Cillian's back was turned, I'd make my escape. That abacor demon was mine.

CHAPTER 26

My foot tapped on the hardwood floor of Cillian's pristine office, my knee unable to stop bouncing. I stared at the clock hung over the headmaster's desk, the sluggish tick-tock of the second hand taunting me with every millimeter it crawled. Cillian hunched over his desk, his bright eyes intent on the computer screen. Every so often, he'd lift his gaze to me and throw me a reassuring glance. I had to repress the urge to snarl at him.

I huffed out a breath, crossing my legs to stop the bouncing. Again my skin itched as if I spent another minute inside it, I'd explode. It was an odd feeling that came over me time and again. It had been less than an hour since Ryder dropped me off, but time had moved at a snail's pace since I watched him walk out the door.

As if last night's rejection hadn't been bad enough, now I had to deal with his brutal rebuff regarding the mission. Wrapping my arms around myself, I fully indulged in my pity party for one.

Cillian cleared his throat and settled his brilliant azure eyes on me. A few months ago, it would have had my insides in knots, but now the hot bachelor had become my headmaster, and I saw him in a completely different light. He was still gorgeous though—I wasn't blind.

"I haven't forgotten about that mark," he said, his gaze dipping down to my chest. "I'd hoped Ryder could have gotten the answers we needed from the Underworld, but since he didn't, I've begun to research other avenues."

Unbidden, my fingers trailed along the puckered, heated skin. "Thanks, Cillian, I appreciate it."

He stood, his long legs eating up the space between us until he stopped just in front of me. His lips twisted into a half-frown, and the crease between his brows deepened.

"Yes?" I finally said, when the silence got awkward.

He exhaled a long breath and clasped his hands behind his back. "I want you to feel completely comfortable with me, Luna. I know you had a rough start and trusting others may not come easily, but I want you to trust me. With anything. Do you understand?"

I nodded, chewing on my lower lip as heat warmed the tips of my ears. Did he know about my dark magic?

"I care about Kimmie-Jayne deeply and you, as an extension." His lips curled into a sheepish smile. "I'd like it if you considered me an older brother of sorts—a much older brother." He chuckled to himself.

Cillian was like a bazillion years old. He'd never even divulged the exact number on *Hitched*. Apparently, angels were weirdly secretive about their ages.

"Okay," I finally said, incredibly confused by this conversation. Was he trying to get something out of me or was he really just being nice?

He crouched down so his eyes were level with mine. "Coming into powerful abilities is a difficult time for any supernatural. The internal battle between light and dark can be all consuming, and I don't want you to fear coming to me. I may be an angel, but I've behaved less than angelic on more than one occasion. I know Ryder has taken it upon himself to mentor you, but if there's ever a problem, you can always talk to me about it."

Something about his tone when he mentioned my instructor had crimson coating my cheeks. Oh God, what if he knew?

Three sharp knocks at the door had us both spinning toward the entryway. And thankfully, it put an end to this crazy uncomfortable conversation.

Darby peeked his bald head through the crack, scraggly white tufts shooting up like weeds. "Sir, there's been a development."

My eyes shot open, and my head whipped back toward Cillian.

"About the abacor demon?" he asked.

The old man shook his head. "No. One of the first year's conjured up a spitfire demon and half of the students in Professor Marston's class have been badly burnt. The healers could use your help."

"Of course." Cillian hurried toward the door, his magnificent wings bursting from his wide shoulders. Before he shut the door behind him, he spun back. "I'll be back as soon as I can. Stay put. You'll be safe here."

I nodded, schooling my expression into a blank mask while my insides danced a little jig. This was my chance to break out of here.

Plastering my ear to the thick timber, I waited until Cillian's footsteps fell away. The scrape of chair legs against the floor plummeted my soaring hopes. I'd anticipated Darby going with him, but no such luck.

I slumped back against the door, my shoulders sagging. Now what? The massive picture window behind Cillian's desk caught my eye, and I scampered across the room. Leaning over the windowsill to the frozen tundra four floors below, I quickly scrapped that idea.

Another quickly took shape along the outskirts of my mind. The words of the cloaking spell I'd never been able to master flickered in my subconscious. It was a good thing I'd been so bad at magic my first few months here that I had all the time in the world to memorize dozens of enchantments.

Hovering by the door, I squeezed my eyes shut and muttered the mystical words under my breath. "Nascondem, ascondem oblivis." After a few more chants, I glanced down at my uniform shirt and skirt, the bright tartan hue screaming, "Here I am!" Damn, it didn't work.

Gritting my teeth, I drew in a long, cleansing breath and tried again. Warmth spread through my veins and hope flickered in my gut until I opened my eyes. Still totally visible.

Blast it!

I stomped across Cillian's office, cursing my fickle magic. Why couldn't it just come when I wanted it to? I trudged past a mirror, and my head whipped back to the ornate framed glass. Gingerly walking toward it, my eyes widened with every step. Either I'd just died and come back as a vampire, or my spell worked!

I wasn't even sure about the no reflection vampire myth, which meant... I was free! I darted to the door, gently turning the antique brass knob. Holding my breath with every click and squeak, I inched the door open. From the crack, Darby's hunched form coalesced across the way, along with that of a very large security guard.

Crapcicles! I hadn't counted on a guard. And I had no idea what kind of supe he was—besides a humongous one. Unlike the students, security didn't wear handy dandy little pins from their corresponding houses. I eyed the bulky man standing behind Darby's desk trying to assess his supernatural status. If he was a warlock, he might be able to see through my cloaking spell. But those bulging biceps and thick thighs didn't exactly scream warlock—not to be racist or anything. My gut said werewolf or some other shifter, which meant heightened sense of smell and sound. I wasn't exactly sure how much this spell cloaked... dammit!

Steeling my nerves, I forced my feet forward. I had to at least try. I held my breath and opened the door just wide enough to squeeze through. Tiptoeing by Darby's desk, my heart thundered with each measured step. I was certain the pounding was so loud even a human could hear it. Neither of them even glanced in my direction.

Must be the spell...

I hurried across the foyer and raced down the steps, thanking my lucky stars my magic held. I wished I'd asked my professor what the ETA was on one of these things.

The main hall was quiet as I zipped through the corridor; luckily most students were still in class. Now I had to find the abacor demon before Ryder or Cillian found me. Hmm... how was I supposed to do that? Demon tracking wasn't exactly one of my magical abilities. Not yet anyway.

Maybe if I just wandered around it would find me. The symbol on my chest pulsed, hot and angry. Another brilliant idea formed in the recesses of my mind. Yanking my coat from my backpack, I slid it on and headed for the forest. If I were a nasty abacor demon, that would definitely be where I'd be hiding out.

Frigid air slapped me across the face the moment I stepped outside. Pulling my coat tighter around me, I hurried toward the encroaching woods. My teeth chattered with every step, that and the crunch of snow beneath my boots the only sound for miles. As I trudged further away from the path, I cursed myself for not stopping by my dorm room to layer on a few extra sweaters and scarves.

Stupid Fae Winter Court.

The pines thickened around me, and I was forced to weave in between the evergreen monsters to avoid being stuck by an errant branch. I still didn't trust those bastards not to poison me.

Just ahead, muffled voices seeped through the dark copse of trees. I quickly ducked behind a massive bark until I placed all three of them. Drake, Scarlett and Triston. No Ryder, thank goodness.

Emerging from my hiding spot, I traipsed toward them. No one even glanced my way as I approached their huddle. Nice! This cloaking spell was definitely a keeper. Now if I could only figure out how to turn it off...

"Let's circle back toward the main building," said Drake. "Either the abacor isn't out here or he's slipping by our scrying spell."

Scarlett shook her head, holding up a crystal suspended from a leather cord. "It's not the spell. I would've found him by now. Something's shielding him, and it's strong."

Drake's phone buzzed, and he scanned the screen. "Ryder and the others are inside. He just passed team two in the faculty dormitories. It's all clear."

Triston's eyes sharpened, the gilded amber glimmering as he scanned the woods. "It's gotta be out here somewhere."

"Too bad we don't have the half-blood with us, we could use her as bait." Drake snickered.

Bastard! Wrapping my arms around my midsection, I seethed. At least the rising heat chased away the frosty air. Once I'd had a second to cool down, I fully processed his words and a light went off in my jumbled mind. The cloaking spell was keeping the demon from finding me. If I could turn it off, he'd come right to us and we could finally kill the demon scum.

So I sucked it up and did something I really didn't want to do. "Hey guys," I said, raising a hand I was fairly certain no one could see.

Drake spun toward me first as Scarlett and Triston glanced around in circles.

"Luna?" Drake's eyes fixed just above my hairline.

"As insulted as I am about your half-blood remark, you may actually be onto something."

"Where are you?" asked Scarlett, stepping closer as she sniffed the air.

"Apparently, I'm under a really kickass cloaking spell that I can't quite seem to lift."

Triston chuckled, his wolf eyes still searching for me.

"What are you doing out here anyway?" asked Drake. "I thought you were supposed to be hiding out with Cillian." He was only a foot away from me now, pawing blindly at the air between us.

"I convinced Cillian I could be of help so he let me come out to find you."

"Bullshit," barked the prince. "There's no way angel boy would've let you out of his sight. Not Ryder's precious half-blood."

My cheeks warmed, and I was suddenly thankful for the invisibility spell. I wasn't Ryder's anything. "Can you just tell me how to turn off the cloaking thing already? Or do you like standing out here freezing our butts off?"

"You forget the prince is from the Winter Court," said Scarlett. "This is nice weather to him." Her typically pale skin was tinged in pale blue today. Apparently, I wasn't the only one affected by the cold. "I'm with Luna. I say let's do it."

Triston nodded. "Agreed. Let's get this demon killing show on the road."

Drake's lips twisted into a pout, his light irises flickering with light and shadows. "Ryder's going to kill us if anything happens to her."

"So we'll make sure nothing happens to her," said Triston,

shrugging. "It's four of us against one of it. I'm pretty comfortable with those odds."

"Fine," hissed Drake, but his tone conveyed anything but. He turned in my direction with a scowl. "Just will the cloak away."

"What do you mean *will* it?"

"It's your spell—only you can control it. Imagine being seen and you will be."

Sure, easy peasy. I drew in a breath, squeezing my eyes shut and pictured my crimson and black uniform coming to life. *Come on!* A burst of warmth seeped through my veins, and my eyes snapped open.

"Took you long enough," Drake muttered, his cool gaze finally meeting mine. He practically leapt back when he realized how close we were, and I couldn't help the little giggle that fizzled in my chest.

Triston scanned the tree line and licked his lips. "Okay, so now what?"

"Now we wait for the abacor to come to us." My fingers drifted over the mark on my chest. "I have a feeling it won't be long."

CHAPTER 27

D rake held his hand up and a long, thin blade appeared in his palm. A lilac hue matching the prince's irises shimmered across the sword. The weapon seemed to be crafted from faery magic itself. Scarlett spun around, her fangs sliding out from her top lip and revealed short daggers in each hand. Triston held no actual weapon, unless you counted the rows of pointed teeth and razor sharp claws curling from his partially shifted paws.

I suddenly felt severely underweaponed. "You guys have any extra weapons for me?"

Scarlett bent down and hitched up her pant leg, revealing another dagger. She tossed it over and panic exploded in my chest as it whirled end over end toward me. At the last second, my hand whipped out to catch the shiny metal hilt. Phew... those training sessions with Ryder *were* actually paying off.

The sound of snow crunching sent everyone's head spinning toward the darkening forest. Drake's eyes connected with mine, and he nodded. No one moved. I couldn't have even if I wanted. Panic spilled through my veins freezing my muscles in place. Triston raised his elongated furry snout and sniffed the air. Turning to us, his irises blazed, the amber lit up like a thousand flickering flames.

Drake's fingers clamped around my shoulder and he hauled me behind him, raising his sword. The uncharacteristically chivalrous gesture nearly knocked me on my butt. Triston and Scarlett flanked Drake so the three stood in a line, each within arm's reach of the other. Were they going to pull the same stunt Raine had with the marai demon?

A dark blur whipped the tree branches as it hurtled toward us. A sharp shriek rang out in the stillness and sent a wave of goose bumps crashing over my skin.

"Look out!" shouted Drake as the creature pummeled right into the four of us. I jumped back, Drake's body taking the brunt of the hit from the massive black beast. It was like a bowling ball whizzing by four wobbly pins. I staggered but managed to remain on my feet, but my friends hadn't been as lucky. Scarlett had been thrown a few yards back. She pushed herself up, holding her head where a line of blood trickled down her nose. And Triston... where was Triston?

Drake snapped up a few feet behind me, his lilac eyes darker than I'd ever seen them as the hairy creature doubled back around. He thrust his sword at the demon, shoving me behind his back once again.

"Ah, the Fae prince," the abacor hissed. "I'd heard they had you hiding out here, but I couldn't believe it."

"No one's hiding, demon."

A dagger whizzed through the air, burying itself in the abacor's beefy shoulder with a sickening squelch. Scarlett stood a few yards away with the second dagger poised to strike. The monster barely flinched as he jerked the knife out of his arm and tossed it to the ground.

Dang it. Maybe we underestimated this thing.

It let out a ground-shaking howl and charged at Drake, its alabaster horns sharpened to lethal points. My heart leapt to my chest, and I squeezed my eyes shut at the last minute like a big baby.

The crash of metal against bone reverberated across the darkening sky, and I hazarded a peek through my slitted lids. Drake swung his sword in a mighty arc, sparks of lavender and magenta dancing across the blade. The abacor used his moose-like horns to deflect the blows, swinging his massive head back and forth like a wild animal.

The demon closed the distance between them and snorted. Thick, black smoke spewed from his nose and mouth, and Drake began to cough.

"Watch out!" I screamed. "That stuff's lethal!" My hands shot out without my control and my safety bubble appeared, cocooning both Drake and me in its blue haze.

"Thanks," Drake mumbled between coughs.

The abacor swiped at the shimmering orb with its sharp talons, but the invisible walls held. "Come out and play, little ones. Or I'll make you watch as I disembowel your friend." The demon's crimson eyes turned to Scarlett right as she let her second dagger fly.

It zipped through the air, but the abacor swiped it away with its meaty paw. Then he lunged at her.

"No!" I cried out, but my voice was muffled within the safety of my little bubble.

Scarlett snarled, her fangs in full view. She dodged the first and second swipe of his clawed digits. The girl was nothing more than a blur as she zipped around him and beneath his tree-trunk legs.

Another howl erupted from a few yards away, and a gray wolf sprinted toward the battling pair. Leaping into the air, wolf-Triston landed on the demon's hairy back and sank his fangs into the back of its neck.

Scarlett didn't waste a second, revealing another knife strapped to her ankle. Freeing it from its holster, she buried it into the demon's gut as he struggled against a dangling Triston.

"Drop the shield, quick!" shouted Drake.

Right. If only I knew how to do that. Sweat lined my brow as I scrambled to recall the words of the incantation.

Oily, black goo shot out of the demon's extended hand, wrapping itself around Scarlett's midsection. She dropped the dagger and collapsed to the ground, writhing against the magical bindings.

"Luna, just do it!" Drake yelled.

Oh, flying faeries! "I'm trying!"

His fingers wrapped around my hand, a little tighter than I thought necessary and a flash of brilliant purple exploded around us, annihilating our little enclosure. Raw power surged from my hand and tingled over every inch of my flesh as Drake released his hold and sprinted toward the others.

I staggered for a second, the rush of energy making my head spin before I got my legs underneath me and raced after him.

Drake speared the demon in the chest as Triston kept him busy from behind, nipping and snarling at his heels. Scarlett's dark hair, splayed across the white snow, caught my eye. She thrashed wildly as the onyx goo crawled up her torso. "No, no, no!" I slid down beside her and tried to tear away at the mystical binds choking her.

"Don't," she murmured. "You'll just make it spread faster."

"So what do I do?"

"How confident are you in elemental magic?" The onyx ropes tangled around her like poison ivy, climbing higher and higher.

I arched a brow. This was not the time for a lesson in Magic 101.

"I want you to try to freeze it off me."

I glanced around at the veritable winter wonderland stretching around us and nodded quickly. I could do this. I'd seen Drake do it a million times. Sure, he was a winter faery, but how hard could it be?

I dug my fingers into the snow, rubbing the soft powder between my frozen digits. Skimming the surface with my palm, I mumbled, "Venitem icem forae." Icicles crackled between my skin and the frosty ground, energy zapping like a live wire. Raising my hands, I splayed my fingers out and channeled the icy minerals crystallizing over my skin.

Power surged through my veins, filling every nook and cranny of my insides. "Wait!" I cried out. "What if I freeze you too?"

Her lips trembled, the black goo crawling up her neck. "Even if you kill me, I'll come back. This stuff is dark demon magic, and I'm not sure what its effects may be. Now just do it!"

Steeling my nerves, I pressed my lips together and stretched my arms out. Ice shot from my palms, covering Scarlett in a winter blanket. Her pale skin turned light blue then completely frosted over. My breaths came in ragged spurts, but I kept going until every inch of the vile goo was covered in ice.

I lowered my hands and slumped back, my head whirling. "Scarlett?" Her eyes were squeezed shut, tiny icicles coating her long dark lashes. Lowering my ear to her chest, I heard nothing. My own heartbeats stumbled. "It's okay, she's going to be fine," I mumbled to myself. "I just gotta get this stuff off her now."

All around me the sounds of a raging battle continued, wild animals' fangs snapped and earsplitting growls swam around me. But I couldn't focus on that. I had to save my friend.

Grabbing the dagger tucked into my waistband, I slid the blade beneath the now icy black tendrils around her midsection. With a sharp twist of the knife, the coil snapped.

"It worked, Scarlett, it worked!" I quickly repeated the exercise until she was free from the black icy mess. I was about to break into a happy dance when the yelp of Triston's wolf sent my gaze flying in their direction.

The gray animal was splayed out on the snow, deep red gashes covering its furry torso. Drake continued to fight the demon, his sword never letting up, but from the look on his haggard face, he wouldn't last much longer.

My chest tightened as I glanced back and forth between the two. I hated leaving Scarlett like this, but she'd be okay for now. Or at least I hoped. I shot to my feet and darted toward the battle.

Drake spun his head in my direction as I approached, deep lavender rimming his irises. "Go, Luna! Get out of here!" He swung his blade, but the demon jerked back, snarling.

"No, I'm not leaving you."

His eyes were wild, his slick platinum hair plastered to his forehead with sweat. Bloody gashes spattered up and down his torso and arms. A twinge of fear ignited in my chest. I'd never seen the ice prince in such a state, and it sent a rush of panic through my veins.

A nearby whimper made my head spin in the direction of the sound. Triston's naked body lay trembling in the snow. I forced my eyes toward the upper half of his form and bent down beside him. He was pale, and like Drake, had lacerations marring the entire length of his body. But they were healing...

"Are you okay?"

"I will be," he hissed through clenched teeth.

"Is there anything I can do?" I tucked my hands beneath his head and laid it down on my lap, his shaggy brown hair spilling over my knee.

"We have to help Drake," he rasped, his eyes flitting toward the ensuing battle. Squeezing his eyes shut, a golden glow encompassed his body, the warmth seeping into my lap. A few seconds later, his eyelids opened, the amber of his irises already brighter. "Can you help me stand?"

I nodded quickly and wedged my shoulder under his armpit. He pushed himself to stand, and I couldn't help but notice the nasty cuts along his abdomen had nearly healed. New pink skin formed between the lacerations, mending the vicious slices of the demon's horns.

From all The Seven, Triston was the one I'd had least contact with—until now. I shoved away the embarrassing thoughts of his naked body pressed against mine as his legs stopped wobbling, and he righted himself.

"You got a weapon?" he asked, peeling his bare torso from mine.

"Just this." I held up the dagger Scarlett had given me earlier.

He grabbed it and flipped it over in his palm. "I'm too weak to shift so this will have to do." Wrapping his fingers around the metal hilt, he mumbled a few words. When his fingers unclenched, two daggers lay across his palm.

"Wow! How'd you do that?"

"Just a quick duplicating spell. It's the best I could do for now." He handed me a blade and clasped his fingers around my other hand, tugging me toward Drake and the monster. "You think you can conjure me up some sweats?"

I nodded quickly. It wasn't something I'd ever practiced before but how hard could it be? Squeezing my eyes shut, I visualized the training uniforms Triston typically wore. A blast of warmth sparked from my fingertips and when I opened my eyes, the shifter was fully clothed.

"Thanks," he said, already pulling me toward Drake. "You ready?"

"For what exactly?"

"Aeria told me what you girls did in their dorm the other day. I'm going to attempt to replicate it. I just hope we have enough remaining power between the three of us."

I gulped, trailing behind him as he yanked me through the soft snow.

The abacor had Drake cornered against a monstrous oak, its

rows of fangs snapping at the Fae royal. Drake's arms shook from the strain of keeping his sword up. Unlike the prince, the demon didn't show an ounce of exhaustion.

He twisted his beast-like head at our approach, a sinister smile curling back his lips. "There you are my little half-blood." Stepping away from Drake, he trudged toward us. "While I've thoroughly enjoyed myself with the prince, I've grown weary of this game. It's time to end this." He reached out a clawed hand, beckoning me forward.

Drake slumped against the tree, his breaths ragged spurts. "Don't get any closer, Luna."

We hedged the outer rim of trees, slowly moving toward Drake as the abacor loomed closer. Triston had to reach Drake for this to work, and he was still a few yards away.

"Whatever you do, don't let go of my hand," Triston whispered.

I nodded, my eyes fixed on the advancing demon.

"Human, let's not make this any more unpleasant than it needs to be." He ran a claw over his hairy jaw. "You've intrigued me, and though the dark lord wants you dead, I think your unique qualities merit a one-on-one first. So let's make a deal. You come with me, and I'll let your friends live."

"Not a chance," hissed Drake.

Triston crept closer to the prince, and inch-by-agonizing-inch, I followed.

"Who is this dark lord anyway, and what does he want with me?" I was both curious and figured keeping him talking could provide the distraction we needed.

Crimson swirled across the demon's dark pupils. "That is for the dark lord to reveal when the time is right."

Figures I'd get some cryptic mumbo-jumbo. "How about you tell me his name so my friends here know who to come after and kill once we've finished with you?"

His massive chest rumbled in what I swore was a belly

laugh. "You are certainly an entertaining little human. And gutsy. The dark lord will like that."

"Too bad he'll never get to meet her," shouted Drake as Triston's hand clasped around his fingers.

A jolt of electricity ignited in my fingertips and slammed into me like a lighting bolt. It was a good thing Triston was holding me, or I would've ended up flat on my back.

"Now!" yelled Triston.

The foreign words of the spell filled my mind and sprang from my lips, unbidden. "Toree fuocum celis demoniom, toree fuocum celis demoniom!" Fire burst from my core, hemorrhaging through my veins until my whole body vibrated with power.

Drake pointed his sword at the demon, and a blaze of lavender shot from the blade, sending the creature hurtling through the air. His massive dark form hung suspended near the tree line for a moment before plunging down into a sprawling oak with a sickening crunch.

The hair on the back of my neck tingled, and I swiveled around to see a dark shadow emerge from the path leading from the academy. Onyx eyes locked onto mine, sending a shuddering breath through my lungs.

"Let's finish this," growled Triston, snapping my attention back to the fight.

I followed the boys' lead, extending my hand out toward the crumpled form of the demon. "Toree fuocum celis demoniom, toree fuocum celis demoniom!" we shouted in unison.

A brilliant fiery wave burst from our splayed palms, flowing like molten magma. The demon's eyes widened, his gaping maw forming a capital O as the scorching energy rolled over him like a tidal wave.

Hideous shrieks filled the quiet forest as brilliant orange flames consumed the demon's flesh.

Triston released my hand and my knees wobbled, my legs no

more than jelly. The forest went topsy-turvy, the darkening sky appearing beneath my feet and the snow above. Squeezing my eyes shut, I waited for the crash of cold earth, but it never came.

Warm arms enveloped me, crushing me to a firm chest. "I got you, mini minx," a voice rasped, his words like a heated embrace. Cocooned in the familiar intoxicating scent, I let go and let the encroaching darkness consume me.

CHAPTER 28

A spicy musky scent swirled around me as I nuzzled into the soft pillow and silky sheets. My lids were heavy, every muscle in my body sore, but that familiar tantalizing fragrance coaxed them open.

Sunlight streamed in through the picture window. I glanced around the bedroom, my mind hazy, until the *gigantic* bed sparked heated memories. I shot up, throwing the fluffy comforter back.

A pair of bottomless irises stared at me from a chair positioned at the foot of the bed. Ryder raked his hand through his hair, tugging at the wild locks. "You are the most infuriating person I know."

"Right back at ya."

The hint of a smile tugged at his sexy lips. I smoothed down the crumpled comforter to avoid his gaze and what it was doing to my insides.

"You know I should ground you for the rest of the semester for that stunt you pulled."

I arched a brow. "You're not my parent so I'm pretty sure you can't ground me. And I'm not a kid anymore. I *am* eighteen so technically I'm free to do whatever I want. I could walk right out of here if I felt like it." I scooted to the edge of the bed, and my toes barely skimmed the floor. Before I could push myself up, a dark blur stopped me.

Ryder's hands were on my shoulders, his fingertips brushing my sensitive skin. "You should still take it easy. And you're definitely not going anywhere. Not today and not anytime in the near future, not with that mark. And besides, you expended a lot of energy killing that abacor demon—whether you're a kid or an adult." Was it me or was his voice a little breathy?

I glanced up, the limited air between us crackling. "I feel fine," I murmured. *My* voice was definitely breathy.

His dark eyes skimmed over my lips, and I couldn't help my tongue from snaking out to wet them. My entire mouth had gone impossibly dry at his proximity.

He growled and took a step back, releasing me. He muttered something under his breath, but I couldn't make it out beneath the rumble of his throat. My entire traitorous body sagged at his absence.

"Are you going to keep doing these incredibly stupid and risky things? I need to know now if you've got a death wish or something."

I narrowed my eyes at my exasperating instructor, shooting daggers at his annoyingly handsome face. "Of course not. I like living just fine, thanks. I hated being sidelined for no good reason."

He clenched his jaw, the tendon in his perfectly sculpted jaw twitching. "There was a good reason. Your life was at stake, and you're too important to m—to the team. We can't lose you."

My knees wobbled a little, but it could have been an after effect of yesterday's heady magic use. Or maybe it was the searing eyes I was trying to avoid. "I'm sorry," I muttered without looking up. "I wanted to help. My powers are finally starting to emerge, and I thought I could finally do something for once. I hate feeling useless."

He exhaled a sharp breath and tucked his hands in his pockets. "Come on, we have to meet the others in the training room. They've been waiting for you to wake up."

"Okay," I muttered. Man, this guy's mood swings were making my head spin.

After a quick stop at my dorm so I could change, we trudged out into the snow to The Seven's covert training space. Cinder hadn't been in our room, and I missed my best friend. I wanted to see how she was doing and catch her up on everything that had happened. At least the fact that she'd felt well enough to go to class lightened the pressure in my chest.

When we reached the old stone structure, Ryder opened the door and applause filled the cavernous space. I glanced up at The Seven, heat swarming my cheeks. They stood in a line, each wearing simple black sweats and their house pin. Turning back to Ryder, I arched a curious brow. His only response was a one-shouldered shrug and a casual smirk.

Drake stepped forward as we neared, an unreadable smile playing on his lips. He held something pinched between his fingers, but I couldn't tell what it was. "You did well out there yesterday, human. As much as it pains me to admit, I'm not sure that we could've defeated the abacor demon without you."

Triston and Scarlett both nodded behind him. I was beyond relieved to see both of them healthy and back to normal.

"You're much stronger than any of us ever expected, and as unofficial leader of the team"—Drake shot a smirk at Ryder —"I'd like to invite you to be our number eight." He closed the distance between us and handed me a pin in red, white and blue.

My fingers closed around the little trinket as tears filled my eyes. "You made me a human pin?"

He chuckled. "No, I didn't make it, the girls did."

Glancing over at Raine, Aeria and Scarlett, I wasn't sure which was harder to believe.

I smiled, flipping the pin over in my palm. "I love the colors." It was like wearing a tiny American flag, which figures that's what they'd associate with humans.

"So what do you say?" asked Ash, his emerald eyes twinkling.

"Only if we make the Supe Slayer Squad our official name. I like the sound of that better than The Eight."

Scarlett giggled, no doubt remembering our sleepover conversation. Raine rolled her eyes with a scowl, but it seemed less hate filled than usual.

"Whatever you say, human," said Drake with a grin.

Ryder stepped forward from behind me and clapped his hands. "Luna, you'll officially join the team at the start of next semester—once you've passed all your exams."

Ugh. Easier said than done.

"Good, now that that's official, we can all get back to training."

A chorus of grunts rang out behind me.

"You guys did well yesterday considering, but you've got a long way to go. Now with Luna on the team, you'll need to learn to work as a whole new unit." He glanced at his watch. "You've got an hour before class so let's get to work."

My muscles still ached from yesterday, but I forced myself onto the mat with Drake. "What are we working on today, oh fearless leader?"

A big smile lit up his typically expressionless façade. "I like the sound of that. You may refer to me as such from now on."

I rolled my eyes. "In your dreams."

His faery sword appeared in his palm, and he thrust before I could blink. Fae bastard! I dodged just in time to avoid a blade in the gut and darted to the far wall to choose my weapon.

As I marched back toward Drake with a short shiny blade

clenched in my fist, a surge of happiness bubbled in my chest. I'd never really been a part of anything before. There'd always been something missing and somehow these seven supernaturals had filled that void. Maybe Ryder too...

"Hurry up, half-blood!" shouted Drake, pulling me from my musings.

"I'm coming!"

CHAPTER 29

"**I** can't believe you're dragging me to this thing." I stared at my reflection in the mirror as Cinder held a lacey red gown up against my chest. My fingers grazed the silky material, the fine lace more exquisite than anything that existed in the human world.

"Luna, we survived our first semester at Darkhen Academy, and we passed all our exams! We totally deserve a night off to celebrate."

I grimaced. I'd barely passed my exams last week after the abacor demon debacle, not to mention most of my classes, thanks to my fickle magic and one ornery unipeg. And I'd almost gotten myself and Cinder killed a few times. But my roommate's smile and bubbly energy were contagious. "Couldn't we just hang out in the dorm and watch a movie or something?"

"Absolutely not. The end of the semester dances at Darkhen are epic. There's no way we're missing the first one."

I grunted, blowing wisps of blonde hair from my face.

"This dress is going to be perfect on you. Now go try it on." She stuffed the gown in my arms and pushed me toward the bathroom.

After nearly getting killed by the abacor demon, and a week of grueling final exams, I so didn't feel like parading around in a ball gown. Even if it was the most gorgeous thing I'd ever laid eyes on.

I slipped the soft material over my head, and it immediately molded to every curve of my body. The silky lace practically floated over my skin, wrapping me in its smooth embrace. The sweetheart neckline dipped to the perfect spot, showing a little bit of cleavage without being overly scandalous. My fingers brushed over the mark on my chest, its deep crimson shade nearly matching the sultry ruby of the dress.

Luckily, the demons had let up on me this past week. It was almost as if they'd known getting through my exams was torture enough, and they were being polite.

"Are you coming out or what?" Cinder's voice seeped through the cracked door.

I peeked my head out, and she urged me forward.

"Let's see!" She clapped her hands, bouncing on her tiptoes. "You look amazing!" she gushed when I finally came out all the way.

"So do you." The raven-haired beauty wore an emerald green mermaid gown that accentuated her long legs and slender figure. "There's going to be nothing angelic about Raf's intentions when he gets a look at you in that."

Her cheeks flushed, matching the deep pink of her lip-gloss. "Oh, whatever." She handed me a pair of ruby stilettos and smirked. "If anyone's going to have the guys gawking tonight, it's going to be you. I was right, red really is your color."

"Ha! Like any guy will come near me with a broody Ryder glued to my side." My self-appointed demon bodyguard hadn't left me alone for more than a few minutes the past week. I was fairly certain he was skulking outside the door at this very moment.

"Is that really so bad?" She winked as she strapped her heels on. "I don't care what he says, that guy totally wants you. The way he looks at you..." She shivered, her shoulders shuddering. "It's so hot!"

I shook my head, running my fingers through my long hair. "Too bad nothing will ever come of it."

"We'll see about that." She disappeared into the bathroom and returned a minute later with a makeup bag in one hand and a curling iron in the other. "Now let's pretend I'm one of your stylists from *Hitched,* and let's get you camera-ready."

Two sharp knocks at the door sent my heart into overdrive. Sure, demons I could handle, but the idea of a dance had my nerves twisted into a pretzel. Taking one last glance in the mirror, I tore myself away from the stunning stranger staring back at me. Cinder had done an amazing job with my hair and makeup, blonde locks tumbled over my bare shoulders and smoky navy eyeliner brought out the deep blue of my eyes. I didn't look quite as gorgeous as Kimmie-Jayne on TV, but I was pretty damn hot.

"I'll get it!" Cinder burst from the bathroom and darted across the room to the door.

Ash and Raf filled the entryway, both in dark suits. Damn, what was it about these supes being so good looking?

"Wow, you guys clean up nice," I said as I walked toward them.

"You too," stuttered Ash, his emerald eyes sparkling like the most brilliant gemstones as they traveled down my revealing dress.

"We thought we could escort you to the dance," said Raf, his gaze flickering toward my roommate.

"That won't be necessary, gentlemen." Ryder's hulking shadow appeared behind them, and suddenly the uber-attractive guys paled in comparison. A fitted, black tux outlined the demon bad boy's wide shoulders and clung tightly to his powerful chest. Ryder dressed in normal clothes was hot. In a tux, he was devastating.

I had to remind myself to breathe as all the air was forced out of my lungs. Devilish demons, why did he have to be so breathtakingly gorgeous?

His piercing eyes raked over my body, leaving a trail of fire in its scorching wake. I repressed the urge to squirm, clenching my fingers into tight little fists at my sides. Hundreds of glimmering stars shimmered across his impossibly dark eyes as I finally lifted my gaze to meet his.

Ryder locked his jaw back into place and barreled by the guys, offering me his arm. "You look ravishing, mini minx," he whispered against the shell of my ear. A swarm of goose bumps prickled to life down my bare arms.

"Shall we?" Raf's voice tore me away from Ryder's spell, and I glanced up at my roommate who stood arm in arm between Ash and the nephilim.

"Let's go!" she squealed.

The threesome walked in front of us chatting away as I glided down the hallway, locked against Ryder's thick arm. His musky, sandalwood scent swirled around me, and it was impossible to inhale without breathing him in. He was like a drug, and I was hopelessly addicted—a crack fiend desperate for my next fix.

The dense silence between us finally dissipated as we neared the gym. The pounding beats of the music filtered down the hallway, and we quickened our pace to keep up with Cinder.

"I wonder what the theme is this time," she said, craning her head back to me. "It changes every semester, and I heard they bring the royal decorators in from the Winter Court. I can't wait to see it!"

When the double doors opened, my jaw dropped. The gym

from a few hours ago had vanished—the bleachers, barren white walls, and the light parquet floor were nowhere to be seen. Instead, an exquisite rose garden stretched before us. White trellises climbed to the vaulted ceilings, trailing with roses of every color of the rainbow. The fragrant perfume wafted over us as we crossed the threshold, my heels sinking into the lush grass. My head dipped back to take it all in.

Between the winding verdant pathways sat round tables dressed in fine white linens and gilded tableware. Sprinkled over each place setting were more rose petals and a beautiful candelabra adorned the center, flickering flames dancing over the tall, tapered candles.

"Wow, it's amazing," I muttered.

We continued toward the beautiful gazebo in the center of the room where hundreds of bodies wriggled across the dance floor. Every inch of the top of the white gazebo was blanketed in blush roses and leafy hanging vines. Thousands of tiny lights sparkled to life, bathing the dance floor in a warm golden glow.

I was so distracted by the sights, I hadn't felt Ryder's heavy gaze boring into me. I swiveled toward him, and his eyes locked on mine. A half-smile pulled at his lips, something unreadable behind his expression.

When the heavy silence between us became unbearable, I let the first stupid thing on my mind pop out. "I feel like I just stepped foot on the set of *Hitched.*"

He laughed, the smooth sound rumbling his chest. He glanced around and smirked. "I guess you're right. It does remind me of the elaborate parties the producers put together."

"Do you miss it?" My voice cracked. "Do you miss her?" I don't know what made me ask such a loaded question. I blamed the intoxicating fragrances in the air—who knew what sort of mind-altering effect the exotic flowers had on a simple human.

His eyes widened, and he didn't speak for a long minute. Just when I was about to take the question back, his jaw ticked.

"It wasn't real. Not *really* anyway. Being sucked onto a show like that where you're practically forced into these perfect circumstances and then thrown into dramatic situations isn't real life. Don't get me wrong; I had a lot of fun. Getting to know the other guys and of course your half-sister changed my life in more ways than I thought possible. And I'm not saying I didn't care about Kimmie-Jayne because I did, a lot. There was something about her that made me want to become a better man. I think I did actually love her—or as close as I've ever been to loving someone. Do I miss that? Sure. But I wasn't right for her, not really. I don't think I was right for anyone back then." He pressed his lips together and stared out onto the dance floor.

I released the breath I hadn't realized I'd been holding in a slow exhale. Another completely unexpected confession.

An arm came around mine, tugging me away from Ryder. "Come dance with me, Luna girl." Ash's big smile appeared beside me.

Ryder bristled, his hold on my other arm tightening for a split second.

"I promise to stay within your line of sight," Ash said to Ryder. "Believe me, I have no intentions of going up against a demon by myself again."

The tension in my guard's shoulders released, and he relinquished my arm. "I'll have my eyes on you, dragon boy."

Ash saluted our mentor with a chuckle. "Yes, sir." He tugged me onto the dance floor, my eyes firmly fixed on Ryder's lingering gaze.

CHAPTER 30

When we reached the center of packed bodies, I found Cinder and Raf dancing. The handsome dark-haired nephilim was all over my roommate. She laughed as he whispered something in her ear, and my heart soared. Rafael seemed like a good guy, and she deserved only the best.

Ash grabbed my hand and twirled me in a circle, my flowing gown dancing over the shiny wood floor. I whirled and whirled, the DJ's intoxicating rhythm moving my body. We danced forever, the feverish beats spinning in my mind, and for the first time in very long, I totally let loose.

Ash was a maniac, his dance moves cracking me up. He broke into old school break dancing before long, and I thought my cheeks would burst from laughing so hard. Someone had definitely been watching old reruns of MTV on the Azarian broadcast network.

As a circle formed around him, a chilly breath tickled my ear. Spinning around, I nearly smacked right into the ice prince. "Drake!" I cried out. "Geez, you scared me."

"Sorry." He raised his hands up, one clutching a fancy flute with deep lavender liquid. "What's got you so jumpy?"

I couldn't help my gaze flickering toward his glass. The fragrant perfume of the faery wine had already reached my nostrils, and my tongue yearned for another taste. I swallowed to rid my mouth of the odd sensation. "Nothing. I was actually having fun." And it was true. The past hour had flown by, and I hadn't thought about the devil's mark or the demons coming after me once.

"Good," he said, his lips curling into a smile.

Raine appeared a second later in a stunning black sheath dress, her hand clasping onto his shoulder. She threw me a half smile before turning her attention back to the prince. "There you are, Drakey. Come on, let's go dance. I like this one."

I swore he repressed an eye roll before turning to follow her onto the dance floor. I watched them for a moment until Raine pressed her perky breasts up against his chest and began nuzzling his ear. *Bleh.* I did *not* need to see that.

Squeezing my eyes shut, I spun around and weaved my way through the crowd. If I couldn't have the faery wine, I at least needed some sort of beverage.

At the outer edge of the circle amassed around Ash and his killer dance moves, a hand snaked out with a glass flute. Tipping my gaze up, I found Ryder with his typical smirk curving his kissable lips. "I was on my way to find you." He handed me the glass, and I sucked it down without a thought. All that dancing had me parched.

Fizzy bubbles gurgled straight to my head, and my lips puckered at the sour-sweet flavor. "What is this?"

"It's the Azarian version of champagne, only it's made with the glia fruit instead of grapes."

I took another sip and swirled the sparkling liquid around my tongue. "It's pretty tasty."

"And don't worry, it's not like faery wine." He winked.

"Too bad, I guess no kissing tonight then." I slapped my hand over my mouth. *I did not just say that out loud!* What was wrong with me?

The corners of Ryder's lips tilted upward, and mischief glistened in his dark eyes. "It does have the unfortunate side effect of loosening inhibitions."

I narrowed my eyes at him, shooting him a good glare. "Thanks for the warning." I'd already guzzled down the entire glass. "You didn't happen to have any of it, did you?"

He stepped closer, his delicious scent invading my senses. "I'll never tell," he whispered, his lips brushing my earlobe.

Holy demon babies! My toes curled in my sexy stilettos, and I had to force myself not to jump my hot instructor right in the middle of the dance floor.

His hand came around my waist and settled at the small of my back as the tempo of the music slowed. "Dance with me."

He totally did have some of that stuff!

"You look incredible tonight, mini minx. I can't tear my eyes away from you."

"Thanks," I stuttered. I swallowed hard as he closed the distance between us, pulling me into his body. Everything else fell away, the close-packed dancing bodies, the tinkle of toasting glasses, the chatter and even the music.

I thought it was just the all-consuming effect Ryder had on me, but a sweet, smoky scent reached my nostrils a moment later. Magic.

Glancing up, I caught the flicker of a hazy golden orb encasing us. "Are we in a protective bubble or something?"

His lips twitched. "Cloaking spell. I can't get anything by you anymore, can I?"

A tiny pang of hurt jabbed at my heart. He was embarrassed to be seen with me. My lips turned down, and my lost puppy dog expression must have given me away.

He tipped my chin up and forced my eyes to meet his. "Hey.

I'm your teacher. I can't be dancing with you like this in front of the entire academy. It's entirely inappropriate. I may skirt the line when it comes to the rules, but I'm not completely insane. You know that, right?"

A ridiculous smile split my lips as he tugged me back into his chest. I wrapped my arms tight around his neck and leaned my head against his firm pec. His heart thundered beneath the surface.

My brain told me to pull away—that nothing would ever come of this, but my heart told my nosy brain to mind its own business. Making logical decisions just wasn't possible when I was in Ryder's arms.

We swayed to the smooth rhythms seeping into our little bubble, our bodies pressed against each other. Mine molded into his so perfectly it felt like its missing half. My skin tingled everywhere we touched, the sensations zipping over my flesh and setting it ablaze. His chin dipped down and his eyes locked on my lips, flashes of citrine like lightning bolts skimming the dark depths. I sucked in a breath as he inched closer.

The music slowed and then stopped, the sultry tune replaced by a raging beat. As if the song had weaved a magic spell over us, its absence had the opposite effect. Ryder released me and took a step back, and the cloaking spell burst. I could feel its magic as it washed over me. The room sprang back to life, all the vivid sights and sounds on full blast. It was like a bucket of ice over the head.

Something vibrated in Ryder's jacket pocket, and his gaze finally pivoted away from mine. He scanned the screen, and his brows furrowed. "Cillian wants to see you."

"Right now?" I huffed, snapping myself out of the heated moment. "Am I in trouble?" We'd never really had "the talk" after I snuck out of his office to fight the demon. I figured the headmaster was giving me a break because of exams. I couldn't imagine he was pleased that I'd blatantly disobeyed him right after promising to trust him.

"Possibly." His dark eyes sparkled. "Come on, I'll take you."

We marched through the quiet halls to Cillian's office, the music from the gym falling away. Ryder sauntered beside me, my ever-vigilant bodyguard. Every so often, his gaze traveled to mine, his silent intensity boring into me. If I had any hopes of getting over him, I needed to find a way to remove this mark otherwise he'd remain stuck to me like glue. And being near him without being with him was going to break me.

His arm brushed against mine, and tiny sparks crackled along my skin. I paused and Ryder slowed his pace, before finally turning to me and tugging me into a quiet corner. My heart pounded against my ribs as he trapped me in the small recess.

"We've got to get this under control," he whispered, his lips inches from mine.

He'd definitely been drinking that magical champagne. There was no other explanation. "Get what under control?" I hedged.

A mischievous smile twisted his lips up. "This"—he pointed back and forth between his chest and mine—"whatever this is, between us."

I tipped my head back to meet his piercing gaze. "It's nothing, right?"

"It can't be." He shook his head. "Not right now—no matter how we may feel."

My heart thudded erratically. Did he just admit he felt something?

"Cillian would kill me. Literally. And then I'd be forced out of the academy, and I wouldn't be able to protect you or train the others. What we're doing here is important, and we can't risk it failing or else both our worlds will be in deep shit." He paused and licked his lips, his eyes still intent on mine. "I'm obviously having a hard time controlling myself around you. So you have to help me, okay?"

I nodded, chewing on my lower lip, all the words getting stuck in my throat.

"Not helping." He freed my swollen lip from my teeth, and his thumb lingered on my chin. "Gods, Luna, if you only knew what you did to me," he rasped out, his eyes trailing down my revealing neckline.

My core clenched, heat pooling in my lower half.

"This is the last time," he muttered before his lips captured mine. Ryder's massive frame pressed me against the chilly wall as my fingers dug into the soft hair at his nape. His tongue entwined with mine, engaged in a sensual tango ten times more intense than our dance from a few moments ago.

Excitement thrummed through my veins, my heart pounding so hard its fevered beats rushed across my eardrums. He pressed closer, obliterating every inch of space between us, and a little moan escaped my lips. He swallowed it up as he continued his frenzied assault. I arched against him, unable to control my body around him.

My brain flickered to life for a second. Luckily, not every ounce of blood had rushed to my lower half. Ryder was kissing me in the middle of the hall; sure we were tucked into a little nook and everyone was at the dance, but still. If we got caught...

Obviously coming to the same realization I had, he pulled away much too soon. Tucking a loose strand of hair behind my ear, he smiled and tugged on my hand. "Come on. We don't want to keep the headmaster waiting."

The remainder of the walk to Cillian's office passed in a blur as my mind whirled with Ryder's words—and toe-curling kisses. He'd made it clear we couldn't be together, but that he had feelings, and then he'd kissed me like I was the only person left in the world. *That's not confusing...*

I pushed the thoughts aside to a dark corner of my mind marking them "Do Not Open till Christmas—or maybe ever."

When Darby ushered us into the headmaster's office a few minutes later, a strange sensation prickled my skin. A pungent sweet, smoky scent filled my nostrils. Slowly, my head pivoted to a blonde man perched on the leather couch by the fireplace. Unnervingly familiar cobalt eyes met mine, and all the air siphoned from my lungs.

Ryder bristled beside me, moving a few inches closer.

Cillian stood and motioned to the stranger. "Luna, I'm sorry for interrupting the dance, but there's someone here to see you."

The tall, slender man stood, his scrutinizing gaze running over me with laser-like intensity. Power throbbed from his lithe form, thickening the air around him like nothing I'd ever experienced. It was as if a pool of dense magic cloaked his very essence.

A shock of white hair zipped through the neat golden blonde strands, a stark contrast to the brilliant cobalt of his eyes. Sculpted cheekbones and a defined, straight nose rounded out the middle-aged man's handsome face.

A tight-lipped smile finally appeared, and he extended his hand. "It's a pleasure to meet you at long last, Luna Hallows."

I returned the tight-lipped grin, but my fluttering heart betrayed me, ramming against my ribcage with every erratic beat. I knew what was coming next—I could feel the unbending certainty deep within my bones.

"I'm Garrix, your father." His gaze lowered to the symbol mystically carved into my chest. "And I've come to help you get rid of that nasty little mark."

Wilder Revelation

Wilder Legacy

Wilder: The Guardian Series The Complete Collection

ACKNOWLEDGMENTS

A huge and wholehearted thank you to my dedicated readers! I could not do this without you. I love hearing from you and your enthusiasm for the characters and story. You are the best!

A special thank you to my loving and supportive husband who always understood my need for escaping into a good book (or TV show!). He inspires me to try harder and push further every day. And of course my mother who is the guiding force behind everything I do and made me everything I am today. Without her, I literally could not write—because she's also my part-time babysitter! To my father who will always live on in my dreams. And finally, my son, Alexander, who brings an unimaginable amount of joy and adventure to my life everyday.

A big thank you to my new talented graphic designer, Sanja Gombar, for creating a beautiful book cover. A special thank you to my dedicated beta readers/fellow authors Jena, Kristin, Tiea, Michelle and Patrick who have been my sounding board on everything from cover ideas, blurbs, and story details. And all of my beta readers who gave me great ideas, caught spelling errors, and were all around amazing.

Thank you to all my family and friends (especially you,

Robin Wiley!) and new indie author and blogger friends (you're the best Mary Ellen!) who let me bounce ideas off of them and listened to my struggles as an author and self-publisher. I appreciate it more than you all will ever know.

G.K.

ABOUT THE AUTHOR

USA Today Bestselling Author, G.K. De Rosa has always had a passion for all things fantasy and romance. Growing up, she loved to read, devouring books in a single sitting. She attended Catholic school where reading and writing were an intense part of the curriculum, and she credits her amazing teachers for instilling in her a love of storytelling. As an adult, her favorite books were always young adult novels, and she remains a self-proclaimed fifteen year-old at heart. When she's not reading, writing or watching way too many TV shows, she's traveling and eating around the world with her family. G.K. DeRosa currently lives in South Florida with her real life Prince Charming, their son and fur baby, Nico, the German shepherd.

www.gkderosa.com
gkderosa@wilderbook.com